EARTH FORGED

BOOK 7 OF THE GIFTING

Earth Forged

The Gifting Series #7

Guilt hounds Izzy, who caused her sister's injury and subsequent blindness. But no matter how she cares for Simone or what she sacrifices, it doesn't ease the ache in her chest. With Simone and naive Caro, her best friend, Izzy's role as protector is fully realized. The cost? Hiding behind quirkiness, pseudo-joy, and giving up her hopes and dreams. What she needs is a knight in any armor. After all, beggars can't be fussy. She has no idea that armor, in her case, means black military and that a knight could come in any color, specifically bronze.

Oyaz wants to find his life force, his soulmate, and he'd like her to be human. Earth's females are soft, amusing, passionate, and their scents rival a garden of hahyt blossoms. His task is to guard their planet that promises so many salvations for his males. It's a duty he's pleased to perform, one he would die for. When Operations Commander Malo orders Oyaz to retrieve a human female, he's eager to oblige. That it would lead to his salvation is something he couldn't anticipate. What he hadn't planned for is an ambush that costs him more than his memory, the loss of his soulmate.

EARTH FORGED

Now what? Nothing in their training prepared him for this.

And yet, despite not remembering kneeling for Izzy, he longs to claim her with every inch of his soul.

Also by Sevannah Storm

The Blood of Legends Series

The Huntress

The Healer

The Gifting Series

Soul Forged

Fate Forged

Sun Forged

War Forged

Star Forged

Shadow Forged

Earth Forged

Lust Forged

Standalones

Xiaxan Fox

Ire of Silver

The Shikari

Sol Survivor

Contents

CHAPTER ONE

Izzy adjusted her T-shirt—the hem scratched her skin, and the sensation raised the hairs on the back of her neck. Everything irritated her. As lovely as the crisp blue sky was, with happy flocks of birds and tufts of white clouds, she boiled inside. The rage churned her gut and barreled up her throat. Each word she spewed was laced with venom.

Dad met her gaze in the rearview mirror and winked.

She huffed, folding her arms across her chest and focused on the passing scenery.

Mom and Simmy were discussing the merits of Jane Austen's *Emma*.

Izzy gritted her teeth. Ms.-Goody-Two-Shoes Simmy basked in Mom's attention. Her grades were exemplary, whereas Izzy couldn't pass English, her home language. No offense to Austen fans, but she couldn't wrap her head around the way it was written. Shakespeare was as much a mystery.

Give her something to do with her hands, and she could master it. But studying was for the...well, birds.

"What do you think about Emma, pumpkin?" Dad asked.

She grinned. "I don't think about Emma, Dad."

"I'd be happy to give you a crash course, Izzy, so you won't have to read it next year." Simmy flashed a sweet smile and reached across the backseat to squeeze Izzy's arm.

"No, Simmy, Izzy *must* read it. There are no shortcuts in life." Mom twisted to face Izzy. "Perseverance is a necessary trait. Especially with things you hate."

Izzy wrinkled her nose. "Does an audiobook count?"

Mom laughed. "It's not a shortcut when it takes twice as long to listen than to read."

"Mrs. Granger said reading builds your vocabulary. It also helps with comprehension." Simmy dropped those little gems of wisdom then peered out the window as Dad pulled into the parking lot. The park stretched for miles on either side. Colors exploded in the plants, flowers, and the aviary nearby blasted the silence with raucous calls and cries.

Mrs. Granger, Izzy mouthed, pulling a face.

"I saw that." Simmy tapped the window. "If you read more, your grades would improve. If you spent less time doing track, you could focus on studying."

Heat burst across Izzy's face, and she narrowed her eyes, conveying as much hatred as she could muster. "If you did more track, your ass wouldn't be so big."

Mom gasped. "Izzy."

"Language." Dad shook his head, tossing his mop of curls so like Izzy's.

Simmy's face paled then flushed. "My ass can shrink or grow, but your brain will always be the size of a pea."

"Simmy, that was uncalled for." Mom opened the car door. "Izzy's smart, just in a different way."

"Sure she is." Simmy laughed.

Izzy trembled. Her fingernails dug into her palms, and she thumped her thigh before climbing out of the car. When she circled the trunk, Dad was pulling out the picnic basket. Mom clutched the blanket to her chest and raised her face to the warm unfiltered sunlight.

Simmy stood on the verge, overlooking the bank sliding into the surrounding trees. A breeze caught her luxurious mane of blonde curls, so unlike Izzy's tight ringlets. And her ass wasn't big, far from it. Everything about Simmy was perfect, from her long legs to her pretty green eyes she got from Mom.

Izzy had Mom's short height, Dad's curls, and gray eyes, and of course, her stupidity was all her own.

"Here, take the umbrella." Dad dumped the ancient thing in Izzy's arms and strolled past lazy-Simmy by the steps descending to the picnic area. Mom trailed, chatting to Dad about the mocktail she had made as a starter.

Still, Simmy just stood there with her precious Austen clasped in her hand.

Stomping past, Izzy swung the umbrella and whacked her older-sister-by-one-year on the ass.

Simmy squealed, twisted on the spot to rebuke Izzy, but teetered. She threw out her arms to find her balance, sending *Emma* tumbling down the hill. With a cry, she lunged for the book. In slow motion, she tilted and, head-over-heels, followed the book's path.

A grating snap and piercing scream silenced the birds.

Dad bellowed Simmy's name.

Izzy threw down the umbrella and scrambled after her. From where she rolled, farther down lay a row of pine trees. Izzy stretched out her hand as if to warn Simmy, but it was too late. A crunch echoed in her ears when Simmy slammed into a tree, her body like a rag doll.

Whimpering at what she'd done, Izzy sprinted down the bank, using her athleticism to reach her sister.

Blood trickled from a gash on her temple. Her skin was pale and tinged gray.

"Mom!" Izzy flicked her tears aside and gathered Simmy close, patting her cheek to wake her. She scanned her sister's body, searching for injuries, and settled on her ankle twisted into an odd angle.

I did this.

Dad slid the last few yards to stop beside them. Mom hovered at the top of the embankment with her mobile pinned to her ear.

"What happened, pumpkin?" Dad ran his hands over Simmy's legs and hissed when he reached her ankle.

"I whacked her with the umbrella, but not hard. I swear it, Dad. *Emma* fell from her hands, and she went after it." Ice encased Izzy's heart and hardened until it formed a shell. "This is my fault. I did this." The sobs shook her body, and she wailed, unable to slow the tears. "Please, Simmy, please."

"It's okay, pumpkin. Medics are on their way." Dad tried to take Simmy from Izzy, but she hesitated. "Go take care of your mom."

Mom? Izzy whipped her head up, focusing on her mom pacing with her arms wrapped around her torso. Izzy dragged her arms away and let Dad take Simmy from her. With a last glance, she clambered up the hill and gathered *Emma*, tucking the book into the back of her jeans.

"What happened, Izzy?" Mom gripped Izzy's arms the moment she reached the top.

Izzy whimpered. "I whacked her with the umbrella. It's my fault."

Mom jerked back, and her face paled. She opened and closed her mouth while tears trickled free. "Get in the car. We'll...talk about this later."

Dad told her to comfort Mom. She couldn't do it from inside the car. "But—"

"Izzy." Anger hardened Mom's tone.

Izzy gathered the dropped items. The meals and treats spilled out of the picnic basket. The blanket looked like a sad, soggy crepe. And the umbrella lay where she'd thrown it. Climbing into the backseat, she tried not to stare at where Simmy had sat not ten minutes earlier.

The medics arrived and lifted Simmy onto a stretcher. Mom climbed into the ambulance, leaving Dad to deal with Izzy. He sat in the driver's seat and gripped the steering wheel. Resting his temple on it, he sucked in deep breaths before meeting Izzy's gaze in the mirror again.

"Not your fault, pumpkin."

"It is, and you know it. Mom knows it." She pinched her lips and ignored the tears flowing free. "What did the medics say?"

"Broken ankle, that's a given. Concussion, at the worst." Dad started the engine, reversing the car to follow the ambulance.

The scenery whizzed past, blurred by her tears. Dad tried to cheer her up, but his stiff shoulders and strained chuckle implied his heart wasn't in it. She didn't expect it to be, and anything he said highlighted how much this *was* her fault. Not one to pray, she did so now, desperate for help. But not aloud. Shame curled her shoulders, and she shoved her hands between her thighs, hoping the warmth would calm the shivers racking her body.

Dad parked outside Winston Memorial and twisted in his seat. "Simmy will be fine. It's just a broken ankle, pumpkin."

Izzy met his gaze. "And if she dies?"

Dad laughed. "From a concussion?" He climbed out of the car and opened her door, pulling her into a hug. "Come, let's find Mom. She might need a coffee."

"Or wine?" Izzy looped her arm around Dad's waist and let him usher her into the hospital.

Information sent them to Simmy's hospital room where Mom paced. When Dad strolled in, she cried out and threw herself at him. He hugged her, rubbing her back while nuzzling her temple with his chin. She sobbed uncontrollably, her words garbled.

"Monica, calm down. What are you trying to tell me?"

"She's awake." Mom sliced a glance at Izzy and narrowed her eyes. "They took her for tests."

"Yes?" Dad smiled. "All good so far."

Mom pulled away to rub her face. "She can't see, Gerard."

Dad stilled, and his smile faded. "What do you mean?"

"She's blind." Mom wrapped her arms around herself and paced. "They don't know if it's permanent."

Heat and ice took turns to bathe Izzy as her lungs burned. She shook her head. No, this wasn't possible. Dad had said Simmy would be fine. Why? Why wasn't she fine? Izzy threw out a hand, caught the wall, and crumpled to the floor. Her vision blurred, and her cheeks flushed like someone had draped a heated cloth over her head.

A nurse touched Izzy's shoulder, drawing her back to the moment. Mom and Dad stood to the side, watching her. Their stiff postures weren't welcoming. Izzy hitched on a sob. They blamed her.

"I'm so sorry." She chanted it, wrapping her arms around her legs to rock. "I did this."

The nurse returned with a glass of sugar water, urging Izzy to drink. "She's in shock, Mrs. Reeves."

Mom, her cheeks glowing red against her pale skin, leaned over Izzy. "How are you feeling, pumpkin?"

"Feeling?" Izzy jerked. Nausea churned her gut, pain seized her muscles, and her heart screamed as if torn asunder. "How's Simmy?"

"She's just gone through the x-rays for her ankle. The MRI scans reveal a swelling, but nothing wrong with her eyes. They say her sight could return." Mom laced her fingers through Izzy's and tugged. "See for yourself."

Simmy lay in a nearby bed, smiling as she chatted with Dad.

Izzy winced at the bandage around Simmy's head, and the orthopedic boot on her foot. She sucked in a sharp breath, then resisted when Mom tried to pull her toward the bed.

"Pumpkin?" Dad opened his arm.

Izzy lunged to hug him, desperate for his warmth and strength.

"Izzy." Simmy giggled. "Sweet sister."

"She's on pain meds," Dad whispered into Izzy's hair.

"No, Simmy, don't touch your bandage." Mom tucked the blankets under Simmy, pinning her in place.

"But Izzy's here. Why can't I see her?" Simmy pouted then squirmed in the bed. "I'm sleepy, Mom." She moaned when she rubbed her face across the pillow.

"Come, pumpkin. Let your old Dad treat you to a milkshake." He ushered Izzy to the hospital's coffee shop. After ordering for her, he rested his hands on the table. "It wasn't your fault. Simmy told us what happened."

Izzy pinched her lips. The scene replayed. Her hatred when she swung the umbrella. Her wicked glee when Simmy cried out and faced her. But the snap of her ankle had torn away what joy Izzy had relished. The crunch when Simmy's head hit the tree had ripped Izzy's heart out. A hollowness remained.

She yanked the Austen out of her jeans and placed it on the table. Simmy couldn't read it anymore. Izzy stifled a sob and clung to the chocolate milkshake a waitress served.

To be reminded like this that she did love her sister was the hardest lesson she'd ever learned. Never again would she treat Simmy like she had. The resentment was Izzy's alone. Her inability to compete with her perfect sister was her burden to bear.

But taking it too far, endangering Simmy's life because Izzy reacted like a child... that was on her.

Chapter Two

Oyaz slammed his fist into his palm while he paced. This was *not* happening. He raised his gaze to King Xeus, who held a private council on the dais speaking to Madyx's father and Adviser Cales. To the left, Madyx sat on the white Fuyra-stone bench, his knees spread wide on which he rested his elbows. He was pale under his bronze cheeks.

A female's whimpering and sniffling gritted Oyaz's teeth. He swung his head to glare at Lady Azian. The deep purple of her ceremonial wrap enhanced her beauty. Black hair swirled around her, belying her dismay. Had she truly been violated as she alleged, her hair would reflect her emotional state. He snorted. So not intelligent to leave her hair down when she deceived. If she wanted to fool King Xeus with this silly claim of abuse, she should have braided her hair.

Oyaz clenched his jaw. The urge to stomp across to Madyx and berate him again tore through him. His mind had reeled when Madyx had presented his version. How Azian had seduced him, then when he'd left her bed, she'd screamed he'd assaulted her. He'd reacted by gripping her upper arms and shaking her, thus bruising her. The dark marks she'd used to justify her claim.

Had she spoken the truth, great dishonor would have brought Madyx and his father low. Perhaps that had been her goal from the start? Oyaz scowled. So many times he'd pondered her motives and remained puzzled.

Her goal couldn't have been a pairing. For most ladies, it wasn't. Only the Ethera could determine that. So time in each other's arms was all Azian could've hoped for. Unless she birthed a female from their...antics.

Lady Larian, Azian's mother had made demands for reparation, claiming her daughter had been sullied, demeaned, and her honor questioned.

Honor? If only Larian knew of her daughter's poor behavior. Azian had tried to work her wiles on Oyaz, but he'd dismissed her. His last sexual encounter had darkened his soul more than he'd expected for a male fresh from the planet, Gikaet. He and Madyx had known each other since they were damu, had become the best of battle-bonds before experiencing their first battle. They'd just finished their trials into adulthood. Madyx was wilder and a tad younger, his soul not yet in jeopardy. As charming as Azian, they were well suited. But no matter what Oyaz said, Madyx ignored him.

"Mistreating a female is never acceptable, no matter the circumstances," King Xeus said. Beside him, Todyx, Madyx's father folded his arms across his chest, his lips pinched.

Ice shivered across Oyaz's shoulders. This couldn't be good.

Madyx pushed off the bench and strode across to stand before King Xeus. He spread his legs and clasped his hands behind his back, trapping the thick braid brushing his heels.

Oyaz did the same, standing beside Madyx. Todyx stepped off the dais and flanked Madyx.

"To claim such when it is not the truth is also unacceptable." King Xeus gestured to the wailing Lady Azian to join Madyx.

Her cries pierced the great throne room, echoing off the painted, vaulted ceilings.

King Xeus winced, as did they all. "Irritating me will not go well for you, Lady Azian." He clipped the words and faced Madyx. "One month in the Fuyra mines and two feet of honor."

"My King, that is too leni—" A glare from King Xeus silenced Lady Larian.

"Your punishment commences now." King Xeus gestured at Adviser Cales.

"But he is innocent." Oyaz leaped in front of Madyx.

"Is he, Warrior Oyaz? When he ignored your warnings? When he expected such behavior from Lady Azian based on her reputation alone? When he reacted to her manipulation with more anger than an Etterian warrior should display?" King Xeus shook his head. "I am being as lenient and understanding as I can be within our laws."

Madyx said nothing, not even when Oyaz threw a pleading glance at him. He placed his hand on Oyaz's shoulder then trailed Adviser Cales and his father from the throne room.

"Lady Azian, please step forward."

Lady Larian dragged her daughter to stand in front of the dais. Her sniffling had diminished, but she now peppered her whimpers with hiccups. Still, her hair remained tranquil.

"One month in the omeika farms, and two feet of honor. In addition, for your dishonorable behavior—" He held up his hand when she gasped. Her hair shot out in spikes and jabs. "I have taken the rumors into consideration. Many have testified on behalf of Madyx, having experienced similar accusations from you. Do not test me, Lady Azian."

Her mother silenced her with a look.

"You will reattend classes after serving your one month. Perhaps you missed those on comportment and honor." He arched a brow. "Failure to perform well will mean a re-evaluation of your punishment."

He flicked his fingers, and two warriors escorted a wailing Azian from the throne room. Lady Larian scurried after her daughter.

King Xeus slumped and pinched his brow. "Warrior Oyaz, for your wise counsel, I have enrolled you in commander training."

Oyaz jerked back, his eyebrows shooting to his hairline. "My king?" He didn't know what to say. Madyx suffered while he benefited? "My thanks for your confidence in me, but I would prefer to serve alongside Madyx."

King Xeus met his gaze. "It is honorable to make such a request. I cannot, in good conscience, punish a male for acting as a good battle-bond. Your commander training will continue. As to Warrior Madyx, his honor lies in his hands. One month mining Fuyra rock should teach him restraint."

Oyaz pinched his lips. "Thank you, my king."

King Xeus smiled, then dismissed him.

Oyaz thumped his fist against his chest in an Etterian salute and jogged in the direction Madyx had taken. Barreling through the massive gold doors, he veered left to the courtyard from where Adviser Cales meted out the Foot of Honor punishment. Madyx had lost two feet of his braid. Lady Azian wailed as she waited her turn. Her pleas fell on hardened hearts.

"Malia pa," Adviser Cales mumbled, commanding her agitated hair to braid itself. As soon as it did so, he caught the tail and sliced two feet off the end.

She crumpled to the stone paving, her hands touching Adviser Cales's boots. The male stepped back and sauntered off, his tasks done.

He paused beside Oyaz. "Report to the battleship *Phoenix*."

"Thank you, Adviser Cales." Oyaz hesitated, not wanting to miss the chance to bid Madyx farewell. His father pressed his hand to his son's chest and strode off.

"*Phoenix*?" Madyx's breathing was ragged, and sweat dewed his temple.

Oyaz hesitated. "I have been reassigned."

Madyx twitched. "You were punished?" His cheeks darkened, and a pulse ticked at the base of his jaw.

"No." Oyaz couldn't bring himself to reveal the promotion. They were warriors, having yet to decide on their service paths. Madyx had wanted to serve Etteria as a data officer. Oyaz had no preference. Despite not showing an affiliation to data analysis, he would have followed Madyx.

"I expected better of King Xeus," Madyx growled.

Oyaz faced him, his jaw almost dropping. "It is disloyal to speak as such. He could have forced you to spend a year at the mines, Madyx."

"He acted as if this was my fault. I am sick of forgiving females for their dishonorable behavior." He flicked a hand across his shortened braid. "As a male, I must pay for it, while they can do and say whatever they want."

Frowning, Oyaz gripped Madyx's shoulder. He had the right of it, but surely he must have heard Azian's wailing? Witnessed her lose two feet of honor as well? "Did your father—?"

"He is displeased with me. I have brought dishonor on his name." Madyx laughed. "As if I could ever attain a place among our ancestors without battle. I am a data officer in training, what honor awaits me?"

Warriors lingered on the stone walkway outside the clearing. They were ready to escort Madyx to a scimitar. He'd travel to the Fuyra mines to begin his punishment.

"You, my battle-bond, will see me in a month." He splayed his fingers over Oyaz's heart. "And keep the ladies warm for me." Chuckling, he trailed a warrior.

"This way, milady." A warrior gestured to Lady Azian, spurring a fresh wave of sobbing.

"Behave, Azian. You brought this on yourself." Lady Larian kissed her daughter's cheek and flounced off.

"Mother." Her forlorn cry was ignored, and she spun, settled her gaze on Oyaz, and plastered on her sweetest smile.

He snorted. "You heard your mother, Azian. Behave."

She huffed and stomped past the waiting warrior. Her scimitar would deliver her to the omeika farms. Oyaz sighed. Madyx had received the lesser of the two judgments. Mining those ravenous fish was not a task he envied. They tainted Etteria's oceans red yet brought in much revenue as a delicacy. When eaten, their flavor took on the consumer's favorite foods. By serving omeika, a hostess could satisfy all her guests' preferences. At least, Azian would eat omeika while working on the farms.

"This way, Warrior Oyaz."

He twisted and faced the last waiting warrior. "Where is the battleship *Phoenix*?"

"It orbits Yithia. You will travel on board the battleship *Chikara* and serve under Sub-Commander Syna for the duration of your journey. Supreme Commander Xan awaits your service."

Oyaz rolled his right shoulder. Without Madyx beside him, Oyaz was lost, adrift. How he would love to kill a gika now and rid himself of this energy. Instead, he tapped his fingers on his thigh and trailed the warrior to the docking bay southeast of the palace gardens.

He boarded the kuta shuttle, typing on his Optical Data Implant, or O.D.I., embedded in his left wrist. His father and mother needed to be informed of the king's decision and on Oyaz's whereabouts.

The kuta carried him into outer space to the fleet of battleships circling Etteria. What had led to Azian behaving in such a manner? Events in a person's life altered their perception and understanding of honor. Azian's behavior, though not unheard of, wasn't the norm. Females sacrificed their bodies to Etteria in the hopes of bearing daughters. And once a daughter was birthed, the mother would remain with the male who blessed her so. But to move from male to male with no intention of serving Etteria except to incite males against each other, no, that wasn't acceptable.

Azian's beauty had blinded Madyx.

And so he would suffer.

In a month, Oyaz hoped his battle-bond would return a better male.

Chapter Three

Two decades later.

Earth

Year of 2254, September

Izzy typed on her mobile, while slicing glances at Garix and Ronin, looming, casting shadows, eating all her salami and apples. *Listen, Miri, you won't believe the sugar going down. Aliens, my friend. Sexy, tall-as-hell and bronzed aliens. How's things with you?*

Izzy touched base with Miri, her bestie while growing up, at least once a week. Her days were dull, so daily updates weren't feasible. What could she say? Sold out on double fudge again today? Spotted the seventeenth seagull rob a poor tourist? Nope, and she'd just sent a message two days ago. Letting Miri know about this latest development was a must.

The 'how's things with you' was sheer curtesy. Miri spent most of her days on hikes. Look, a tree. Oh, and the same boulder she'd seen last week, month, year? Izzy shuddered. Talk about dull.

Miri's response could take minutes or days, depending on whether she had signal or now. Izzy scored big time when a text buzzed her mobile. *"You've got to be kidding me, Iz. What kind of a news is that?"* The next one pinged as fast. *"Have you been kidnapped? Probed? Shit, do you need a rescue?"*

Izzy giggled. *"Chill. I'm fine. They're big ol' teddy bears. Emphasis on big."*

"Good. My hikes are fully booked for the next six weeks, but I'll take the sat phone with me, just in case. Knowing you, you might need me."

Izzy huffed. She hadn't asked for Miri's help, not since she'd moved to the city. Pinching her lips, she took a moment to admit that Miri might be right. Past experience had taught her dear friend to be prepared when it came to Izzy. When she'd spilled paint on Mom's couch, Miri had been scrubbing right beside Izzy.

"Thanks, babe. Appreciate it."

She beamed at Garix and tossed the mobile onto the couch. One moment, no one stood by the door to the enclosed balcony. Next, Caro clung to Malo whose intense expression focused on Caro's face. Izzy wanted to gawk at that much chemistry, instead, she fell on her trusted overreaction.

"Holy shit," she squealed. "You can't go around evaporating, then bam, coming back. Give a girl a warning, please."

She fanned her flaming cheeks for poor Caro, Izzy's roommate and bestie, looked smitten and dazed. Her blue gaze was distant, and her fingers trembled when she swept aside her brown hair. She left dark-and-sensual Malo for the safety of her bedroom, abandoning Izzy. Like being around three alien warriors was the norm for Izzy. She snorted and dipped her head when Malo arched a black-winged brow at her. His ice blue eyes seemed to pierce through her, as if everything she'd done, thought, dreamed were on display. She tucked her legs under her and raised her chin, meeting his gaze. Confidence or fearlessness could be feigned.

"Izzy, sweetheart, could you come here for a sec?" Caro called.

Izzy leaped off the couch and bolted for Caro's bedroom, grateful for the reprieve. "What is it?" She popped her head around the door.

"I need your help." Her friend beckoned from the bathroom.

Izzy giggled and entered the room, closed the door then tiptoed into the bathroom. Caro snapped the door shut, then ran the basin's taps at maximum. What was this?

"I need to talk to you," she whispered.

Izzy smirked, dragging her gaze from the flowing water. "I can see that."

"They have excellent hearing." Caro shoved Izzy onto the closed toilet. Like a good girl, Izzy stayed seated and clasped her hands between her thighs. A few minutes passed as Caro paced.

"Firstly, they believe in soulmates. They call them Dar Eths."

"What?" Izzy squeaked. "For real for real?" She laughed and applauded, delighted by this news. Soulmates were the stuff of dreams, soap operas, and romcoms. Nothing wrong with that delusion. Every girl needed something to hope for, even if it was an impossibility. "That's awesome."

"Yes and no." Caro winced.

Izzy gaped. She squirmed on the seat. "Malo's yours?"

"According to him." Caro clasped her cheeks, going from pale to flushed.

From delusion to reality? Hell yes. Izzy mumbled, "Hot jam and buttered toast."

"He's given me time to think about it."

Izzy froze, then fire exploded from her chest outward. "What? Why? What's there to think about?" She pointed at the door. "Are you insane? You snatch that man up this instant, Caro. He's the best thing that's ever happened to you."

Caro waved her hands, trying to get Izzy to lower her voice. "It's not that easy." She snuck glances at the door, as if Malo would burst into the bathroom. Although, Izzy could imagine it with ease. A steel door would be no hindrance.

She grabbed Caro's hands and squeezed. "Babe, I know you're scared, I see that, but to not grasp this opportunity for happily-ever-after? Then you take one for the team. You do this for all women on this planet who would snap him up on his offer in a heartbeat."

Caro paled. "I would love forever with him, Izzy."

Wait? What was happening here? Caro was deadly serious. "Do you think I could have a soulmate?" Izzy's breath lodged in her throat. Was it so simple? Could she just choose an Etterian? Claim one?

Caro grinned. "You want one?"

"Hell, yes. To be loved forever, to be treated as if I matter?" Izzy tilted her head to the side on a sigh. Whatever she needed to do, consider it done.

"Malo said he knew the moment he met me. Since Garix and Ronin remain protective and haven't tried to kiss you, I would say neither of them is your soulmate."

"Right, so I just have to find my alien." Izzy rolled her eyes. "Not daunting at all."

Caro gazed at her reflection in the mirror above the basin. "I can't believe I'm considering this."

"If you don't do this, Caro, I'll be so furious with you. Even Simmy will be disappointed."

"Simmy would not," Caro gasped.

"Then think of your aunt." Izzy wagged a finger in Caro's face. "She didn't raise a fool, Caroline Masterson."

Caro flinched. "That's a low blow."

Izzy hugged Caro, crushing her for a second before releasing her. "Not at all, babe. Your aunt would have dragged you onto the spaceship by your ears." She grimaced. "She was stronger than she looked." Izzy rubbed her ear. "Caro, I've seen how Malo stares at you. He's smitten."

"Smitten?" Caro cupped her mouth which smothered her chuckle.

"He sniffs you, for tart's sake. He's always touching and kissing you. And he punched your ex in the face. What more do you need?"

Caro jerked back. "You know about Gary?"

"He was crying like a baby when we went for coffee. He tried to get the E.A.F. to arrest Garix and Ronin, pointing at their uniform and making demands." Thankfully, Earth Armed Forces, the global police, hadn't been called.

Caro beamed.

"Now, hurry up." Izzy switched off the water then left the bathroom and bedroom. When she stepped into the lounge, three men gazed at her. Right. She ran her hands over her hips and offered a small smile. "She'll be out soon."

Garix grumbled something to Malo, then glanced at Izzy. "I shall cleanse. Lady Izabelle's care is yours."

She squeaked when he vanished. It boggled the mind, it did. Made her distrust her eye sight too. What could she say? Prior to Etterians, something or someone disappearing before her eyes was pure magic—the kind with rabbits and hats.

Realizing she was gawking, she lowered her chin to her chest. Her stomach gurgled, reminding her she hadn't eaten since a breakfast protein bar.

"Caro, are you ready?" Izzy called. "I'm starving."

"I'm here," Caro trudged into the lounge as if she wasn't happy about having soulmate.

Hell, Izzy would be ecstatic. Foolish woman. No more dating. No more broken hearts, hopes, dreams. Stuck with a man who'd treasure her no matter— She glanced at Malo. Did someone's weight matter to these aliens.

"I'm running out of shoes," Caro said. "Where's Garix?"

"He went to *cleanse*." Izzy bit into an apple, and hummed. She savored the crunchy tart flesh for a moment, then leaned across, grabbed another apple and tossed it at Ronin. "He waited for you two to return before evaporating. Said something about ensuring I'm safe." She paused when Ronin and Malo didn't respond. Their frowns ramped the tension in the air. Angling her head, she pressed the cool apple to her chin then summoned her false joyfulness. "I almost died. There was bacteria on the counter. Oh, heavens, thank you, my heroes." She threw a hand over her temple in a melodramatic pose, her sigh exaggerated. Exhaustion dipped her shoulders. A vacation sounded awesome.

Caro snorted.

"You mock our need to protect you, Izzy," Malo said, his frown thunderous to behold.

Izzy froze and raised a wide-eyed gaze. Shit, had she just pissed off the alien ambassador. A glance confirmed Caro had stiffened too. "We're in our apartment, Malo," Izzy said around a bite of the apple. "There are no wild animals, no attackers, just a pain-in-my-ass neighbor." She peered at him then forced a sweet smile. "I'm sorry if I've offended."

"We may be *too* overprotective, but your safety matters to us," he said in a gentle tone.

"It matters more to Garix. He is large for an Etterian male. Your size calls forth his protective instincts," Ronin said, who tossed an apple core and plucked another apple from the basket.

"Thank you for explaining. I'll try to be more understanding," Izzy said. Poor Garix, gentle giant meets sassy her? She winced, admitting she'd need to be careful when teasing the man. Despite deciding that, her mouth ran away with her. "But if he doesn't get his ass here soon, I'll need to be rushed to the hospital. My stomach's swallowing me whole."

"She's joking, just Izzy being Izzy." Caro waved her hands at Ronin and Malo, who looked like they were about to call for medical assistance. "And you, can it. You ate enough yesterday, so much so there should be two of you."

"Garix and Ronin ate more than their share." Izzy pouted while licking her thumb. "I had to suck the butter from my fingers to avoid starvation."

Caro arched a brow. "You would've licked your fingers anyway. Now get us two taxis, and allow Malo and Ronin a little peace."

Finally, action. Izzy tossed the apple and bounced out of the apartment, slamming the door behind her. She skipped down the stairs, content to do that than sit and wait with two men staring at her. What, was she supposed to break into a dance number, jazz hands and all? Just once, she'd like to meet a man who didn't rely on her to entertain him. Being joyful twenty-four-seven was a soul sucking pain in her ass. Pushing on the front door, she stepped onto the solar-paneled walkway and raised her gaze to the shimmering dome. Behind that was the bright sunlight of a sunny sky. So pretty, and for a moment, she could pretend all was right in her world. That she was normal, that her life had meaning, that she wasn't a tight bundle of anxiety-driven habits, and that, somehow, she was loved.

Sighing, she dragged her gaze to the cars whizzing by and held up two fingers. As expected, two taxis pulled to a halt. She dipped her head in and commanded each S.A.D.I. to start their meters. Then she faced the façade of her apartment building and folded her arms. Time ticked by, with no Caro appearing.

Gritting her teeth, Izzy dipped her head through the windows and instructed the S.A.D.I.'s to wait. She took the stairs two steps at a time and burst along the parapeted walkway to where Garix guarded the apartment door. She spared him a glance before stepping inside. What the hell? Malo had Caro in his embrace. Her dear friend's cheeks were the color of ripe peaches. Ronin tapped on the holographic numbers rising from his forearm. That they'd kept Izzy waiting proved the very point that she didn't matter...to anyone.

"Guys, the taxis won't wait forever, y'know," she said from the door. Garix hovered behind her, his great bulk casting her in shadow.

Ronin marched across to her, his flickering forearm forgotten. Assuming Caro and Malo would follow, Izzy squeezed between Garix and the door. With two towering Etterians trailing her, she marched along the walkway. A glance behind showed the gaping apartment door.

"Flaming nipples," she hissed then screamed, "Caroline."

When a giggling Caro and a dazed Malo slammed the apartment door behind them, Izzy stomped down the stairs to the taxis. "About damned time," she huffed when Caro finally exited the building.

Without another word, Izzy ushered Garix and Ronin into a taxi. Squashed between them, she let their grumblings roll over her. Chaotic thoughts pointed to one thing, that change was coming, and the pessimistic part of her expected it to be bad. Regardless, her life would no longer be the same.

"What is it, *ensa*?" Garix shifted to the right, as close to the door as possible.

She frowned. Did he have a problem with her body touching his?

"I must apologize, Lady Izzy, I did not mean to crush you." He grimaced and tried to plaster his great bulk to the door again.

She stiffened then slumped, while tears pressed to the backs of her eyes. Here was a man as destroyed as herself due their sizes. She squeezed his arm and plastered on a watery smile. "You're not, my big ol' teddy bear." She took a deep breath. "In fact, I find you presence comforting."

He blinked then relaxed. "You do?"

"Yup." She popped the 'p.' "Nothing and no one would hurt me with you near."

He studied her, harrumphed and faced ahead.

"Garix thinks you lie." Ronin scowled.

She gasped. "I do not. It's rude to imply—"

"I do not imply," Ronin snapped.

She held up her scrawny arm. "Look at me. Only someone awfully strong and big can get through Garix to reach me. I doubt such a person exists." She cupped Garix's cheek to hold his gaze. "And for that certainty, I'm at peace, content in the knowledge that you *can* protect me."

"My size does not bother you?" he asked, a brow arched.

"Does my size bother you?" she asked, arching a brow to mimic his.

He grinned. "No, *ensa*."

"Good." She dropped her hand and squeezed between him and Ronin, pressing her shoulders to the seat. The breakfast place she'd chosen made the biggest stack of protein pancakes. She was sure they'd appreciate the buttery goodness. A future loomed of her feeding Ronin and Garix while Caro and Malo lived a happy life. Izzy would have to find contentment in that, in being the aunt and not the mother, to being the maid of honor but never the bride.

Chapter Four

BLAH BLAH, ALIENS WANT *a chance to date human women*. Izzy scanned the crowd filled with journalists and mad hatters eager to flash their boobs at said aliens. She barely listened to Caro standing on the platform, since she sounded like a pimp. The thing was, the alien man had to fall to a knee first. No amount of pimping or boobs flashed would snare him.

Izzy snorted. She would be front and center if that was all it took.

The sun was a gorgeous pale yellow, warm against her upturned face. After the massive breakfast she'd consumed, along with killing time with Ronin and Garix, she was ready for a nap.

She sighed, leaned to the right, and rested her temple on Garix's massive, bronzed bicep.

Etterians.

Tall with dark-blue eyes and thick, black braids down to their heels, wearing military gear like they were bikers.

Gorgeous and desperate for human women, or so they claimed.

Caro had snagged one.

Izzy wanted to pout, to curse the fates. Then again, who would want to deal with the bundle of trouble she was?

She and Garix stood to the rear of the crowd, amid stranglers. Not once did she study those around her, except to catch glimpses of hooded men. That didn't alarm her. With the press present, not all would want to expose their identities. She shivered. Besides, with the Etterians looming, who would mess with her.

"*Ensa?*" Garix arched a brow. "Are you unwell?"

Oh, the dear, sweet, teddy bear. Seven feet of solid muscle and all heart. He wasn't hers either. She smothered a giggle in his bulky bicep. Had he been, with her shortness and his tallness, they would've made a funny picture in family photos. And Ronin was on his own mission, grumbling at her, or guarding her with a vengeance as if his life depended on it. Said man, wearing a formidable scowl, paced toward the dais then back to Garix.

Rubbing her belly, she swallowed a yawn. Last night's disaster of a movie and club visit, with Malo brawling in front of a coffee shop and Garix complaining about 'Earthian' mating rituals, had been entertaining but exhausting. Still, they'd reacted to her in a dress better than any man she'd dated.

Smiling, she studied Malo and the way he gazed at Caro, as if she was his air, joy, future, and hope. That's what Izzy wanted, not the sweet concern in Garix's eyes because her tininess alarmed his seven-foot self or Ronin who tolerated her out of duty as an older brother would.

The crowd jeered, closed in, and blocked her view, so she shuffled to the left, rising on her tippy-toes to see Caro.

An arm snaked around her collarbone, and she frowned. "Garix, you don't need—"

A bang pierced the air beside her, ringing her ears.

Chaos erupted. The crowd squealed and scattered, clearing a path to the dais. The pounding of feet on the solar-paneled parking lot overwhelmed Izzy's thoughts. Caro had slumped to the ground with a red stain on her blouse. Izzy gasped, then struggled against Garix's grip. It didn't loosen. Instead, it tightened and tugged her back. She could barely breathe. Digging in her nails got her nowhere. She froze when Malo's face contorted in a roar, his sorrow so potent, it silenced the panicked crowd for a second. Trying to reach her bestie, Izzy fought, grasping at Garix's arm. She blinked. Instead of choking her, the huge Etterian leaped onto the dais to stand beside Ronin.

Ice drenched Izzy's spine. As if she were underwater, time slowed, and she dipped her focus to a silver-gray arm. Who the hell? She rasped Garix's name, not sure whether he'd hear her, but she had to try. Daring a glance at her attacker, she blinked at the humanoid shark, his sabretooth fangs dimpling his wide bottom lip. Oh, hell, no. She wasn't going with that.

Slumping, she tried to make her petite-self heavier, but when the sharkman didn't slow its backward run, she dug her heels and nails in. Neither worked to release her. A glance at the dais showed Ronin with his strange weapon drawn. Garix scanned the crowd. No doubt looking for her, the idiot. She was half-tempted to re-move her nails from the sharkman's arm and wave. Hell, might as well add "cooey" to that, like she was out on a picnic and merely wanted to catch a friend's attention.

Seeing no help coming from anyone, humans and Etterians alike, she gritted her teeth. Typical. Want something done properly...

Twisting, she opened her mouth wide and sank her teeth into the slimy fish-like flesh of the bastard's arm. Rotten, mercury-infested, castor oil coated her tongue.

The creature hissed, and in an instant, she was free. Not that she ran. She fell to her hands and knees and gagged like a cat unable to spit out a furball. Tears burned behind her eyes as shivers racked her body. When black boots disturbed the dust at her splayed hands, she stumbled back, planning on crawling her way to freedom.

"Ensa."

At Garix's deep timbre, every muscle in her body melted, along with her tear ducts. And into his arms he swept her, as if she weighed nothing more than a tub of ice cream. A gag followed, worsened by his jarring when he sprinted onto the dais to where Malo kneeled. Caro was nowhere, and the abject sorrow darkening Malo's face meant bad news.

Izzy knew that look, had seen it in her father's eyes. Then, it had been her fault.

"Where's Caro?" That high-pitched voice drenched with panic couldn't be hers? "Garix?" She wiggled in his arms, desperate to be released. What was she? A sack of potatoes?

"She has been taken, *ensa*."

Izzy gaped, gagged, wiped the drool off her bottom lip with a flick of a wrist, then gagged again. "Malo will find her, right?" Nausea wrenched her gut. She shuddered, trying to keep down the bile climbing up her throat.

Garix patted her shoulder. "You did well, escaping that Yithian."

Gag. "Sure, then why do I feel horrible?" Shiver.

"Izzy, what did you do?" Ronin narrowed his gaze on her.

She raised her chin, despite the gag-reflex spasming. "I bit him."

"Alodon's balls, female," Ronin roared. "Are you insane?"

"Get her to medical." Malo's stoic voice sliced through her panic. He stumbled to his feet and tapped his forearm. "Afax, four to medical."

"Port?" Gag. "Oh, hell, no. I'm not getting—" Tingles assaulted her body, added to the shivers taking turns to lambaste her, the sharp twists of nausea, and the *hoo-whack* of the gagging. "—zapped."

The bright sunlight was gone, the cacophony of the dispersing crowd silenced. She stood in the middle of a gray-walled room, with trestle tables to one side, a sparring mat on the other, and Garix ushering her to a blinding-white room in the corner.

"Medic Brynr," Garix growled, "Lady Izzy needs attention."

An older male scurried forward with a 1920's cellular phone. It flickered lights, and had she seen it in an antique store, she might have thought it was used to shave her privates.

"I do not see an injury." Brynr scowled, running the shaver over her.

Two gags followed, and she clung to Garix, hoping to stop the advancing twitches.

He curled an arm around her, drawing her against his warm body. "She bit a Yithian."

The older male stilled, widened his eyes, and played with the device.

The *hoo-whack* stopped mid-way, and the churning nausea faded. Score one to the shaver. She slumped, only now registering the fine layer of sweat coating her skin. "What the flaming nipples just happened?"

Poor Brynr jumped back as if she'd punched him.

"Sorry, Brynr, thank you for healing me." She offered him the sweetest smile she could muster, then faced Garix, poking him in his chest with a pointed finger. Pain burned her knuckle since he was harder than he looked, but with the way red circled her vision, she didn't care.

"What," Poke. "Just." Jab. "Happened?" She curled her finger into her palm, hoping she hadn't broken it.

A rumble swept through the room, reminding her they weren't alone. Many blue gazes fixed on her, but she glared at them, sidled to the right, and used Garix's massive frame to shield herself.

"So help me, Garix. You better start spilling the beans, or I'll..." Shit. She chewed on her lip. If only she had an Etterian handbook. A dramatic pause would follow while she scanned the 'How to threaten an alien' section. "Cry?" She arched a hopeful brow at him. That worked on human men, might do the trick on aliens too.

"Ensa, you know what happened. Malo saw the Yithian grab you, thus was not focused on his Dar Eth. When she was harmed with your Earthian—"

"Human," she huffed.

He squeezed his eyes shut for a second. "—weapon, he rushed to reach her, but by then, they had ported—"

"Zapped." She shivered, and a phantom gag itched her throat.

"—her. She is gone. Operations Commander Malo will find her. He can do nothing else with the Ethera driving him."

"The what now?" Izzy rubbed her brow, swearing a grandmother of headaches was forming. A dull throb pulsed behind her left eye. "Spill." Spinning, she strode to Brynr. She gestured to her eye. "Headache."

He shook his head but was wise not to say anything. Scanning her with his shaver, the intense throbbing eased, and her eye stopped watering.

"Thank you. Garix...? I'm waiting. What's this Ethera?" She faced him, raised her pointed finger, then thought better of it. Thankfully, a tear slipped out—the remnants of the headache. Adding an overdramatic sniffle and a trembling bottom lip had the poor man darting across to her.

And she was airborne, crushed against his massive chest while he patted her head as if she was a kitten. With her face squished against his armor, she was lucky she could breathe. Right. She shouldn't use womanly wiles when everything she touched didn't end well. Case in point.

"It is what sparks an Eth finding his Dar Eth."

"Oh. Then why couldn't you just tell me? And you can let me down."

He dropped her, but before she could scramble or squeal, he caught her at the last minute. It happened so fast, her thick mass of hair bounced, covering her face. She harrumphed, wishing she could smack his arm for manhandling her.

"Where's Malo and Ronin?" She studied the men watching her, pretty sure she knew Ronin's face well enough to spot him.

"Searching for Caro."

Right. She folded her arms across her chest. "How?" When Garix opened his mouth to speak, she halted him with a twirl of a finger. "Pack up...ship and haul ass after what? What if the sharkman—"

"Yithian."

"—didn't leave Earth?" She glared. "How long's this going to take?"

"As long as it takes."

She smacked his arm and winced. "Damn..." She bit her lip, having been about to call him a mountain. "What can I do?" Falling into pacing, she focused on the metallic floor instead of the 'crowd.'

When Garix didn't respond, she chanced a peek.

His bronzed brow was furrowed with his dark eyebrows sinking as if she'd asked him to explain the meaning of life. "Why would you want to help?"

She threw her hands up and muffled a squeal. "Caro is my bestie, mine to protect, to cherish, as expected of friends. What would you do if your friend—"

"Battle-bond."

She glared again. "—was shot then zapped?"

"I would track him on his O.D.I."

She sighed. Did he have to sound logical? "His what now?"

Garix touched his forearm and those holographic letters leaped into life. "Optical Data Implant."

Aliens and their newfangled technology, though she had to admit to seeing similar or even exact images on billboards and digi-mags. Tech and her didn't get along well. It was yet another way for her to mess things up.

She held up a hand, curled into a fist, then thought twice about punching him. Pulling her hair out only made it grow back curlier, so that was out. She sucked in a calming breath. "Okay, let me explain it like this. I. Need. To. Know. How. Malo's. Going. To. Find. Caro." Squeezing the bridge of her nose helped for a second.

"With the help of a data officer. He will scan all ship frequencies in the area. That alone will confirm whether Caro is on your homeworld or not. In addition, since a Yithian tried to take you, this implies Yithia is involved. Malo will waste no time in traveling there. If the Maker blesses this mission, he may find Caro en route."

"Travel?" Izzy squeaked. "How...how far is this Yithia?"

"Two weeks."

"Holy...shit," she whispered. Space travel wasn't for the fainthearted. "So, there's nothing I can do but wait for news?"

"Yes."

A familiar helplessness settled on her. The only way to deal with it was to keep herself busy. She could be alone for fourteen days.

As if on cue, Garix's stomach gurgled. "Hungry?"

No, she wasn't. Not in the slightest. She forced a smile. Anything in her mouth would be better than the lingering vile sharkman taste. "Pizza?"

Garix's eyelids fluttered, and the slow sensual smile he blessed her with snatched what air remained in her lungs.

"Grizzly," she huffed. "Then let's head home." She grabbed his wrists and peered around him at their audience.

"Ensa—"

He was going to argue with her about this? She had a right to go home. Or was she a prisoner? "Garix, I'm tired. Caro's been kidnapped. You've just told me I'm useless. On top of it all, I bit a Yithian. I want *my* home and bed."

He studied her, tapped his O.D.I., then snaked an arm around her.

Her eyes widened as it dawned on her what he was about to do. "Garix, no. Not the zapping thingy. Can't we take a spaceship—"

The idiot chuckled. "You are a *damu* with your fear, Izzy. It is just porting."

She swallowed the bile rising to choke her.

"Two to port to Lady Izzy's housing unit."

Tingles assaulted her again, and that phantom *hoo-whack* tickled her throat. Finding herself standing in her living room did little to hold back the wrenching nausea. While Garix dug in the fridge, she pulled her phone out of her pocket and placed an order for many large boxes of pizza.

"I'm off to shower," she called. And maybe twelve mouth gargles would remove the oily fishiness clinging to her teeth.

He grunted and chewed on a stick of salami while sprawled on the couch. He looked as if he had nowhere else he needed to be. If he was going to stay, the couch wouldn't do for a permanent bed. And with Caro gone for who knew how long, Izzy might as well set him up in her room...for now. Two weeks to Yithia and that long back? She sniffed and choked back a sob.

Sadness drooped her lips, her eyes darkened, and in the reflection in the bathroom mirror, a solitary tear streaked down a pale cheek.

Too much had changed too fast, and she didn't know how to deal with it.

Chapter Five

Days later.

Earth

Izzy scooped another spoonful of lemon sorbet into her mouth, swearing upside-down, she could still taste the alien's arm from when she bit him. Here she was, in her ice cream parlor while a Malo chased after a vanished Caro. Who knew where across the galaxies and damn stars he'd find her. Not that Izzy doubted he would either. The man had reeked of danger. What worried her was how long before Caro was safe. All knew, time mattered in kidnapping cases.

She sighed. From harrowing days to this. Outside the sky was its usual blue, the clouds were wisps of shredded cotton wool, and the variegated blue waves crashed across the sand. And here she sat, with her elbows on the counter, watching folks live their marvelous lives.

"Argh, I have eaten too much."

She whipped her gaze at Garix hovering in the office doorway. "You say that every day."

He harumphed, even as he ran his dark blue gaze over the flavors available while rubbing his flat-as-a-pancake stomach.

"Listen here, big guy, if you didn't bring in the masses, you'd have to start paying. No one on this planet can afford to feed you." She wagged a finger at him.

Seven feet of bronze muscle in military black dominated the small store. And yet, he refused to leave her, claiming she needed protection. Showing him her teeth had made no impact, like biting hadn't saved her life. Shrugging, she scooped his favorite—black cherry—into a new container. Without him, she would be bored up to her eyeballs. As predicted, he lived with her, now occupying Caro's too-small bed. His legs dangling off the bed was hilarious, which was why Izzy hadn't ordered a longer bed for him.

"Anything yet?" She asked him at least five times a day if he'd heard about Caro.

"Nothing. Not since Ronin messaged that they were going dark on all comms."

Right. Garix had mentioned that already. She studied him, curling her lips in suspicion. "You'd tell me the moment you hear?"

"Of course." He said it with confidence, but still, she wasn't sure he would.

The clock in her office ticked closer to lunchtime when mamas, blushing teenagers, or plastic housewives flooded her store to ogle Garix. Not one had brought him to his knee—the sign he had found his soulmate or Dar Eth. Caro had her Malo, who hunted her with a single-minded determination that scattered Izzy's wits. That's what she wanted. An alien of her own, with those ice-blue eyes, his obsidian hair down to his heels, and shoulders broad enough to handle her sass.

She had no one, nothing, except Garix's friendship.

"How about pizza tonight?" She wiggled her eyebrows. "I want cheese, four kinds of toppings, and maybe deep base?"

He rumbled around the spoon hanging from his mouth and pressed his palm to the glass counter.

"Thought we could visit my sister?" She bounced around the counter to offer him the black cherry and throw a pout at him. Although, she shouldn't have bothered when he didn't understand most of her expressions.

"Your sister? As in blood-bond?" He arched a brow.

"Yup." She grabbed the waste bin and wheeled it toward the double glass doors. "Going to the incinerator before the rush hour hits."

He trailed her.

She paused, raising her face to meet his gaze. "No, don't follow. It's out back."

He frowned. "Ensa, it is my honor to guard you."

"But, Garix, if you follow me, then I have to lock up the store. I need you here to handle the customers." She fluttered her eyelashes with mock innocence. A moment's privacy would be wonderful since the only alone-time she had was when she used the bathroom.

He grimaced, and a shadow darkened his eyes.

"Listen, sweetcakes, if for some strange coincidence, a gray shark-man—"

"Yithian."

She huffed since he was missing the point. "If a *Yithian* should attempt another kidnapping, I'll holler like a pregnant heifer, screaming blue murder, enough to draw the crowds."

His eyelids fluttered at her choice of words as his O.D.I. hurried to educate him.

She bolted out the store. Giggling at how mean she'd been to pull that on him, she skip-jogged along the glass façade to the rear of her shop where the waste incinerator dominated the back wall. Massive pipes traveled underground for the gasses generated by the fast-tracked decomposition process. Caro had tried to explain it all, but Izzy wasn't a smart cookie like her physicist bestie.

"Izzy."

Ducking her head at Garix's roar, she clipped the bin in place, and hit the red button, tapping her foot as it did its thing.

"At last."

She squeaked and faced the man standing too close for comfort. Peering around him, she frowned, wondering how he'd managed to sneak up on her. So much for hollering like a heifer. His brown hair fell across his forehead in greasy clumps, sticking up at the ends, as if he'd just rolled out of bed. She ran her gaze over the slept-in pants and button-up shirt he wore.

"Thomas Tenet from What's Hot digi-mag. How do you feel about these alien warriors taking our women?" He held his forearm closer to her face, the flickering light under the skin indicated he was recording. Hmph, it looked like an O.D.I. How out of date was she?

She glared at him. Damn journalists. "No comment." Facing the incinerator, she waited for the light to switch to green, then punched the start button.

"And where is Caroline Masterson? Have they kidnapped her? Is she working the brothels on the far side of the galaxy we have yet to map?

Izzy growled, shoving her hands into her pockets, ready to bitch slap the man. Couldn't they leave her alone? The countless times they harassed her, posed as customers in her shop in the hopes of nailing a comment, and still, she'd said nothing. She gritted her teeth, gathering the tattered remnants of her patience. With an arched brow at him, hoping to appear unperturbed, she dusted non-existent lint off her parlor uniform, patted her hair barely restrained in a hairnet, and wrapped her fingers around the bin's handle. He lunged between the bin and the sidewalk, his eyes wide. His cheeks trembled, and for a second, she thought he might burst into tears like a toddler who'd dropped their ice cream.

"Please, I just want to know what happened," Thomas whined. "The media vids show you being attacked by a two-legged shark. Did you know—?"

"Attacked? More like an attempted kidnapping." Her vision blurred red with black spots around the edges. She jerked as she tried to hogtie her emotions when she never did so, never kept anything inside. "I bit the alien ass, that's what I did. After they shot Caro with an antique pistol—"

She snapped her lips shut, and with a violent nudge to his abdomen, wheeled the bin past him.

Then, as anger set her chest ablaze, she faced him. "Etterians are trying to protect us. There's a spaceship chasing after whoever has Caro. I don't know if it's the sharks, I just know there are people out there eager to farm us for whatever gain. I'm going to side with the most powerful race, but that's just me. I don't have plans to die anytime soon, but hey, if you want to chase away a stronger and more advanced species, leave me out of it."

She rounded the corner and slammed into Garix, bouncing off his hard stomach. He caught her by the elbow while glaring at Thomas.

"Are you well, *ensa*?" Garix's deep voice soothed her ruffled feathers.

She released a long sigh. "Just an irritating journalist, Garix."

"Why do you have a bodyguard? Are they manipulating or drugging you?" Thomas held up his arm as he inched nearer to her and farther from Garix.

"Garix is my friend, you ass. Besides, why would I need protection?" She raised her chin and sauntered off, leaving Garix to pull the bin behind them.

"You are my friend too," Garix said as he clipped the bin in place behind the counter. "The closest I have are battle-bonds. It pleases me you think of me as such, Izzy."

She snorted, despite the sting of tears. Her one bestie was too far away for comfort, and visiting her sister sent Izzy into the dark side. She closed her eyes to calm the slithering oily guilt that wouldn't leave her, no matter what she tried. A lifetime of making amends couldn't fix what she'd done.

Blinking at Garix, she forced a smile. "Like I would let just anyone live with me."

Unable to resist, she threw her arms around his waist, as best she could with their height differences. He patted her shoulder since they had yet to discuss human social etiquette. At least, he no longer ate a stick of salami like a bar of chocolate. Well, not in front of her. Small steps.

"When someone hugs you, you wrap an arm around them."

He chuckled. "I know what a hug is, *ensa*." Sliding his hands under her armpits, he hoisted her as if she was a six-year-old, pinning her against his chest. Her feet dangled. "Better." He squeezed, and she swore she heard a rib crack.

"Can't. Breathe."

He released her, and gravity took over, yet when her sneakers touched down, nothing jarred except where he gripped her upper arms. Sure, she was small, but did he have to manhandle her like a doll?

"Does Earth have giant females?" He scanned her, then draped his arm across her shoulders. Her knees almost buckled under the added weight.

"Does Etteria have tiny males?" She grinned.

Giggling preceded the ding of the shop bell. Garix bolted for the safety of the office. Teenagers barreled in, their school bags hanging off their shoulders. They rose on their tippy-toes to sneak a peek at him through the glass. Izzy considered ordering him a bigger apron and forcing him to stand behind the counter.

She laughed. There was no way she could get all his hair into a net, and he would eat while he served. Sighing, she pulled on a fresh pair of disposable gloves and waited for the estrogen masses to get their fill of him.

Maybe she should close shop early today. Gone was the sense of accomplishment she'd enjoyed when she'd first bought the ice cream parlor. At that time, a steady income and mostly something to do had been her motives, but with Caro out there in the unknown, where did Izzy fit into the picture?

She couldn't abandon Caro, nor could she leave Simmy on Earth. Miri could survive anywhere, so Izzy didn't feel guilt about an even greater distance between them. They had the kind of friendship that time and absence didn't diminish.

And if Izzy found her soulmate, her Eth, then what?

The shop had to go.

She scanned the turquoise-pink walls, the various trays of sorbet or ice cream, and the swirly patterns on the tiled flooring. Papa and Milly's next door had once asked her to sell. A trip there this afternoon would give her some sort of direction.

If they bought Cheery Cherry, then the universe, the fates, and the powers-that-be had decided. Izzy would be happy with that. Then all she had to do was convince Simmy to fly the galaxy with her and Caro. Her sister could sculpt anywhere.

To leave all this behind? Izzy released a slow breath, as if an anchor-like heaviness was taken off her shoulders.

She bit her inner cheek as a wave of despair trembled the polite smile she wore. A relocation for Simmy meant relearning the layout of her new home. Could Izzy do that to her sister? Would Simmy fight her on this?

"Oh, death by chocolate, please, two scoops in a cup." A young mother rested a hand on the counter with her card clutched between her fingers. Clinging to her jeans was a small girl, pigtails flying along with her tutu as she twirled. "And strawberry in a cone, one scoop."

When Izzy circled the counter to offer the girl the cone, she'd vanished. A squeal reached her from the office where she tugged on Garix's hand, begging him to play.

Her mom gasped and hurried to intercept. "Cindy, sweetheart, leave the nice man alone."

Garix exited the office, carrying the little girl as if she were a bomb about to explode. His eyes were wide, and a smile teased his gaping mouth.

"Spin me." Cindy giggled. "Mama, I can touch the ceiling." She stretched to brush her fingers across the pink stars Izzy had spent days painting.

"I'm so sorry," the mom said, wringing her hands as she peered at Garix, but having to tilt her head back to maintain eye contact.

"Having fun, Garix?" Izzy teased, offering the girl her ice cream, fully expecting a messy Etterian warrior to emerge from this.

With one arm looped around his neck, Cindy licked her ice cream before wiping it across Garix's mouth. "Yummy."

"Oh." The mom's face contorted in dismay. "She's learning to share."

"Don't worry about it. Garix's a natural with children." Izzy laughed when he glared at her while pink ice cream dripped off his chin.

The teenagers sighed as one when he lowered the girl into her mom's outstretched arms. Izzy offered him the towel hanging from her back pocket. He took it with a flick of a wrist and disappeared into the office again.

The mom clasped her daughter's hand, ensuring no more disappearances would occur. "I'm truly sorry—"

"I'm not. Here's yours." Izzy handed over the cup, accepted payment, then waved at Cindy as they left the store. Now that was fun. Eyeing the simpering teenagers, Izzy arched a brow. "Who's next?"

Chapter Six

Etterian Battleship Valiant
Speeding away from Etteria
The common
12254 Years, 9th to 10th Month

SEATED IN THE COMMON, with his kreso cooling and momaberry sauce congealing, Oyaz nursed a hot chocolate as he waded through endless communications. Flicking a finger, he scrolled through the holographic texts his O.D.I. displayed.

He paused mid-comm and raised his head. Something had disturbed his concentration. With their advanced hearing, it was rude to eavesdrop, yet one word had snagged his attention. He tilted his head to listen.

"...Macera..."

Following the voice, he narrowed on a warrior sipping giyua juice, an empty plate before him.

Oyaz pushed off his seat, crossed the common, and flattened his palm on the Maloidian steel table. "What about Macy?"

"Supreme Commander Oyaz." The warrior saluted with a fist against his chest.

Oyaz winced at having broken protocol. "My apologies for listening in, warrior. What of Macera?"

"Queen Macera is King Xeus's Dar Eth."

Oyaz grinned, the smile claiming him before he could thwart it. "Truly?"

"Yes, which bodes well for us, Supreme Commander."

Oyaz rubbed the spot over his heart. "That it does. You too may find your Dar Eth, warrior. We need only protect Earth."

Sauntering off, he headed for his quarters, wanting privacy to comm Macy. Why hadn't she, Nuos, or Azan let him know? Scowling, he paused in front of the large display vid mounted to the wall in his quarters.

"Macera Mitchell." Nothing happened. Not a flicker or a connection. "Pilot Krist, what is the meaning of this?"

The male's face appeared on the vid. "My apologies, Supreme Commander, all communication with the queen follows the same protocol as with King Xeus. Patching you through to Adviser Cales."

Oyaz gritted his teeth, and his nostrils flared. She was *his* frie nd... He sighed. And not his queen? Drawing in calming breaths, he worked through his unusual reaction. The last time he'd been so volatile was when Macy had demonstrated how to slow dance. Thankfully, he and Illan had talked her out of ever doing that in front of his males.

"Supreme Commander Oyaz, how may I assist?" Cales focused on his O.D.I., but when Oyaz hesitated, Cales raised his gaze.

"I wish to..." Oyaz grimaced. "Chat with Macy... Queen Macera."

"Chat?" Cales's eyelids fluttered. "Yes, of course. My queen is with the children. Let me convey your request. I am certain she will comm you as soon as possible."

Cales's image vanished.

Oyaz shook his head. Macy had been so worried there wasn't an Eth for her, that she wasn't beautiful like the other human females...women.

"Nuos et Dinuos."

Pink sunlight bathed Nuos's face when he answered the comm. "Supreme Commander Oyaz."

"How is Macy?" What Oyaz wanted to demand was an explanation for their silence.

"She is well. Calls me a gorilla." Nuos chuckled. "King Xeus has rescheduled her training sessions to later in the day."

"Why would the king involve himself?"

Nuos's eyes widened, and warmth burst through Oyaz's chest. *Yes. At last.*

"I commed you with the news, Supreme Commander." Nuos frowned. "Macy insisted, leaned over my shoulder, and told me what to say. Said she was too lazy to type."

"What news?" Oyaz activated his O.D.I. to scan through his comms. There, under low priority, waited a comm from Nuos. "My apologies, Nuos. I had yet to see it."

The warrior smiled. His easy emotions were indicative of the time he spent among human women. "She was most disappointed when you did not respond." He tilted his arm for Oyaz to catch a glimpse of Macy jumping from one leg to another, her hair blazing around her when she spun. "They are playing a game called hopscotch."

At her bright smile and joyful laughter, the tension in Oyaz's shoulders eased. "I will read your comm and respond."

"Thank you, Supreme Commander."

Oyaz ended the call, dropped into the closest comfy, and ignored it as it adjusted to the shape of his backside. He chuckled when he skimmed through her comm, hearing her voice in his head as he read it. She was well and happy. That was all that mattered.

He drafted a quick response, more formal as he congratulated her on finding her Eth.

Leaping off the comfy, he strode into the cleansing room, stripping his armor with efficient movements. He stepped under the spray, intending it to be a short cleanse. Restlessness plagued him, yet the void had been held at bay the last week, his life filled with too much for it to grow, to strengthen, to remind him he was alone. Unclipping his hair, he let it unravel and tipped his face into the water. He was en route to Earth, to assist where needed. As daunting as it was with so many females available, it was a matter of time before he found his Dar Eth.

As he mused over the available options, what color hair she might have, her general size, he settled on one definite. She had to be as energetic and joyful as Macy. The time he had spent with her on board the *Phoenix*, he would always cherish.

"Supreme Commander Oyaz, urgent transmission from Prince Enyl," Pilot Krist's voice reverberated from the O.D.I.

Oyaz touched his forehead to the cold white tiles of the cleansing room while the water flowed over him. "Does the prince require a visual?"

"I do not, Oyaz." The voice was Prince Enyl's.

Oyaz winced and stifled a grumble.

"Is he cleansing? Sounds like a shower," a human woman's softer voice came through.

This time, Oyaz didn't bother smothering his dismay.

"Yes, he is cleansing." Enyl's voice hardened. "End your cleanse, Oyaz."

"His showering doesn't bother me," Princess Oriana said. "Just tell him about Malo. Quit waffling."

Waffling? Oyaz's closed his eyes and bit his lip to swallow a chuckle. Prince Enyl's protectiveness toward his Dar Eth was renowned, as was Princess Oriana's stubborn streak.

"Waffling? You will pay for that later," the poor prince threatened.

"I look forward to it." The princess's voice turned breathless.

Oyaz coughed. It was a career-ending move to laugh at one's superior. "With what may I be of assistance, my prince and princess?"

"Operations Commander Malo has been attacked," Prince Enyl announced.

Oyaz jerked, stunned to hear of this. *Humans? Yithians? Who would dare?*

"He was on Earth in an ambassadorial role," Princess Oriana interjected.

"We need you there, Supreme Commander," his prince ordered. "I want this situation contained—"

"And you get those bastards, Oyaz," Princess Oriana blurted.

Prince Enyl sighed. "Adviser Cales will forward what information we have."

A smile twitched Oyaz's lips again. "Understood."

"I do not know why I let you talk?" Prince Enyl whispered.

"Because you love me...and my mouth," she rasped.

Neither realized Oyaz could hear them loud and clear. "Will that be all, my prince?"

The transmission ended on a throaty moan.

Oyaz laughed and finished the cleanse. Malo? As an ambassador? What had led to such a decision? He was the most unsuitable male to act as a diplomat when his go-to was to inflict the maximum amount of pain.

Oyaz didn't air dry by pushing the blue button on the cleanse console. Instead, he traipsed across his quarters, naked and dripping wet. Sprawling onto his bed, he activated his O.D.I.'s holographic buttons and punched in new instructions. This would ensure Krist increased their speed to maximum, destination as before, Earth, but faster.

He browsed through the data, how and why Malo had been tasked, their objectives. Oyaz frowned. Yes, it made sense to send Malo, if Etteria didn't trust humans. En route to Earth already, his hands were tied as to immediate assistance. Malo could handle tracking down who'd attacked him. It wouldn't surprise Oyaz when he reached Earth that Malo had resolved everything. But he would do as his prince asked and 'contain' the situation.

He sent off a message to the *Gladio*, informing the pilot that he was on his way. The response was swift and as confounding. Joy struck, bright and warming, that Malo had found his Dar Eth. It was her he was hunting, stolen from his embrace. They still didn't know who'd attacked him, though he was well. And as a precaution, they were heading to Yithia on the scimitar. Oyaz added the message to the report. Adviser Cales would no doubt see it.

Oyaz winced when he caught the time on his O.D.I. His next shift would start soon, and he'd yet to find his rest. He stared at the ceiling, trying to wrap his mind around all that had transpired in the past two weeks. The rescuing of prisoners from a captured Yithian slave ship had been the catalyst for the craziness that had become his life. Unexpectantly, three human females had taken the ship, followed by one of the females sparking his Supreme Commander Xan's Ethera. Since Princess Oriana and Prince Enyl's pairing, humans had triggered the lifeforce bond with more and more Etterian males. Oyaz did want a soulmate—Macy's word, not his, but acceptable, nonetheless.

Two Durn had also been on that ship. Only a few hundred of their species existed after a plague ravished their planet. Their highly intelligent, strategic minds were valued, and their lost culture mourned. Xan had escorted them to Issneen to meet with King Xeus.

Thankfully, Oyaz had made it to Etteria, with the sole focus of ensuring his treasured friend Macy was protected. After which, he and Medic Flad had transferred to the closest battleship *Valiant* heading to Earth.

Fortunately or unfortunately, he was undecided on which one, Oyaz had also been promoted to Supreme Commander and given the *Valiant* to command.

As part of the fleet of Etterian battleships, the king tasked them to guard Earth against future Yithian abductions. Now this. Operations Commander Malo, known for his elite skills in interrogation, negotiation, and infiltration, was head of their espionage units. He'd acted as the ambassador and had been attacked by unknown forces. If they'd known who was behind this, Prince Enyl would have changed the *Valiant's* destination.

Oyaz frowned. The tricky nature of this situation didn't sit well. Complications meant unpredictability. With a sigh, he pressed a few buttons on his O.D.I. and let the soothing sounds of Beethoven fill his room. Macy had introduced him to music after she had discovered it in the Etterian's informational database on the subject of Earth. It was something he would need to thank her for when next he saw her.

Once he'd called her friend, but with her status changed, her happiness and protection secured, he had to free her from their friendship.

He rubbed his chest where the restlessness settled. His experiences with her had solidified his decision to find his soulmate sooner. Earth was the first step. Once there, he would offer his assistance to the *Gladio* and Malo, and perhaps, Maker willing, stumble upon his Dar Eth.

Chapter Seven

"Garix?" Izzy poked her head through the office door. "I'm heading over to chat with Papa. Shop's closed. Wanna stay or come with?"

Garix deactivated the glowing keys shining on his arm and rose. Pink drops of ice cream had hardened on his uniform. She smiled. She should feel guilty for doing that to him, but these men...males had to learn to live a little. He was tons less a stick-up-the-ass now than when she'd first met him.

Slipping inside the cool interior of the diner, she waved at the waiter behind the counter. "Papa?"

Following the pointed finger, she rapped on the No-Entry door and waited. All gazes stuck to Garix like flies to shit, the poor guy. Her chat with Papa wouldn't be long, then she could whisk Garix away for something delicious. Slicing a glance at her gigantic friend, she chuckled as she rocked on her toes. He sniffed the air like a bloodhound.

"Get us a table." She pictured mountains of barbecued ribs squeezing her into the corner of a booth, Garix's cheeks smeared and his fingers sticky. "We'll eat here tonight."

He beamed and chose the closest booth.

She pounded on the door again. "Listen, Papa, I don't have all day, and you're going to want to hear me out." She huffed. "I'm aging here."

"Patience, Izzy." Papa opened the door. His ponderous belly swayed him when he slipped behind his desk.

"You still interested in the Cheery Cherry?"

He stilled and blessed her with wide, hopeful eyes. "Sure thing."

She hitched a thumb in the direction of her shop. "Make me an offer."

He rattled off a number, more than she'd expected. Without giving herself time to doubt her decision, she held out her wrist for payment. Once the receipt of funds was confirmed, she transferred the deed.

"Done. Want my ice cream stock?"

He shook his head, his grin conquering his cherubic face.

"All right, I'll make a plan with those. Garix and I'll be having dinner here at Papa and Milly's. I'll clear out my things afterward and leave the keys on the counter."

"On the house. I insist, Izzy."

She laughed. "You'll regret that. Garix eats enough for five men."

Papa rose on his toes to peek at Garix and grimaced, shaking the metal toothpick clamped between his lips. "Fine. Half price."

With that done, she weaved across the restaurant to where Garix waited. She slid into the booth and swiped the menu, even though she planned on ordering the usual. "Don't choose something with more than two patties. Makes eating it a nightmare." Though, with his massive hands, he might manage it.

"What did you just do, Izzy?"

She smiled over the top of the menu, then lowered it. "I sold my shop."

He gaped. "Why?"

"If I choose to go with Caro after Malo rescues her or I find my Eth, I won't need my shop."

"It is logical." Garix tapped the flattened menu. "What do you recommend?"

She winked at him. "Anything with bacon on it."

"I love bacon."

"I know. Listen, Garix. I have tubs of ice cream to remove from the shop, do you think we could share it with your men?"

"Males. And yes. They would appreciate the flavors. Many have yet to taste Earthian food."

"Human food. But how do we get it there, Garix? And please don't say zapping." She shivered. The ice-cold tingles of dematerializing slammed across her mind as she struggled to understand how it could separate her particles from Garix's. She couldn't shake the thought that he had parts of her in him, and she had parts of him in her, even if only on a molecular level.

"A shuttle."

She pressed a hand to her chest, as if that would still her pounding heartbeat, and blinked away the tears. The last time she'd been on his battleship was after Caro's disappearance days ago. Despite Malo roaring like a wounded animal, then becoming a wall of stone, he'd still tasked Medic Brynr to scan Izzy. Biting a shark was supposedly dangerous. She suppressed a gag. It was vile, that's what it was. She gulped the chilled water the waiter placed on the table.

"Any news—"

"None." Garix didn't look up from the menu. "Malo's pushing the scimitar's engines to their limits. And, according to Data Officer Tias, Malo's also called in all favors owed to him."

She blinked at Garix. What did that even mean? What favors? And who was Tias? She opened her mouth to ask, but Garix rattled off a five-burger order to the gaping waiter. She tried not to giggle. After Garix included chocolate brownies for dessert, she ordered a plate of fries and a chocolate milkshake with the promise of thinking about joining him for the brownies.

When they were alone, she clasped her hands and arched a brow at Garix. "And Tias is?"

"A data officer tracks, interrogates, and sifts through data. Any ship in the vicinity, any chatter on the navigational systems and buzz feeds, anything regarding Caro will be communicated to Malo." Garix studied her hands and mimicked her stance, even though his shoulders remained stiff, his back ramrod straight.

"You mentioned favors." She sighed. Getting information from him was like pulling teeth.

Garix leaned back, his gaze calculating. "Malo is not an ambassador but someone with...other skills."

She frowned. "Like a stripper? Or a mechanic?"

Garix's eyelids fluttered. He grimaced. "Operations Commander Malo et Dalo is trained to gather...information from those who do not wish to share."

"Oh," she gasped. *As in a spy?* She rolled her top lip over the bottom. "Well, then, I guess his 'other' skills are better for finding Caro."

Garix said no more, so Izzy did the same, even though she wanted to know if Garix was a spy too. Instead, she rushed off a text to Miri.

Listen, babe, sold my shop. Will explain later.

Miri's response was quick. *Why?*

Izzy grinned. *Why what? Selling or explaining?*

Izzy.

Imagining Miri's pointed glare, Izzy giggled. *Time for a change, M.*

As long as you thought it through. What does Simmy think?

Izzy frowned. Why should Simmy's opinion matter? As far as Izzy knew, her sister's art had made her wealthy. On top of this, their parents had taken care of her future. The inheritance had been unbalanced, but that made sense. Simmy couldn't work. And what monies Izzy had received had gone into the Cheery Cherry.

I haven't told her. Exhaustion slumped her shoulders, and she sagged in her seat.

Good, Miri said. *It's about time you thought of yourself first.*

Izzy blinked back a tear. *Aw, thanks, honey bunch.*

She was halfway through the fries saturated in salt when an image of her face flashed on the TV above the counter. When Thomas Tenet's smug smile conquered the screen, the last bite soured in her mouth.

"Oh, jam and buttered toast." Shoving the plate aside, she rested her temple on the table and cursed, using foul words Caro had forbidden.

"What is it?" Garix leaped off the chair and spun, his body stiff as if he prepared for battle, brandishing a ketchup-laden fry as if it were a sword.

"I'm on the news." She gestured to the TV. Her face flushed, and had Tenet appeared beside her, she would have punched him in the balls.

'I bit the alien ass' flashed in bold red. Right there was her legacy, her five minutes of fame. Her parents would be so proud.

"Just finish eating, Garix. Chill. There's nothing you can do that will ease my mortification. Oh, the abject burn of it." She threw her arms over her head.

"It'll be forgotten by tomorrow, Izzy." Papa patted her on the shoulder. "Here, as a parting gift."

The rich aroma of chocolaty gooeyness with a hint of snow snapped her gaze up. She beamed like a long-lost lover at a large piece of brownie. "Ah, Papa, thank you." She flicked a tear aside and squeezed his hand. Color stained his cheeks before he hurried away.

Garix grinned, eyeing her dessert like a salivating Cerberus. When he reached for it, she smacked his hand.

"You're getting your own. This one's mine." She always shared with him, and his gaping mouth slithered guilt—her familiar dark friend—into her chest, cinching her until air was scarce. She sucked in a deep breath. "Fine, but you're sharing yours."

With his untouched fork, he dived into the brownie, even scooping ice cream. His moans and rumbles softened her resolve, and she smiled at him like a proud mama. He loved his food, and she couldn't castigate him for it. As tall as she was small, they shared the insecurities that went with their sizes. It explained why they'd clicked, why she considered him a close friend in so short a time.

"It won't take long to pack. So, when you're done, you summon, call, order—whatever term you use—a shuttle."

He licked his fork before biting into his fourth burger. Two empty milkshake glasses sat to the side, and as she waited for him to finish eating, she slurped hers, content to watch him.

"How long do you think you'll guard me?"

He stilled in mid-chew. A frown knitted his brow. "I choose to stay with you, Izzy. It is honorable to protect you."

"I'm not questioning your honor or motives, teddy bear, just want to know if we should upgrade the shower."

"You do not like porting, I know. But, Izzy, your Earth water is harsh on my hair."

She blinked, the gurgle of laughter bubbling up meant she was about to hurt his feelings. Dipping her chin to her chest, she took great gulps of air to swallow the giggles. "Your...*hair*?"

"Laugh if you must, *ensa*, but this night, you shall use my cleansing room and see for yourself."

She huffed. "I'll take your word for it." When he narrowed his gorgeous blue eyes on her, she muttered, "Fine."

As soon as the waiter slid another brownie onto the table, Garix shoved his half-eaten fifth burger aside and tore into the sugary goodness. Where he put it, she'd stopped wondering, believing that his species had mastered black holes, and Garix now carried one inside his stomach.

Her phone rang with Simmy's ringtone. Angling her butt, she tugged it out of her back pocket and pressed it to her ear. "Hey, sis."

"Mind telling me why I have journalists pounding on my door, Izabelle Reeves?"

Ice chilled Izzy's spine, and a knot formed in her stomach. A wave of nausea followed, and she pinned a fist to her chest, trying to hold back the urge to throw up.

"What?" she squeaked, sitting up straight.

"I'm not letting them in, of course. Still, I'm trying to finish the order for the gallery. I can't concentrate." Simmy sighed. Izzy couldn't help but picture her sister pinching her brow. "I'll head to the base-ment, but you sort this shit out, you hear me, Izzy."

Wincing, she hurried to answer. "I'm on it."

After Simmy hung up, Garix waited for Izzy to speak, calmly licking his spoon with his gaze on her.

"How do I fix this, Garix?" She tossed the phone on the seat beside her and dropped her face into her hands.

"We could port her to the *Gladio*."

"No." She pressed the heel of her palms into her eyes, willing the tears to stay away. "No, that won't work. She's a sculptor, and moving her from her studio never goes well." A whimper slipped past her de-fenses. She clenched her jaw and leaned her head against the backrest.

"We will discuss this with Sub-Commander Vorn. He could task a few males to guard her home."

Warmth swept through her, and she lunged across the table to kiss his cheek. "You're the best, Garix. Now, let's pay and get those tubs of ice cream to your needy males."

"Needy?" He frowned.

She patted his arm before he slipped from the booth. "As in starving for some sweetness."

"Fair enough, *ensa*."

While she paid the bill, she bounced on her toes and swung her ass to a mental tune. Music was forbidden, so what played in the restaurant's speakers were ambient sounds. The wild calls amid the cacophony of a jungle wasn't something she could dance to.

After a tearful hug farewell, with Papa doing the crying, Izzy packed her office while Garix commed the *Gladio*.

"Trav and Eriz are en route."

She grinned, wiping her nose on her sleeve before clearing the computer's search history. Digging out a pen from the back of the drawer, she wrote the password on a paper napkin and draped it across the touchpad keyboard embedded in the steel desk. "I don't have personal things in the office, but I thought I should check. So, it's just the ice cream."

Looping around to the back, she slipped on a hairnet for the last time and dived into the walk-in freezer to load boxes of ice cream onto a trolley. With Garix's help, it didn't take long to stack them in the front. The tubs in the display had to have their lids in order to travel. She made swift work of adding those to the growing mountain of ice cream.

"Izzy, this is Operative Eriz." Garix gestured to a male who rounded the corner of her shop, coming from the incinerator.

"Hi." She waved and studied him, looking for a weakness in his knees.

He ran his gaze over her, then gathered the first few boxes.

Right, not my Eth either. Sighing, she tried to take a tub or two, but Garix nudged her toward the shop.

"I hate it when you're so bossy," she grumbled, but she wandered the shop, making sure she'd done all she could think of. No cash meant no tallying after a day's sales. Peeling off the hairnet, she tossed it into the waste bin, draped the apron over the counter, and left the keys on top of it.

Garix waited for her outside, saying nothing when she closed the glass doors. The darkness inside the shop taunted her, adding doubts to her chaotic thoughts. Her future wasn't certain, and she had to be prepared to act at a moment's notice. Best to end things smoothly, rather than let her ice cream go to waste.

With his hand on her back, Garix ushered her to the shuttle. The dark-gray metal shimmered, painted silver by the moonlight. It hovered too high off the ground. He gripped her waist and lifted her before she could swat at his hands.

"Damn grizzly, bossy, and a manhandler." She glared at him.

He blessed her with an unrepentant smile. "Operative Trav, this is my Izzy."

The male at the console nodded but said nothing as he flew his fingers over the glowing keys. Garix tugged her to a seat and strapped her in when the doors closed, sealing off the compartment. Her boxes had been placed in a smaller storage area, separated from them by a thin metallic mesh wall.

Dark stars filled the massive display screens to the front of the shuttle, and after a slight jarring when they breached the atmosphere, a massive black shape formed in the center. Parts of it glimmered as the shuttle had, but it sat there like a void.

"*Gladio*?" she asked, despite knowing. Porting removed the wonder of traveling through space to a battleship. "It's beautiful."

She couldn't judge the size from this distance, but as they approached, she realized they headed for an opening the size of her pinky nail. By then, the void engulfed the screens, sending her senses into a panic. If it wasn't for the hum of the shuttle's engines, she might have lost her mind.

Trav spun and reversed into a bay. As he touched down, the massive doors closed, cutting off with dull, gray metal the beauty of space.

The shuttle door swished open, and males boarded, unpacking while sneaking glances at her.

She patted her hair, the mass of it falling across her shoulders. Accepting that she looked a fright with nothing she could do about it, she trailed Garix. He helped her down, and in his beautiful language, barked instructions.

When another male growled at them, Garix pushed her behind his back, shielding her. She peeked around his torso, assessing the glowering male whose tone dripped with fury. His chiseled jawline, those dark blue eyes, and the way his nostrils flared had her sighing like a woman offered too many chocolates. Leaning her back against Garix's, she scanned the bay, smiling at the males rushing around. They were all gorgeous and sexy like they were bred for human women. Tall, broad-shouldered, and in military black, their braided hair whipped around as they worked. Granny's nipples, she should open an ice cream parlor right there. The view was spectacular.

"Izzy?" Garix's voice intruded, and she hummed a response. "You scent aroused."

Males paused in mid-stride, under the weight of crates, with tools in their hands to...*sniff* her. Heat exploded in her stomach, burning upward to scald her cheeks.

"Sorry." She ducked her head into the curve of Garix's back.

"Shall we?" Chuckling at her, he led her from the bay, along passages lined in gray metal with grated flooring and dim lighting. She lost track of direction, with nothing but walls to guide her.

He paused outside a door. "Females are not allowed in the barracks. Pilot Vyar has assigned an officer quarters to you for the duration of your stay."

Placing his palm to the panel beside the door swished it open into a well-designed space. White organic-looking chairs dominated the endless gray. To the right was another door in the wall, to the rear was a small counter with two black glass surfaces embedded in it, and to the left, another door. She stumbled across the threshold when Garix nudged her.

"Is it to your liking, *ensa*?"

"It's... gray." She winced. "And clean."

Laughing, he barked in his language, and the walls shimmered to pink.

"Oh." She skipped across the room to touch the closest wall. "Make it blue, purple, no, green."

"Later. Come, Izzy."

When he approached the door to the right, it opened into a bathroom the size of her bedroom—a massive shower sat in the corner, and two buttons were on the wall.

"The spray will begin when you step under it and at a few degrees hotter than your core. The water contains all you need. It will soap and wash your hair, and if you gargle with it, your teeth as well."

"Wow," she whispered, raising wide eyes to his.

"Press the blue button to dry and the gray button for a toweling wrap." He abandoned her with the door closing behind him. "Want a coffee?"

"Please," she bellowed through the walls while eyeing the glassless cubicle. *Right. Shower. How hard could it be?*

Chapter Eight

Orbiting Earth
Etterian battleship, Gladio

"Garix?" Izzy gripped the robe closed and left the bathroom.

The blow dryer in the ceiling had blasted her so hard, she swore her curls surrounded her like a halo. But when she accessed her reflection in the mirror above the basin, her hair fell down her back in soft waves, as if a hairstylist had spent hours taming it. The silken strands slid through her fingers. She got it now and agreed with him. For her hair, she would shower here every day if she had a choice.

"This thing's massive." While flapping her elbows like a startled chicken, she settled her gaze on the male sitting in the white chair.

"Press the ends together," he said around a stick of salami as if he hadn't just eaten five burgers. So much for learning how not to eat cold meats.

"I did." She wiggled her hand to show she had to hold it or expose herself.

He bounded out of the chair, clamped the salami between his teeth, and pinned the edges of the robe together. It adjusted, drawing a squeak from her when it clung to her curves like she was vacuum-sealed.

"Thanks." She crossed to the table and raised the mug to her lips. After a few sips, she chose a chair. When it caressed her ass, she screamed and bolted, almost spilling the coffee. "What the hell?"

A rumbling preceded a guffaw. Garix rested his temple on his hands as he laughed. "Oh, *ensa*, you are precious."

"That was mean," she huffed and slid into a chair, letting it cup her ass.

"Repayment for the pink ice cream."

Heat crept up her throat, but she shrugged. "You loved it."

"The female *damu was* adorable." He bit into the salami.

"Little girl." She gestured to the front door. "Now, what did that angry male have to say?"

Garix tensed, and a formidable scowl darkened his features. "Sub-Commander Vorn was not pleased that I commandeered a shuttle for ice cream."

She fake-gasped. "He doesn't have his priorities straight."

Garix grinned. "I assumed Trav or Eriz would follow protocol and request the shuttle's usage. With Malo, he values initiative, dedication, obedience. Who takes a shuttle is not a concern."

"Perhaps he lets Vorn worry about those things?"

Garix tilted his head, and a slow smile swept across his lips and warmed his eyes. "You may be right, *ensa*."

She cradled her cup. "We still have to ask about Simmy."

"I did. Sub-Commander Vorn has tasked Trav to look into it. Without Data Officer Tias, we are shorthanded."

She slumped, letting the tension ease from between her shoulders. "Thank you, my friend. Now shower or cleanse, whatever you call it."

He hesitated.

"I'm fine. Or will your males storm this room and steal me away?" Damn, she hoped so. She almost faced the door with too much eagerness.

"You are right again, Izzy. As I leave you alone each night to cleanse, I should not need to be so vigilant on the *Gladio*."

The bathroom door swished shut behind him, and moments later, the shower activated. Running her hand through her hair, she tugged strands down her chest while sipping the coffee. With Simmy protected, the shop sold, there wasn't much Izzy could do. Take up needlepoint? Oil painting? Stain glassing? Sighing, she unraveled her legs to tuck them under her again, each time jarring the chair as it struggled to adjust to her movements.

The front door opened without warning, and in strolled grumpy-faced Vorn. He scowled when he settled his gaze on her. "Where is Garix?"

She pointed to the bathroom.

The male spread his legs to assume a military stance, his hands clasped behind his back.

She froze. "Wait. You speak English?"

"Of course, milady."

She glared at him, then slid the coffee onto the table when her enjoyment of it had evaporated. "So, speaking in Etterian in front of me was an act of rudeness on your part?"

He growled, and a pulse ticked at the base of his jaw. "Etterian business is not meant for female ears."

She gasped, jerking back as if he slapped her. "Is that because I'm human or because you think me too stupid to understand?" She cursed him under her breath, uncaring that he could hear every word. Calling him a slimy snake and an asshat hardened his jaw until she expected it to snap.

"Inform Garix that a sec-drone has been deployed. Your sister does not warrant the use of my males."

"What?" She blinked. Ice drenched her shower-heated body. Pissing off the sub-commander might not have been the best strategy. "A drone? But—"

"It is done, milady." The door closed on his leaving ass.

"Fuck." She bounded to her feet and bolted for the door, screaming at its smooth surface. "Asshole. May you never get a Dar Eth, or if you do, she's an asshat too."

"Izzy?" Garix hovered in the bathroom doorway, wearing a robe over his drenched body with his unbraided hair darting around him.

"The fuckhead sent a sec-drone. Simmy's life didn't warrant warriors to guard her." A wail clogged her throat. Her knees failed her and dropped her to the floor. She allowed the sobs and tears to own her. Her thoughts stilled. Incapacitating sorrow engulfed her.

"A sec-drone will notify us if there is a disturbance." Garix gathered her in his arms and tugged her onto his lap when he sank into a chair.

"Garix, my friend, you don't understand." She wiped the tears off her cheeks and gripped the lapels of his robe. "Simmy's blind."

His eyelids fluttered, and she froze, surprised he didn't understand the word.

"How...how is this possible? Has Earth not yet learned eye growth, healing, or replacement?" He clenched his jaw. "And you told Vorn this?"

"I didn't get a chance. He insulted me, called me stupid, then left." And no, she didn't feel guilty simplifying their pointless discussion into a handful of words.

Rising, Garix let her legs fall to the floor before setting her aside. "I will speak with him, reveal the ramifications if we do not protect Simmy."

Beaming, Izzy threw her arms around him and wiped her damp cheeks across his robe. "Thank you."

He strode to the flat surfaces on the counter, punched it, and a new uniform appeared. She gawked, but couldn't ask when he stormed past her and disappeared into the bathroom. He emerged a minute later, brushed the hair off her temple, and abandoned her with a "Wait here."

She did, pacing and wringing her hands. If Vorn didn't help, she couldn't reach out to Malo. He had to find Caro, and whining to him was the equivalent of complaining to a parent. She could fight her own battles. She slapped her fist into her palm, planning how best to protect Simmy. Garix and her could do it if he let her have a blaster.

She winced. They looked heavy, but with two hands, she could hold it, aim, and fire. Sighing, she acknowledged journalists weren't high on the danger chart. Now if they'd been sharks, Vorn would be all over the house. She snorted. *What an ass-freaking-hat.*

The door opened for Garix, and the smile he wore bathed her with relief.

"And?" She bounced on her toes, unable to stand still.

"Vorn wants nothing to do with you."

"Oh," she squeaked, then darted around Garix to scream down the passage. "Well, the feeling's mutual, dickhead."

"Izzy."

"Sorry, Garix." She pressed her fingers to her cheeks, hoping to hide how hot they burned. "So, why the smile?"

"He handed you over to the arriving Supreme Commander. Oyaz has had dealings with human females—"

"Women."

"—before." Garix narrowed his gaze on her. "Vyar is patching us through." He gestured to the screen dominating one wall. "Come, Izzy, share why you think Simmy must be protected." Pausing, he pinched her chin, forcing her to focus on him. "And behave."

She huffed. "When have I never—?"

He arched a brow at the open front door.

Right.

"SUPREME COMMANDER OYAZ, I need your counsel."

Oyaz raised his head when the display vid flickered in the comm room on board the *Valiant*. Sub-Commander Vorn's face appeared. The darkness swirling in his eyes and staining his cheeks indicated an irate male.

"How may I assist, Vorn?"

"I am grateful we have found Dar Eths. Maker, I swear I am, but she...drives me crazy with her *damu*-like behavior and her uncontrollable tongue."

Oyaz blinked at the flustered male. "Perhaps you should explain the issue?"

"Lady Izzy is spreading her sensual scent wherever she goes, has my males using shuttles without permission, and gorging themselves on ice cream."

"Oh?" Oyaz understood the problem. The female tempted Vorn when his dark blue eyes meant she was not his Dar Eth. "They do smell incredible, Vorn. I cannot assist with that. You will have to bear it as an Etterian warrior. Never let it be said that we cannot endure."

The male grimaced. "The issue is Lady Simmy, her sister. Lady Izzy believes her to be in danger, but the sec-drone shows no threat other than overeager Earthians seeking answers."

Oyaz frowned, pushed out of the comfy, and approached the display vid. He spread his legs and gripped his hands behind his back. "Why does she think her sister is in danger?"

"As Elite Warrior Garix explained, Lady Izzy bit the Yithian who tried to abduct her. This would have remained unknown had her name not been revealed on their buzz."

Oyaz stilled. Only by clenching his jaw did he swallow a bark of laughter. "Lady Izzy bit a Yithian? Is she well?"

"She has seen a medic. If the Yithians discover her name, they will find her sister."

A valid concern. "So, why not deploy two warriors to guard?"

"I do not see the value when the sec-drone's surveillance does not justify it."

Human women were irrational when the safety of others played a role. Oyaz would've deployed two males anyway. It was best to be overcautious. "My question remains, Vorn, how may I assist?"

"Please speak to the female, calm her and perhaps, make her see reason, but be aware, Supreme Commander, she is volatile." Vorn pinched his brow, realized he did so, and lowered his hand in haste.

"Very well, I shall speak to her."

Vorn's shoulders slumped a fraction. "My gratitude. Pilot Vyar will patch you through to Garix."

The screen flickered to a view of an officer's quarters and Garix, whose gaze slanted sideways before he focused on the display vid. "Supreme Commander Oyaz, thank you for assisting."

Oyaz scanned the room and frowned at not seeing a human. "Where is Lady Izzy?"

"I sent her to dress."

Oyaz closed the distance between himself and the console, peering into the dark blue eyes of an unmated Etterian male. So, not a pairing.

"Is he on?" a voice with a sweet lilt preceded the woman sliding into the display vid's line of sight.

Oyaz stepped back but didn't remove his focus, absorbing the wealth of curls surrounding a small face with large gray eyes dominating her features. A plump mouth twitched on an ever-present smile, and laugh lines crinkled the corners of her eyes. Her sand-colored hair, tinted with darker hues, framed a beautiful face.

Then she smiled, and the staccato of his heart deafened him.

"Izzy, this is Supreme Commander Oyaz." Garix gestured to the display vid.

"A pleasure to meet you." She held up a palm, as if to halt any words he might speak. "It's my fault you had to mediate, and I might or might not be sorry, but he's an ass."

Stunned by her words, Oyaz could do nothing but gape. After clearing his throat, he gathered his wits about him, recalling how Macy had kept him on his toes. "Who is?"

"Vorn, the dickhead." Izzy huffed.

Oyaz's eyelids fluttered, and he winced. This was what Vorn had meant by an uncontrollable tongue. "And how did he earn such an...insult?"

"He spoke Etterian around me even though he knows English, then when I asked why, he said certain business wasn't meant for female ears. The arrogant ass, like I'm stupid or something." She folded her arms across her chest. Her pink tunic bulged, proving her more feminine than her size implied.

Rocking on his toes, Oyaz wished he could peer inside the display vid to admire all of her, not just the top half. Returning to the matter at hand, he inclined his head, acknowledging her opinion without agreeing with it.

"Sub-Commander Vorn explained his motives behind using the sec-drone."

"Did he tell you why I want her guarded? Y'know, fuck it." She threw her hands into the air and paced, disappearing off and on the edge of the screen. Her hair bounced as she cursed, and her eyes swirled a lovely gray. "Garix and I can do it. For the love of Earth, just give me a blaster, maybe a smaller one. And a shuttle. I hate porting, hate the

I'm-missing-parts-of-my-DNA feel of it." She paused to shove her face closer to the vid. "She's blind. Did asshat mention that?"

Oyaz's eyelids fluttered as his O.D.I. hurried to explain the antiquated word. "How...how is this possible?"

"Yeah, I heard the whole why-hasn't-Earth-evolved speech. Does it matter? She's alone, surrounded by journalists, and if those damned sharkmen get their hands on her, she's at their mercy. I'm not willing to take that risk, Supreme Commander."

Oyaz stared, unable to cease doing so. Izzy was exquisite, so vibrant, full of life and energy. "Share her location, and I will task males to guard her."

Her eyes widened, and the brightest smile warmed her face, flushing her cheeks a delicate pink. "You promise?"

He grinned. "Yes."

She squealed, jumping up and down while clinging to Garix's arm. "Thank you, Supreme Commander."

She pressed her lips to the display vid in a kiss and scattered Oyaz's senses. His chest exploded with warmth, sending tingles spiraling outward. As a reaction, it was odd and unknown, until the heat settled in his groin, echoing the pleasure his morning chore called forth.

Alodon's balls, I lust after her.

Stunned again, he dipped his head to hide his flaring nostrils and gaping mouth. "Call me when you are alone," he said to Garix in Etterian and ended the comm.

It took minutes before a comm came through. By then, Oyaz had altered the temperature regulator in his armor, adjusted the tightness of his breeches, and paced the narrow confines of the comm room. His reaction baffled him, for had she been his Dar Eth, he would have fallen to a knee. Since that hadn't happened, then desiring an unclaimed woman was irrational.

He drew in calming breaths, ignored his males tossing concerned glances at him, and faced the display vid. The bulkhead behind Garix was from the passage. He must have slipped out and used the nearest vid.

"Your thoughts, Elite Warrior Garix."

"If it proves necessary, relocating Lady Simmy will be a challenge. The female...woman is familiar with her home. On the other hand, a medic must scan her to assess whether we can heal her."

Oyaz ran a thumb along the edge of his jaw. "And are the Yithians a threat?"

"I would be if someone bit me." Garix chuckled. "Regardless, if we can secure a fem...woman, we should. Her Eth will appreciate our efforts."

"Agreed. I will discuss this with Vorn and choose two warriors to patrol. You will be informed of their names and their time of arrival."

Garix thumped his chest in salute. "Thank you, Supreme Commander."

Oyaz leaned closer, almost as if to whisper. "One more thing, Garix, why do you guard Lady Izzy? Is she in danger, as well?"

The male stood taller, and his chest expanded along with the smile he wore. "She is my friend."

Oyaz's thoughts flew to Macy. Guarding her had become second nature to him, affection for her a given. "I understand. I am but a day away, Garix. Comm me if the situation changes."

When the comm ended, he staggered back and settled into a comfy.

What in Alodon's hell had just happened?

Chapter Nine

Orbiting Earth
Etterian battleship, Gladio

WHEN GARIX RUSHED OUT of the quarters, abandoning her without a backward glance, Izzy collapsed into the nearest chair, gratitude warring with the explosion of heat in her belly.

His name 'Oyaz' sounded so exotic. She shivered, reveling in the tingles racing across her skin and puckering her nipples. Holy balls of fire, he was gorgeous.

Humming, she replayed the call, wondering if she had made a fool of herself again. With a slam of a fist into her palm, she leaped to pace, but her gaze snagged on the lifeless black screen.

Etterians shared similar features: long braided hair linked to their honor, broad shoulders, and sculpted bodies. When Garix exercised with his greatsword, she had to admit to peeking—and salivating.

Yet, when Oyaz's face had appeared on the screen, her senses burst into life, while she struggled to latch onto her zooming thoughts.

Closing her eyes, she recalled the shape of his wide forehead, raven-winged eyebrows above hooded dark blue eyes. His long, perky nose ended on wide full lips that broke into smiles as easily as Garix did. His cheeks narrowed into a chiseled jaw, with one dimple forming, slanting his smile. Flustered, her words had stuck to her tongue.

And he had listened to her, as if she mattered. He hadn't treated her like a child.

She sniffed, fighting the swell of disappointment making her eyes water. She wasn't his Dar Eth. His eyes hadn't changed color to that mesmerizing crystal blue like Malo's. Then again, once Oyaz met her, he wouldn't want her either, not someone so petite. She had to find a shorter Etterian, if such a male existed.

Not wanting Garix to see her tears, she hurried to the bathroom and spent a few minutes trying to figure out how to activate the water at the basin. Giving up, she shoved her hand in the cubicle and squealed when the spray drenched her.

Giggling at her silliness, she pressed the blue button and let the hot air dry her damp robe, hair, and cheeks. When she gathered her discarded clothes, she raised them for a sniff, then jerked back. There was no way she could wear those until she washed them.

"Izzy?"

"In here." She strolled through the door with her clothes tucked under her arm and a fake smile plastered on her face. Dumping her clothes on a chair with the sneakers balanced on top, she flicked a thumb at the rectangles on the counter. "How did you order your uniform? Did you call it from storage? And can we leave for home? I need to call Simmy."

"Come."

Izzy gawked when Garix took her through the functions of a replicator, for non-edible items, and the rehydrator which carried a menu spanning species, not just of Earth. He had altered the strange symbols into English and waited for her to try it out. At first, she couldn't think of a single thing she wanted. Her cold coffee sat on the table. She was still full from dinner, and whatever she chose would forever be compared to Eve's choice. Izzy might be the first woman to eat from the Garden of the Rehydrator. Snickering, she punched in an apple and gasped at the bold red fruit that materialized before her.

"Granny's nipples, Garix, this's amazing." She snatched it off the counter and squeezed, testing its texture. With one bite, she closed her eyes on a moan. It crunched as she chewed, and the sweet juices coated her mouth like a real apple would.

"Now, comm Simmy." He gestured to the black screen. "Speak her full name, and the system will use the nearest capable device to open a connection."

Izzy gaped with her mouth full, then whooped, swinging her hips while dancing on the spot. "So easy?"

He chuckled. "Yes."

"How much does it cost?" She had money, but maybe not enough for an intergalactic call.

He guided her hand to his mouth for a quick bite of her apple, taking half of it. "No cost. Etteria pays for whatever we need."

She stilled with a finger across her lips, struggling to swallow past the apple caught in her throat. "Free?" she squeaked. Tears pooled at the corners of her eyes. She coughed to clear her airway.

He wrapped his massive mitt around her hand and towed her with the gentlest of tugs. "Speak your sister's name."

She squared her shoulders, positioned herself in the middle, and leaned forward until her lips were an inch from the screen. "Simone Elora Reeves."

The screen flickered and filled with a view of a ceiling.

"Simmy?"

A scream followed, then Simmy's wide gray eyes filled the rectangle. "What the hell?"

"Sorry, sis. I'm calling with news." Izzy giggled, tossing her hands high as she did a quick jig. "Are the journalists still bothering you?"

Simmy huffed, placed the phone down, and carried on working on her art. Izzy was used to this. As a blind person, face to face meant nothing to Simmy unless Izzy was in the room with her.

"They've camped on my porch. The fucking audacity."

Izzy winced. Sure, she swore when the situation called for it, but years with curse-sensitive Caro had made her aware of her 'unladylike' vocabulary.

"Well, I spoke to Oyaz..." She sighed, just saying his name exploded butterflies in her chest.

Simmy reached across the phone for a palette knife. "Who?"

"Supreme Commander Oyaz. He will send two warriors to chase away the mean journalists and ensure no one bothers you."

"What?" Simmy's face appeared again. Anger furrowed her brow and twisted her lips. "Are you fucking insane, Izabelle? I don't want anyone. Just peace and quiet. What has this world come to that even that's threatened?"

"You won't know they're there, Simmy." She tossed a glance at Garix and grimaced. "Um, there might be a bigger threat than the humans."

"Humans?" Simmy jerked as if Izzy had slapped her.

"Yeah, I bit an alien, and now that they know my name, it's a matter of time…" She was the worst sister. Simmy should just cut all ties. Not knowing Izzy was the safest for her. "I'm sorry."

"Why did you bite someone? You're not making any sense." Simmy pinched her brow as if she warded off a headache.

"He tried to take Izzy, Lady Simmy."

Her sister gaped before color exploded across her cheeks. "Who the fuck? You're not alone?"

"Sorry, it's Garix. I've mentioned him, haven't I? He's my Etterian friend." She frowned. The conversations she had with Simmy were always short and never sweet. "Regardless, we're on Iceberg status."

"Aliens, warriors, Etterians…and now a fucking iceberg? I'm not falling in with that shit, Izzy."

Curling her sticky fingers into fists as fury shook her limbs, Izzy fought the urge to stomp and roar, going Sister-zilla on Simmy's ass. "I don't care how you feel about this. Your safety's at stake. If a man says the password, you're to go with him."

Simmy parted her mouth, but Izzy had had enough. Couldn't her sister tell she was only trying to live up to the promise she made Dad? Why did she have to make things difficult?

Izzy's face caught alight, inflaming her cheeks to her hairline. "Fuck it, I'm done. Go get kidnapped by sharklike men. Go be their sex slave. You're more than up for it, virgin and all." At Simmy's wince, Izzy glared at Garix. "End the call…please."

"End comm."

The screen flickered to black again, but the fire still burned along her veins. She was ready to murder Simmy. As Izzy fell into a pace-skip, her limbs twitching, she cast a pleading glance at Garix. "I have to...walk, run, jump, do...something."

Frowning, Garix ran a gaze over her and headed for the replicator. He returned and shoved workout clothes at her. "Change."

She bolted into the bathroom, tossed aside the robe, then yanked on yoga pants, and a tight tank. Scowling at herself in the mirror, she bounced on her toes, jiggling her breasts. So like a man not to realize she needed...support. With an arm across her chest, she headed for the replicator and punched in sports-bra requirements. When the black garment formed, she snatched it and disappeared into the bathroom again. After contorting herself into the contraption, she peeled the tank on again, and bounced, testing the bra's give.

Satisfied, she skip-jogged to where Garix waited by the front door.

Izzy spat her hair out of her mouth, and with a flick of a wrist, wiped the sweat dripping into her eye. She glared at Garix and swung forward punches, keeping her legs spread, her weight on her front foot, and her thumbs tucked under her fists—as he'd taught her.

Exhaustion tremored her limbs, and her knees weakened by the second.

"Still hitting like a girl?" she huffed, pummeling his palms.

Air tickled her spine. The training mat was smack damn in the middle of the common. Riveted, many males ogled her like the latest space opera Love and Supernovas where Milisande had just discovered her husband in bed with her sister.

Izzy rolled her shoulders, trying to focus with her face so hot. Waves of nausea churned, along with spells of dizziness. She'd been about to call it a day when Garix said she punched like a *damu*. The ass. And he chuckled, enjoying her pathetic attempts to prove him wrong.

"Granny's nipples, I'm done." Her arms fell to her sides, and she couldn't draw the energy to lift them.

Her audience stamped their booted feet, the reverberation rippling through the mat and up her bare toes. She pasted on a wide grin, faced them, and did the most ladylike curtsey she could muster without fainting like a damsel-in-distress.

She ignored the bitchy thoughts that said she looked like a drowned rat with the way her hair clung to her sweat-drenched skin. Fuck it, her appearance didn't matter. A bottle of water, a shower, and the sweet softness of a pillow were all she wanted.

Garix said nothing when he led her to their quarters. She didn't bother asking for a shuttle to return home lest he suggested a porting. Not in the mood to be dematerialized, she opted to pinch her lips shut and shuffle behind him.

He called forth a metal container of water from the rehydrator, and after she downed it, relishing the cool liquid soothing her parched throat, she trudged into the bathroom. The shower was hotter than normal, but she stood there, let it wash the sweat off her body and ease some of the stiffness settling into her muscles. Forgoing the blow dryer, she pulled on a clean robe, wincing as shards of pain protested any movement. She stumbled across the lounge, through the other door, and onto the massive bed.

Where Garix slept wasn't her problem.

But when he woke her ten minutes later, she groaned, tossing curses and threats at him. "Flaming nipples, go away."

"Come now, *ensa*, Supreme Commander Oyaz has commed."

Argh. She didn't move, didn't twinge. Every inch of her throbbed, twanged, pulsed, and tremored. And now the sexiest Etterian she knew had called. Her inner girl squealed, spiking joy. She lay there, letting it bathe her in welcome warmth until her toes tingled. She whimpered, even her toesie wosies hurt.

"What did he say?" she mumbled into the pillow, then huffed to blow her hair out of her eyes.

"He is waiting to speak to you."

"What?" She bolted upright then slithered into the same sprawl Garix had found her in. "I'm in agony. I'll call him back."

"Ensa, come. I will order you coffee while you cleanse."

He said coffee, the evil alien. "Meanie." But she wiggled a leg off the side of the bed, let it fall to the floor, then with a grunt, pushed herself up. Every step jarred forth a gasp, as if someone had locked her knees.

"Who calls at this time of night, Garix?" She whirled on the spot and cried out when fire lanced down her thighs. Closing her eyes against the sting of tears, she willed herself to remain immobile. "Is Simmy all right?"

"Lady Simmy is fine." Garix placed a hand between Izzy's shoulder blades, his touch hot and soothing, even as he nudged her to the bathroom. "It is ten in the morning, Izzy."

"What?"

Garix laughing earned another glare from her. "Shall I add pain medication to your cleanse?"

She gaped, letting her mouth fall into an 'oh.' "You can do that?"

He frowned. "Yes."

She smacked his arm. "And you tell me this now? Here I've been dying, my muscles spasming."

"This is not normal for Earth?" he asked before shoving her into the bathroom.

"No. Duh." She huffed then offered a weak smile. "Please to the pain meds. I want to feel nothing."

Garix snorted. "A little is all you need, Izzy."

The bathroom door shut behind her. After using the toilet, she removed the robe and draped it over the closed toilet seat. She stepped under the shower's spray. When the heated water flowed over her, she moaned and rested her temple on the white tiles.

She imagined the stiffness and constant aches spiraling down the drain. By the time she climbed out, using her limbs didn't hurt as much. With a smile, she spun so that the blow dryer reached all of her while she tested the ability to move. Slight stiffness and pulsing pain lingered, but not enough to incapacitate her.

Snapping the robe in place, and with one glance at the mirror, she shrugged. Sure, her hair didn't look like her aura was powered by the electrical company, but her face and her size hadn't changed. Only extensive surgery and a shit ton of tokens could alter those.

Her Eth either liked her as she was, or he could...go suck it.

With an eye roll at her flushed face, she left the bathroom, accepted the coffee Garix held for her, and positioned herself in front of the screen. He activated it while she took the first sip. She groaned when the smoky flavor and its heat warmed her tongue, burned down her throat, and set her insides on fire. All good. She hummed.

Opening her eyes, she jerked back at finding Oyaz's gaze fixed on her. "Greetings, Lady Izzy."

"Morning," she mumbled, dipping her chin to hide her inflamed face. "Just Izzy, or Izabelle, though only Simmy uses the latter, especially when she's pissed with me." Which had been most of her life, well...since the incident.

She pinched her lips, ceasing her chatter. His swirling dark blue eyes and unflinching gaze unnerved her. She shuffled on her feet and gritted her teeth against a wave of pain as her shower-heated body cooled.

"Surveillance—" Oyaz cleared his throat, but when he spoke again, his voice was as hoarse as she remembered. "—is concerning."

Unable to stop her reaction, she shivered. She tightened her grip on the cup and forced herself not to break eye contact.

Oyaz's focus shifted for a second to her hands before meeting her gaze again. "The sec-drone indicates movement around Lady Simmy's housing unit. The heat signatures do not align with the humans outside."

"Alodon's balls," Garix growled. "Do you suspect Yithians, Supreme Commander?"

"Yes. You had a right to be concerned, Lady...Izabelle. I arrive in a few hours and will collect Lady Simmy."

Relief soaked through Izzy. She leaned a shoulder against Garix's chest. "Thank you." Offering a smile was all she could do to repay Oyaz. "I put her on high alert last night. When you arrive, tell her 'Titanic.' She should leave with you without too much arguing."

Oyaz arched a delicate brow. Her fingers twitched with the urge to trace it. "Titanic?" His enviably long eyelashes fluttered. A slow smile curved his delicious mouth and sent her heart into apoplexy.

She pinned the mug to her chest, hoping to calm the erratic pounding of her heart and an influx of suicidal butterflies consuming her insides. Biting her bottom lip kept the gasp trapped in her throat.

"Titanic," he rasped. "Apt. Very well, Izabelle, I will comm when we are en route with your sister onboard." His gaze hardened, a pulse ticked at the edge of his chiseled jaw, and he barked something in Etterian at Garix.

When a similar tick formed on Garix's jaw, she frowned. Facing Oyaz, she opened her mouth to ask, but the screen faded to black. "What did he say?"

"He wants to speak to me alone." Garix bolted for the front door, abandoning her. "Eat something." The door sealed behind him.

She slumped against the wall, feeling as if her womanly bits had been put through the wringer.

Flaming nipples, Oyaz was hotter-than-hell sexy. And the way he'd said her name was like the brushing of his fingers along her skin. She hadn't even demanded she go with. Trapped on this battleship, she couldn't leave without Garrix and grumpy Vorn agreeing or unless they zapped her. And if Oyaz was closer to Simmy, diverting to fetch Izzy would only delay the rescue.

Which meant she would meet him soon, face to face. Tingles assailed her body to her toes, curling them. "Get yourself together, Izzy. You can't melt at his feet like a teenager."

Pushing herself off the wall with a small whimper, she downed the coffee and plodded to the rehydrator. What she wanted was bacon and loads of it. If she was to meet the male, she needed fortification. Alcohol might have been a better choice, but she had to have her wits about her.

Then after breakfast, she'd practice forming a polite smile in the mirror.

IZABELLE'S GROAN OF APPRECIATION shouldn't have blazed fire along Oyaz's veins to nestle in his groin. Nor should her image have come to mind while he attended to his chore that morning. None of his reactions to her made sense.

Nor did he understand the fury pounding his heart and tensing every muscle in his body. Why was she in pain? Dark circles under her eyes and her pale skin beneath her glowing cheeks attested to this. No woman should be abused, ever, and never by an Etterian male. He fell into pacing, hoping to ease the tension and regulate his breathing.

"Supreme Commander," Garix said as soon as Oyaz answered the comm.

Slamming his palms onto the console, he shoved his face to within an inch of the display vid. "Why in Alodon's hell is Izabelle in pain?"

Garix winced at Oyaz's roar.

He sucked in a sharp inhale, fighting for calm, for control. Yet it eluded his grasping fingers. "Explain, now, Garix, or I will have Adviser Cales slice your hair off at the scalp."

Garix's jaw tightened. "Izzy sparred last night. Her body is not used to it."

Air whooshed out of Oyaz's lungs while he blinked at Garix. As per Oyaz's role with Macy, Garix performed a similar one. Yet Macy's grumbling and complaints had been humorous, not so with Izabelle. Maker, he loved the way her name rolled off his tongue. Pinching his brow, he squeezed, trying to hold back a growing ache farther down his body. "My apologies, Elite Warrior Garix. You have served honorably."

The male's shoulders relaxed.

"Trav and Eriz guard Lady Simmy from afar. They confirm the presence of footprints in the sand outside her glass openings—"

"Windows, Supreme Commander."

Oyaz nodded, thankful for the correction. "Yet cannot confirm sighting intruders other than the humans. Elite Warrior Danic and I will retrieve Lady Simmy. Trav and Eriz will patrol the path between the shuttle and the woman."

"I appreciate your efforts, Supreme Commander."

Oyaz ended the comm and left, stomping to the common. What he needed was a hot chocolate and Beethoven.

With a steaming cup of Earth's delicious beverage, he shared his music choice with the viewing deck and slid onto a bench while the soothing notes filled the space. Planets passed by on the display vids, the kaleidoscope as mesmerizing as other galaxies, but his thoughts circled to wide gray eyes dominating a small face.

Electric excitement stiffened his muscles, as if he prepared for battle. Warmth reached every molecule and squeezed the air from his lungs. He would meet her soon, then perhaps this restlessness, this dishonorable lust would leave him.

He could but hope.

Chapter Ten

"WHAT?" SIMONE'S LAUGHING EYES and wide smile implied Izzy was teasing her. "What do you mean someone spied on me?"

"Oyaz says there are footprints outside your windows, and the heat signatures weren't human." Izzy was too scatter-brained for her own good, and Simmy was the calm one. But the past few days had more than ruined her sister's perfect, routine life.

She flicked a dismissive hand. "That's impossible. I would have heard something."

Izzy arched a brow, then snorted, like her sister knew what to listen for. "What would they sound like, Garix?"

"The Yithian language is a sequence of hisses," he said, licking his lips before taking a long pull from his iced coffee.

Simmy's face paled, then her cheeks bloomed. "Fuck. I could strangle you with my bare hands."

Well, that was confirmation. Izzy laughed, having heard that threat too many times for it to have any meaning. "As to what? Using a garrote?"

Simmy's face mottled.

Swallowing her laughter, Izzy said, "Chill, sis, it's just until the threat's minimized. After that, you can return to your idyllic life."

Simmy folded her arms across her chest. "Remind me again why I'm in danger."

"Caro and I were with Malo when shots were fired. It was crazy-scary at the time." Izzy jumped up to pace, her long gypsy skirt swishing around her as her hips swayed wild in her agitation.

"Who's Malo?"

Izzy faced the screen with a scowl. "Dammit, Simmy. That's what you ask about? Not that someone shot at us?" She huffed. "Malo is..." Looking for guidance, she sliced her gaze to Garix who downed his coffee, watching over her as her ever-vigilant guard.

She loved that about him, but affection for him contradicted the maelstrom consuming her. Sure, she was a child to them, but she would be damned if she took this lying down. Those silver shark bastards had taken her bestie and tried to take her too. Targeting Simmy was O.U.T. She wouldn't stand for it, not an effing chance in hell.

Bending over, she flicked her mass of riotous curls, trying to keep them off her face. She needed a cut, something to tame her hair, and despite the wonderful water onboard, it was still unruly. Now wasn't the time though, yet it was the one thing she could change, one thing out of many irritations.

"Malo's a gorgeous alien, and an Etterian warrior, to be precise. He and Caro formed a bond, and now he's chasing after a kidnapped Caro."

"Kidnapped?" Simmy squeaked.

"Haven't you been listening to me?" Izzy squealed and yanked on her hair, hoping the sharp painful bites on her scalp would calm her.

"They tried to take me too, and when the damn news got ahold of my name, it put you in danger. Listen, Simmy, I'm going to say this once." She drew in a deep breath. "Titanic."

Simmy shook her head enough to tug her pale hair free from its bun. "I'm not going. You're being paranoid again, Izzy." She paused. "Wait, yesterday, you said aliens? What do they look like? No, never mind. Did they kidnap Caro?" She huffed and threw her gaze toward the ceiling. "Fine, I'll be ready."

Izzy danced, wiggling her ass, not that she wasn't above kidnapping her sister if need be. "If you hear anything, head into the tunnel."

"All right, Izzy, but you owe me big."

Didn't she already and wouldn't she always? Tears burned her eyes, but she swallowed past the lump in her throat and forced a smile. "Add it to my tab. You know the drill. Love you, sis. End comm." She kept her smile in place while waiting for the image to fade. Despite Simmy not being able to see it, she could hear it in Izzy's voice.

"Tunnel?" When the screen flickered off, Garix asked with a black eyebrow dipped in confusion.

She trailed a gaze over the defined edges of his cheekbones, his square jawline, and wide forehead above his dark-blue almond-shaped eyes. He was too handsome and too intimidating, but he was as soft as a big old teddy bear.

"Yeah, she'll leave the lights on, lock all the doors, then sneak through the hidden passage to the tool shed at the back of the yard."

"Alodon's balls." He scowled.

She shrugged. "Paranoid of me, but she's living alone due to her stubbornness. I built that tunnel myself. Took me months, had to study drainage and housing schematics to make sure I didn't hit a pipe and drown. Worth it though." She studied her palms, the calluses having taken as long to fade.

"You are a good sister." Garix's words struck true.

She winced as pain lanced through her. Yeah, sure. Good sisters didn't push their sister down an embankment. She blinked back the tears. She'd happily trade places with Simmy, had wished she could for years.

"What was iceberg for?"

"That's to put her on alert. I know I'm overly paranoid, Garix, but if you knew how Simmy lost her sight..." She chewed on her lip, pulling her hands into fists to stop the tremors.

He rose and hugged her, crushing her face against his sternum. His awkward patting and the comfort he offered helped her draw in a calming breath.

"I sensed no anger or resentment in her voice or expressions. I do not think she blames you, *minus susa*."

"I blame me." Izzy yanked herself out of his arms, aware she did so only because he let her. "Nothing will change that." She stomped to the rehydrator to request a bottle of water. Once she had taken a few sips, she faced him again.

"You wouldn't need 'Titanic' if I was on the shuttle, but I know you won't let me go." She stuck out her tongue at him. "Blah blah, human women are special," she mocked in a deep voice. "I'll be waiting in the docking bay, and if you say one word about that, I'll sneak onto a shuttle, and to fly it, I'll sweet talk someone with promises of ice cream and...other things."

As threats go, that was an empty one. Hiding from an Etterian was as crazy as finding her soulmate, her Eth, in a sea of bronze faces. She gripped her hip and raised her chin to show her determination.

"Etterian males obey me without question. Why can you not do as asked?" He glowered at her. "We ensure your safety, Izzy."

"Because Etterians don't ask. You order. Humans are never submissive, unless we want to be." She dipped her chin to her chest to hide her sadness. If Caro was here, she'd laugh and ease the tension in Izzy's shoulders.

"My face and height should make you cower, why is it you do not?" The poor male looked horribly lost.

"Do you want me to cower, Garix? To fear you when you raise your voice?" She placed her hand over his heart, raising her gaze to meet his.

"No, susa, I would not want any female to fear me. However, a healthy respect for my authority and the effort I have put in to be able to defend little ones such as yourself? That I do demand."

He *had* saved her and became her friend since they'd ported to the battleship like something out of a sci-fi movie.

"I'm sorry, Garix." She threw her arms around him for a hug. "I didn't mean to disrespect you. I've been caring for Simmy for years." Leaning back with her fingers on his forearms, she smiled. "It's hard to trust someone else with her protection."

"That I can understand."

"Good, now do you think Oyaz will mess this up?" Her breath caught. Oyaz had the look of someone more than capable of mastering anything. His confidence, his calm, the way he smiled...wait, that had nothing to do with ability. But, oh, his lips...

"Supreme Commander Oyaz is an excellent warrior." Garix frowned again.

"You act like there are no bad apples in the barrel." She shook her head. "Just let him know about the tunnel and the details. You'll be with me in the shuttle bay, right?"

"Yes," Garix said while punching on his arm-thingy.

She clapped, bouncing on her toes, and blessing her poor friend with a wide grin. "Would you like a chocolate mousse?"

"What?" His eyelids flickered as his O.D.I. updated him. He gasped, and a slow, sensual smile spread his lips.

She ordered from the rehydrator as promised. Surrounded by gorgeous and untouchable aliens was like an all-paid vacation to Temptationville. Except she was celibate, with no sex or love on the itinerary for her.

Cursed, that's what she was.

Chapter Eleven

Oyaz stared at his O.D.I. in disbelief. Who in Alodon's hell would build a tunnel under a housing unit? He shook his head at the ingenuity of human women. At least, Lady Simmy burrowing deeper confirmed the presence of intruders. He and his four males were en route, keeping to the shadows of the dark green trees, and dodging the strange boxes on wheels thumping and glowing. Scans had revealed that humans lived inside, no doubt waiting for Lady Simmy to emerge or for Izabelle to arrive.

The solo moon was waning, the minimal light concealing them even more. No breeze stirred the air. Tapping his O.D.I, he indicated to the ground unit to stay alert as they neared the white structure. He directed them to scout ahead and re-join at the shed.

"Anything?" he asked Trav who fell into position beside him.

"Just those footprints. Unmistakable, Supreme Commander."

Oyaz grimaced. "Seen Lady Simmy?"

Trav stared ahead. "Not once. Scans reveal she remains underground."

Oyaz paused at the sight of the housing unit's gaping front door. On instinct, he altered his plans. Garix's latest information had stated all doors would be locked. And since Princess Oriana had told Oyaz to 'get the bastards,' he would follow her orders, as well. He flung out a hand, striking Danic's chest to halt him. His armor and chest muscle muffled the slap.

"New plan. Get the human woman to the shuttle. I will take care of the intruders." Oyaz pointed to the opened door. "Tell Lady Simmy, 'Titanic.'"

Danic frowned before skirting the housing unit, keeping to the shadows, and staying true to his target.

"Trav, guard the front. Eriz, take the back."

Oyaz crept to the front door, muting his footsteps as expected. All Etterians trained to be light on their feet, but as a warrior, he had access to advanced armor that assisted by utilizing a planet's gravity. To an observer, he'd look like he glided just above the stone floor circling the home. He stilled to listen in the doorway. Hissing flowed from one room to another as Yithians tore through the rooms. He scowled, not liking this turn of events. Since they had yet to notice him, he punched his O.D.I. and activated the Yithian Language Protocol.

"He will be happy with any female. We have wasted enough time looking for this one," said a Yithian.

A bang followed. "She bit one of us, Sdion. That is most promising."

Sdion's hiss was long, pronounced, showing his displeasure. "She is not here, Agma."

Anger coursed through Oyaz, raising the sensitivity of his skin. He altered the temperature regulator of his armor and sneaked closer.

Izabelle had bitten a Yithian, which meant these two referred to her. Trembling with barely contained fury, he peered through the crack between the door and its frame. Noting their location within the room, he slid around the door and stepped into the light.

The Yithians spun in slow motion, their mouths gaping. He fired two blasts in quick succession, stunning them. They collapsed to the floor.

Holding his finger on his O.D.I, Oyaz spoke to the unit's channel, "Two Yithians to transport, Operative Trav."

Turning to leave, he slammed into the metal door. Fire burned along his temple, making his left eye water. He cursed under his breath. No wonder Etterians had changed the design of their doors. He had no idea the danger they could pose. Ignoring the pulsing agony and the wet heat of his blood, he dragged the two bodies to the front of the house.

Trav met him at the door and took the weight of a Yithian. Oyaz acknowledged the assistance with a grunt, his eye twitching and stinging. Once they crossed the green grass around the housing unit, he flung the Yithian over his shoulder and jogged along the shadows. Glances to the side confirmed their unnoticed passing until he reached the ground marking that indicated the cloaked shuttle's location. Dripping blood hindered the vision in his eye.

The shuttle door opened, revealing the unlit compartment within. Oyaz rushed up the ramp and dumped the Yithian on the metal grated floor, none too gently. Trav did the same.

Oyaz narrowed his gaze on Eriz seated at the console. "Is Lady Simmy—?"

"Onboard, but Danic is down." Eriz gestured to the enclosed section at the rear of the shuttle.

Oyaz jerked back. Had there been more than two Yithians? "What—?"

"Lady Simmy hit him with a harvest tool," Eriz growled. "I scanned him with a med-gun, but he has yet to awaken."

As Eriz launched the shuttle, Trav raised a med-gun to Oyaz's temple, but he brushed the male aside. "It is a cut, nothing more. A medic will attend to it soon enough."

He strode the short distance to the back, rubbing the blood out of his eye with his palm. He entered the storage room and halted. A human woman with a wealth of blonde hair pressed a cloth to Danic's temple on what looked to be a fading bruise.

"I'm sorry," she whispered, startling Oyaz, for he hadn't made a sound. "I didn't mean to hit him. I was in the tunnel listening to the hisses in my home when he came up behind me."

Oyaz frowned. How could she have heard Danic approach her?

"He whispered the password before passing out." Removing the cloth, she unfolded and refolded it. She dribbled water onto it from a bottle she clenched between her thighs before placing the wet cloth on Danic's temple.

If Oyaz hadn't known she was sightless, he wouldn't have been able to discern so based solely on her movements. "Your actions are understandable, Lady Simmy."

She sighed, her shoulders dropping. "I'll apologize to your soldier as soon as he wakes up."

"His name is Danic. I will escort you to medical myself."

"Thank you, and perhaps have your injury attended to as well?" she asked with a raised eyebrow while staring at the bulkhead to the right of his position.

"You can scent my blood," he stated.

She twisted her body in his general direction and offered him a small smile, her white eyes pretty in her pale face.

"I assume my sister will be awaiting my arrival?" Her chuckle was warm. "You don't need to answer that. She'll be there. Izzy can only be herself." She offered him another smile. "Thank you for fetching me." And she returned to her task.

He was dismissed but not in a bad way. "We will arrive shortly," he told her and removed himself from the tiny room. He faced his males. "Well done this day."

They acknowledged his praise with a quick bow of their heads. Oyaz lowered himself onto a seat. He gingerly tested his temple and winced. The pulsing pain added to his uncharacteristic impatience. Via his O.D.I, he updated Vorn and Garix on the status of the mission, specifically referring to the prisoners.

Oyaz had another mission to return to—assisting Malo. Perhaps these Yithian could reveal who'd taken Malo's Dar Eth. Not trained in espionage, Oyaz would let Vorn do the interrogation. He grunted. This diversion may just be what he needed.

THE SHUTTLE TOUCHED DOWN on the metal-grated floor of the bay, and the doors opened onto the pressurized area. As Oyaz waved his males past, a human woman ran toward them. Her hair cascaded around her in wild disarray, her familiar gray eyes were wide with excitement, and she bore the sweetest of smiles. He admired her pensive face, the gentle swell of her breasts, and a waist he could span with his hands. Beauty bolted toward him, colorful, vivacious, like an exotic creature.

White pleasurable heat exploded through him. He thrust out a hand for support and to prevent the sharp, intense pain from bringing him to his knees. Instead of the metal bulkhead stopping his descent, his hand slid, and he hit the grate with one knee.

He groaned, the wound in his temple all but forgotten. At the pinnacle of the fiery onslaught, a vision of Izabelle appeared. She was on her knees, her curved backside offered to him, her feminine folds glistening, her back arched with her curls everywhere. She wriggled before meeting his gaze.

"Oyaz, please," she gasped, her gray eyes hooded, and her lips parted.

He shuddered as the pain merged into unadulterated pleasure, and his malehood hardened to its full length. Gritting his teeth, he clenched a fist, struggling to rein in his tight control. He tried to stand, but his knees refused to lock.

"Flaming nipples, Oyaz, are you all right?" Her voice rippled through him. Her every word caressed his hypersensitive nerves.

"Izzy?" Lady Simmy called.

"Simmy, I have a hurt soldier here. Do you need me, or can I help Oyaz first?" Izabelle's hand on his shoulder summoned a shiver.

"I have an injured man too," Simmy said. "We can chat later."

Oyaz grumbled at having been called hurt and his rank ignored. He was injured. There was a difference. And he wasn't *just* a soldier.

Izabelle's warmth and scent were at his side, drawing him from his irritation. She lifted his arm, no small feat as muscled as it was, and slid under it as if to help him to rise. But as her body pressed to his, he groaned and tightened said arm. He crushed her to him, bringing her around to pin to his chest, with her backside dropping onto his bent knee. Her hand fluttered, and the gentle sensation teased him through the armor. With her scent surrounding him and her luscious backside on his knee, he forced himself to look at her.

Her gray eyes were wide in her small face. Dark blonde eyebrows rose with concern but not fear. He liked that she didn't fear him. Her tiny nose tapered to full lips and a pointy chin. *Stubborn.* Riotous dark blonde curls tumbled around her. *Untamed.*

"Am I harming you?" he asked as soon as he realized how tiny she was. Although, as his gaze traveled the shape of her breasts, tiny did not mean immature. She was a ripe human woman.

Her mouth parted at his words, then a splash of pink stained her cheeks. "No."

When the sweetness of her arousal assaulted his nose, he squeezed his eyes shut and trembled, drawing in deep breaths to memorize her scent, regardless of how detrimental it was to his control.

And he had longed for this?

"If you release me, we can get you to a medic." At her concern, he snapped his eyes open to smile at her.

"Supreme Commander Oyaz, might I suggest releasing Izzy?" Garix loomed, his warning clear in his stiff posture and clenched fists.

Vorn stood beside him, his eyes narrowing as he assessed the situation. "Operative Trav has informed me about the...prisoners and their involvement in Lady Caroline's disappearance." With a fist to his chest, he spun on his heel and strode off. Males carried the unconscious Yithians behind him.

"Izzy?" Garix inched closer.

Dragging his gaze from Izabelle's upturned face, Oyaz met Garix's. The male froze then grinned and threw out two hands as if to appease. "Congratulations, Supreme Commander."

So, it is true. Oyaz tightened his grip on his Dar Eth, enough to trap her, not enough to harm her.

"Why don't we both find a medic?" his human woman suggested. She brushed a hand across his chest in a caress that was in no way soothing.

"I am fine," he said, then grimaced at his hoarse voice. Awareness of his surroundings flooded back. He glanced at Garix's understanding expression, the fear emanating from Lady Simmy standing just behind them, and settled on Izabelle's furrowed brow. "See to Elite Warrior Danic. Lady Simmy hit him with a harvest tool," he said to Garix.

Izabelle's gray eyes widened, then crinkled with humor. Her reaction tugged on something in Oyaz's chest.

"A spade?" she asked then laughed. "Proud of you, sis."

"Not funny," Lady Simmy mumbled, edging into the open compartment with a hand on the bulkhead while Garix carried Danic over his shoulder.

Izabelle wiggled, indicating she wanted up. Oyaz forced his fingers to release her. It went against every fiber in his being to do so.

She jumped up and circled him. "We'll talk about this later," she whispered in his ear, sending darts of white lust through him. Before he could snatch her into his arms again, she hugged her sister. "You didn't hit him with the sharp edge, sis?"

"Of course not, the flat end. I'm not a monster."

Izabelle looped an arm through Lady Simmy's before escorting her off the shuttle. Oyaz struggled to his feet and watched helplessly as his Dar Eth strolled away from him.

"What the hell just happened?" Lady Simmy asked to which Izabelle shrugged. "Where is my soldier? Your man said he'd take me to medical."

Izabelle gasped and snuck a glance at Oyaz. "He's not my—"

"I did indeed say I would, Lady Simmy." Oyaz bolted forward, testing his weight on his weakened knees.

IZABELLE JERKED AT OYAZ'S smoky voice from just over her shoulder. Damn, he moved fast. He was huge yet so light on his feet. And when she said huge, she didn't mean as big as Garix. Still, his presence stretched out and brushed along her senses. He might as well press his sculpted chest against her back. She stilled and tried not to peek. Curious how tall he was compared to her, she snuck a glance at his chest without meeting his gaze. She estimated that her mouth would be at the height of his nipples. Nipples. What color would they be? She sighed, enjoying the tingling warmth soaking her core.

He growled behind her before sliding his fingers down Simmy's arm to her hand, guiding it to his forearm. "It is this way."

Simmy shifted closer to him, pulled away from Izzy, and allowed him to lead her.

At her sister's unusual behavior, Izzy's eyebrows shot up. Simmy didn't trust easily. With the narrow passage and Garix ahead of them, Izzy followed. Not that she minded. The view was spectacular. Oyaz had a backside like nothing shed seen. It was probably tight enough to bounce a quarter off it. She chuckled at that imagery.

"I can scent you, female."

She gasped, and her panties drenched again. Damn. Now *that* was sexy. He growled and took in a deep breath, expanding his chest, and hummed.

Heat exploded across her face and tied her tongue.

"I would say get a room, but you're my guide," Simmy said.

Izzy pinched her lips—she doubted she could speak without sounding like a call sex operator. Frowning, she dipped her chin to her chest. Why did he affect her so? Perhaps it was the decisive way he'd pulled her against his body, as if he desired her and was strong enough to take what he wanted. That was indescribably magnificent.

They crossed a packed common to medical—same as on the *Gladio*. The medic, who wasn't Brynr, rushed forward to guide Simmy to where Danic lay.

"He will recover, milady. You hit him hard enough to cause sleep and nothing more. I have treated the swelling and bruising and expect him to awaken soon."

"Thank you." Simmy smiled and ran her fingers along the bed, over Danic's hand, forearm, and upper arm, across his collarbone to his neck and jaw, and finally into the locks at his temple.

"May I assess you as well, milady?"

She frowned. "I'm fine, but you can see to him?" She gestured in the direction of Oyaz before burying her fingers in Danic's hair again.

"Certainly, milady." The medic crossed the room to Oyaz. "Supreme Commander Oyaz, please allow me to attend to your injury."

Oyaz seated himself on a lowered bed. His gaze settled on Izzy and didn't budge. Under his intense scrutiny, she shivered but tried to hide her reaction. She liked his smoldering ice blue eyes and the tiny smirk on his firm, lickable lips. Hot jam and buttered toast. She wanted to run kisses along his razor-sharp square jaw and graze her teeth across the pulse in his neck.

Wait. Ice blue eyes? Was he someone's soulmate? Disappointment dropped in her stomach like a led balloon. No, she would ask him first before she gave in to despair.

The medic blocked her view, so she crept closer. Her heart stuttered when Oyaz's gaze followed her.

When the medic darted around medical, tidying things, Izzy rested a hand on the bed beside Oyaz. "I'm sorry you were hurt."

"My fault, Izabelle." He closed his eyes, and a dreamy smile claimed his mouth. Rubbing his chest, he flicked his eyes open and settled his gaze on her again. A potent emotion swirled in their depths, but she couldn't read it.

"Please, milady. Etterians no longer encounter loss of sight in any form. It would be my honor to assess whether your sight can be restored."

Izzy's breath caught, and she dragged her gaze from Oyaz.

Simmy's head whipped up to look in the direction of the medic. "Return my sight?"

Izzy had never considered that a possibility, that the Etterians could heal where Earth's medicine had failed. She'd assumed, judging by Garix's shock, that they could heal eye injuries as soon as they occurred but never long-term injuries. "You can do that?"

"Yes, milady."

Simmy shook her head while a tear slid down her cheek.

Izzy's mouth fell open in disbelief. Was she insane?

"My answer is no, Izzy. I'm not disrupting my life again."

Izzy took a steadying breath, ready to argue her sister into capitulating. "But—"

"I tell you what." Simmy tilted her head and settled an unseeing gaze on Izzy. "Forgive yourself, and I'll consider it."

Izzy jerked back as if slapped. Something tight, heavy, and dark cinched her chest. What Simmy asked was...impossible. Izzy curled her hands into fists, keeping her shoulders stiff lest she broke down and cried. "Simone, please."

"Fixing my eyes won't magically undo what you think you did, Izzy. Forgive yourself first. Then maybe we can try." Simmy lowered her focus to Danic.

Izzy recognized that expression, one of determination.

Her vision blurred. Tears cascaded down her cheeks unchecked. As shards of cold agony pierced her heart, she choked back a sob and ran.

"Ensa?"

With a whimper, she dodged Garix's outstretched hand, weaved through the males gathered to see Simmy, and sprinted along the passages, no destination in mind.

Chapter Twelve

Oyaz vaulted off the bed to go after Izabelle, not liking the sorrow pouring off her. It lacerated his chest with great swaths of pain.

"Please give her time to grieve, Supreme Commander. She has blamed herself all these years." Lady Simmy 'faced' Danic and sighed. "I love her, but she has to let this go. She'll never be able to fully commit to you if she is guilt-bound to me."

"I understand." Oyaz strode to the comm room, fighting himself each step of the way. The Ethera compelled him to bathe in Izabelle's presence, still, he was an Etterian warrior, a Supreme Commander with duties to perform. Once there, he initiated a communication with the prince.

"My prince," he said as soon as the comm was accepted.

"Oyaz, Malo pursues an Etterian scimitar, abandoning his role on Earth."

Oyaz gritted his teeth. Enyl had discovered more information before he could. Already, he was failing his mission.

"It is as it should be when our Dar Eths are priority," Enyl continued. "Still, without Cales and Citus on Earth, our peace negotiations have stagnated."

"Their arrival is imminent, my prince. This day, Yithians tracked a human woman on Earth. One mentioned any females would do." A phantom ache pulsed in his temple. Oyaz rubbed the healed wound and grimaced at the blood stains on his palm.

Enyl frowned, darkness settling in his crystalline eyes. "This is distressing news, Oyaz. I will speak to my father. Our warnings at the G.C. have gone unheeded."

"I believe so, my prince. The Global Council are not known for their decisiveness. I have captured the two Yithians. Sub-Commander Vorn will attend to them in Malo's absence."

"Good. Continue guarding Earth, and be vigilant, Oyaz."

"For Etteria, as always, my prince." He thumped his chest.

"Congratulations on your Dar Eth." Oriana stepped in front of the vid screen, peering into Oyaz's eyes. Her crimson hair and Ferusi-green eyes were striking as always. "Don't endanger yourself without cause; she needs you now more than you know."

"Thank you, my princess." He did ache to find Izabelle.

Enyl looped an arm around Oriana's shoulders. "I agree. I would recommend you rely on your second-in-command. I did not have my full faculties at the beginning of my Ethera."

Oriana chuckled. "He still doesn't."

Enyl growled at her, but she hugged him, burying her nose in the curve of his neck.

Speaking of Etterian matters, Oyaz said, "I have not yet chosen a sub-commander."

Enyl didn't look away from Oriana's upturned face. "I would recommend Elite Warrior Aaro. His record is impressive."

Aaro? Oyaz furrowed his brow. "Thank you for your recommendation, my prince."

"Which is a polite way to say, 'butt out.'" Oriana laughed.

Oyaz flashed a grin just as the vid screen flickered black. With a sigh, he punched instructions on his O.D.I. and summoned Aaro. The male would have to be shuttled from the *Kushin* to Malo's *Gladio*.

"Pilot, locate Vorn."

The pilot pressed buttons on the multi-lit console. "Sub-Commander Vorn is in interrogation, Supreme Commander."

Oyaz rapped his fingers on the console, eager to be elsewhere. "Status on Danic."

"Doing well, Supreme Commander, but has not awoken yet."

"Location of the human woman, Izabelle." Oyaz stifled the shiver saying her name sent through him.

"The viewing deck, Supreme Commander."

Oyaz reined in a smile. She had chosen a secluded spot. "Have accommodation allocated to my males and for the human woman, Lady Simmy. Location of Lady Izabelle's quarters?"

"The one she shares with Elite Warrior Garix?" The pilot arched a brow.

Oyaz stilled, then growled, "Relocate Garix to the barracks. Send through all locations as soon as you have assigned them." His reflection on the display vid revealed a frightening scowl. He softened it when he glanced at the pilot. "Thank you."

"At your service, Supreme Commander."

Oyaz grunted, left the comm, and hurried to Izabelle. His long strides were a little more determined than usual. Garix hovered outside the viewing deck, lunged into pacing, before he halted, peered through the door then paced again. The male should be honored for his dedication, his protection of Oyaz's Dar Eth. But in her mind she wasn't his yet, making their relationship tremulous.

"Thank you for the relocation, Supreme Commander." Garix held a fist to his chest. "As much as she brings me joy, when she is this sad, I confess, I know not how to handle it."

Oyaz stood in the doorway.

Izabelle leaned against a bulkhead with her forehead and palm pressed to a display vid. Her cheeks were red, her eyes swollen, and yet he had never seen a more beautiful creature. He took a moment to absorb her, his salvation and lifeforce. His breath hitched when her lips trembled, and he fought the temptation to calm them with his own. Her delicate hand stroked the vid as if to soothe it, as she had caressed his chest.

"As her Eth, I must learn," he grumbled to Garix.

"May the Maker bless your efforts," Garix said. "It brings me joy she found you. Take care, Supreme Commander, she believes her size is a deterrent."

Oyaz placed his hand on Garix's shoulder. "My thanks for the information. Her stature does not bother me at all." Releasing the male, Oyaz glanced at Izzy. "Have the data officer scan the housing unit. I want it secured." He stepped through the door and waited for it to close. His gaze he fixed on her.

She glanced up and caught him staring, but she didn't react. Instead, she returned her focus to the surrounding stars on the display vids lining the side of the viewing deck.

He strode across the open space and scooped her into his arms. She squeaked her surprise, but when he assumed her seat and held her against his chest, she melted into him. Her hand rose to his chest again, and he realized, that was where it always needed to be. The gesture showed her trust and acceptance.

"It will work out, *ensa*," he said while rubbing his jaw over the crown of her head. The scent of her engulfed him, and he allowed the flame of lust to rip through him. Nothing had ever scented as enticing as Izabelle.

"How can you know, Oyaz?" She buried her face against his chest, even as her fingers flexed. Every move she made settled into his mind, formed memories and cherished moments.

"Lady Simmy will be healed sooner or later. You have only to be patient."

Izabelle shifted back to meet his gaze, her eyes wide with hope. She cupped his cheek, running her thumb across it. "You promise?" she asked like a *damu*.

Unable to resist, he nuzzled her palm, relishing the soft texture of her fingers against his skin. His heart stuttered at the wide range of emotions bombarding him. *Maker.*

"I cannot promise. Life is too uncertain," he said in a gruff voice, opening his eyes to stare into hers—the gray so like sun-kissed Maloidian steel.

"I know." Her unexpected bright smile spread across her face like the magnus sun's rising.

His arms convulsed, and he tightened them around her curvy body.

"Do you do this often?" She stroked a finger along his jaw, dangerously close to touching his lips. They tingled in anticipation. "Pulling women into your arms? Not that I mind," she rasped. "You do it with such decisiveness."

"No, females are scarce and a precious resource."

Her gaze snagged on his mouth, and as the gray of her eyes darkened, his breathing thinned. He wanted nothing more than to kiss her, to ease the bottom lip she nibbled on.

Distracted, she ran a thumb over his eyebrow. "You don't know any females? How's this possible?"

"I do know a human woman. Macy is my friend and my king 's...wife."

"What? She married the king?" Izabelle bounced, her luscious backside rubbing against Oyaz's hard arousal.

Sinking into the fiery need burning outward from his groin, he squeezed his eyes shut. His teeth pressed on his bottom lip while he struggled to control his reactions.

"An honest to goodness king? Is she his soulmate?"

He stilled, his heart slammed into his chest, and he leveled his gaze on her. "You know about soulmates?"

"Yes, Caro explained. She's Malo's, according to him."

"She *is* Malo's Dar Eth as he *is* her Eth," Oyaz said, attempting to calm his heartbeat. His Izabelle was full of pleasant surprises.

"Do you think I have a soulmate, Oyaz?" She dipped her chin, unable to hide her sadness. "Not a single male has kneeled for me."

Thank the Maker. They would have stolen her from him.

"You want one?" He gathered her closer, his fingers flexing where he gripped her hips.

"Hot jam and buttered toast. I want one something fierce." She laughed, squirming against him with boundless energy. "How does it happen or work? Does a man just choose me, and bam, he's mine?"

"No, he must see all of you, then the Ethera brings him to his knees." That was the only explanation why her face on the display vid hadn't triggered the bond. He replayed the moment he admired her curves when she'd run toward the shuttle. The pain had been worse than losing his eye *and* regrowing it...combined.

She focused on the collar of his armor where she stroked his skin. Her delicate touch pebbled the nearest nipple. Without realizing it, she seduced him.

Clearing his throat, he snagged her gaze, ensuring she listened. "Then a pleasurable pain will burst through him, changing his eyes to ice blue."

She froze and realization dawned. "Oyaz?" she squeaked, rising to cup his face. She stared into his eyes with her mouth gaping, the pink recesses tempting him to close the distance. "That's why you're hugging me?"

"I cannot stop holding you, *ensa.*"

She worried her bottom lip with her tiny teeth, then squared her shoulders as she gathered her courage. "Because you're mine?"

"Yes." Such a small word had such meaning.

A joy so bold, so exquisite spread across her face. "You're my soul-mate."

She squealed in excitement then laughed, the sound husky and liberating. Shuffling off his lap, she tugged on his arms until he stood before her. She feathered her hands over his chest, hips, the base of his spine, and his long fingers she laced with hers. "You're so big."

"Yet you do not fear me," he said, inflamed at her touch, his knees weakening again.

"No. You're not unhappy with me, are you? Being so small?" She lifted her face to his, her need for assurance in her furrowed brow and sad eyes.

He lifted her off her feet, crushing her to his chest. She was light, her weight negligible. His armor was able to resist blades and Gika acid, but he imagined he could sense the softness of her breasts.

"I will never be unhappy you are mine, Izabelle. You have blessed me, more than you will ever know."

She smiled, her eyes shimmered, and she snuggled into him, tucking her face in the curve of his neck. Like Oriana had done to Enyl. The swell of unknown emotions expanded Oyaz's chest to a snapping point. No wonder Enyl allowed Oriana's open affection. The experience was addictive.

"What now?" Izabelle's lips brushed across his neck as she spoke, sparking a shiver.

"If you were Etterian, I would take you to my quarters and claim you."

She gasped, and the musk scent of her arousal teased his nose. She would like that, his Dar Eth. Decisive she had called it.

He winced, disbelieving what he was about to say. With how she had mourned Lady Simmy's decision and having bitten a Yithian, forcing himself on her now would be cruel, not after all she had endured in too short a time. He wanted their connection to be memorable and not fleeting, so learning how to control his reactions might be wise. "However, since you are human, I will follow the examples my males have set."

She tilted back with a frown marring her pale brow.

"Xan and Quin did not complete their pairing immediately." He groaned. Izabelle was in his arms and so pliant. All he had to do was lower his mouth to hers. The Ethera urged him to succumb to the temptation. "But, Maker, Izabelle, I want to kiss every inch of you."

Pink splashed across her cheeks, and her breathing was shallow. She wiggled, forcing him to tighten his arms around her.

"Lift me higher."

He obeyed, curious as to why. Brushing her mouth across his wasn't expected, and he growled, wanting her to do it again. Her lips were so soft that he disbelieved the sensation. And as she hovered, peering into his eyes, her breath fanning his chin was warm, tempting. But one kiss wouldn't be enough, and if he knew the taste of her, along with the Ethera's compulsion, he couldn't give her the time she needed.

"Going slow for my benefit's honorable, Oyaz." She plucked his bottom lip with her thumb. "If I was an Etterian woman, what would you do?"

He closed his eyes to envision it. "Izabelle, you would be beneath me and without garments, your hair spread across my pillow, my face between your breasts." Meeting her gaze, he sighed. "I do not know the difference between humans and Etterians, so claiming you in a forceful manner would have to wait until tomorrow."

She frowned. "Why?"

"Our first time should be slow as I learn our differences. Tomorrow, I will have more confidence." His explanation didn't ease her confusion.

"But why wait?"

He chuckled at her ignorance. "Females can only enjoy a mating once a day."

A wicked smile warmed her eyes and shot darts of heat to his groin. He groaned, succumbed to the compulsion, and slashed his mouth across hers, diving his tongue between her lips. Oh, the taste of her. *Maker.* He'd known kissing her would be this addictive, so hot and exotic. He shuddered, tilting his head to deepen the kiss when she dug her fingers in his hair.

He broke away and held his temple against hers. "Do not smile at me like that again. Please, Izabelle."

She ignored his plea, offered him another sensual smile, then snatched a sweet, short kiss. "Human women don't have the same limitations."

"Truly?" He shook his head. Why had no one mentioned this to him?

"Yes, and if you hurry, we can discover the anatomical differences together." The pink on her cheeks darkened.

She couldn't mean... He spread his legs wider, trying to ease the solid Fuyra of his arousal. "Izabelle..."

"Oyaz..." She laughed, throwing her head back to do so. Her hair tickled his arms, and he shifted so it could do so indefinitely.

"We can wait." His breath caught at the thought of sinking into her now, again, and—as she had promised—again.

Her hot mouth on his neck, the graze of her teeth along his skin, scattered his heartbeat, and he bolted. "Where are your quarters?"

With a nip on the left side of his neck, she whispered, "Go left." And thus, she directed him, with each bite sending heat burning along his veins.

He slapped his palm on the panel beside her door, and once inside, pinned her to the bulkhead, gripping her knee to widen her legs for his hips to nestle. A rumble vibrated his chest at his malehood pressing against her entrance.

His kiss was brutal and demanding, with swipes and delves of his tongue as he learned the sweet crevices of her mouth. Her gasps and moans were music to his ears, rivaling his precious Beethoven. Her fingernails grazing his neck, stroking his hair, and tugging on his braid splintered what control he had.

Still, he needed to cleanse the blood off him.

He broke the kiss and crushed her in his arms as they fought for breath. "I must cleanse, my Dar Eth." Wincing, he snatched another hard but quick kiss. "I scent my blood."

She glided her palms over his shoulders to his upper arms. "I'll be waiting."

He released her knees and stepped back, careful to let her slide down than drop her. Her flushed cheeks, the sparkle in her gray eyes, her parted mouth, and heaving breasts became a cherished image the longer he admired her.

"Oyaz?" She arched a brow.

He chuckled and created distance between him lest he succumb again.

"Hot jam and buttered toast," she whispered just as the cleansing room door shut behind him.

Chapter Thirteen

IZZY PACED, HER SKIRTS swishing as much as her thoughts and emotions whirled. Her inner voice squealed, deafening the erratic beating of her heart. She had an Eth. Oyaz, the male she had lost her mind over, was hers. After a few fist pumps, she broke into a dance, as overwhelming waves of joy tumbled through her. When had she ever been this happy?

But therein lay the dilemma. She was about to *do* him on their 'first date.' Did it matter? She was nine years away from being forty, and it had been ages, like in centuries—she huffed—since she last had sex. Doing Marcus against the wall of the Cheery Cherry's office didn't count. Especially when he'd escaped off-world. Earth Armed Forces had harassed her for weeks.

Thankfully, the ass had stolen from her too, so they ruled her out as an accomplice. While slamming her against the office wall, he had siphoned money off the paychip in her wrist. Now, that had been an expensive lesson. She'd avoided men since then.

But Oyaz wasn't Marcus, who now wiled away his days in Mars' penal colony.

Oyaz's heated kisses, his gentle caresses, and those swirling ice blue eyes said he wanted her. And to second guess this when she'd been praying for it, now that was silly. Besides, it was the year 2254. And the sexual revolution somewhere in the 1900s had freed women like her to sleep around willy-nilly. She wouldn't mind a little willy and a lot of nilly.

Giggling, she pressed her fingers to her tender lips. No way on this battleship did Oyaz have a small…um, appendage.

Granny's nipples, would he fit?

Slapping her thigh and relishing the tingling sting of it saved her from succumbing to the tendril of fear coiling around her lungs. Women gave birth, dilating to ten centimeters. She wrapped her arms around her torso. Just thinking about Oyaz doing anything to her set her senses alight. Excitement bounced her, sparked tingles, pooled fiery need in her core, and dampened her panties. She was a goner for sure.

Gasping, she gathered her dirty clothes still stacked on the chair and hurried into the bedroom. Spinning, she scanned for a place to stuff them. Ridges on the top right of a panel drew her notice, and she lunged, rebalanced her overloaded arms, and touched the grooves. The panel glided open, revealing shelves. Grinning like a cat that found the canary, she shoved the clothes to the rear of the shelf. Sighing, she peeled her jeans from the middle, dug in the pockets for her phone, and returned the jeans to the pile. The door closed when she stepped back. Convenient.

Beside the bed, she placed the phone after checking she had about thirty percent battery life. Not that there was a way to charge it onboard a battleship. Aliens didn't have Earth's antiquated technology, not with that glowing-in-the-arm thing.

"Izabelle?" Oyaz's husky voice snatched her breath.

She hurried out of the bedroom. Then she slammed to a halt with her slippers squeaking on the metallic flooring.

In a robe, split wide down his chest, stood...her male.

Holy flaming nipples.

Her gaze roamed freely, lingering too long on the bronzed caramel of his chest, the flexing of his fingers, to his toes peeking out the bottom of the robe. His unbound hair swirled around him like a man underwater. While staring at her, he whispered something, and his hair braided itself. He swung it, caught the tail, then clipped it.

He drew in a deep inhale, expanding his chest until she prayed the robe would slip off and bare all. Her heart had long since lost its rhythm, and her lungs burned, urging her to breathe.

His nostrils flared, and a deep rumble traveled from his belly to his throat. "You scent...incredible." With a few massive strides, he swooped her into his arms and carried her to the bedroom.

He lowered her to the bed until her knees touched down. With gentleness, his fingers lingered on her hips before he slid his hands up her back to dive into her hair.

"Soft." Dipping his head, he buried his face in the curls, then gathered a few to rub along his cheek. "Undress, *ensa*, if you want to keep your garments."

She squeaked. Would he strip them from her if she didn't? Heat swelled, churning, and she pinched her thighs together against the growing ache.

A slow sensual smile curled his mouth, one dimple appeared in his cheek, and his blue eyes warmed. "As you wish." With a flick of his wrists, her shirt flapped open, scattering the tiny buttons.

She quivered, digging her fingers into his robe as her breath whooshed out of her. Had she known, had she even thought of it, she might have chosen something sexier than a plain white serviceable bra. The smallest mercy was that her panties matched.

His focus settled on her breasts. She glanced away, not willing to peek at his reaction. *Too small, right?*

"Maker, Izabelle."

At his whisper, she flicked her gaze up. He rested a trembling hand above her cleavage. His touch spread warmth, while the intensity in his eyes snagged her focus. A bomb could explode beside her, and she wouldn't miss his fascinated daze.

"So...beautiful." He ran a finger lower and hooked the clasp of her bra, then with a jerk, it too parted.

His breath hitched when her breasts bounced free. With the slowest of motions, he swept the torn shirt and bra off her. The cool air against her heated skin puckered her nipples. But when he feathered his palms across the peaks, they hardened into diamonds, shriveling the areolas around them. She whimpered, throwing her head back as pleasure barreled through her. Ogling his face through hooded eyes, she arched into his hands, desperate for his touch.

When he closed around a globe, he brushed his mouth across hers. At the swipe of her tongue along his bottom lip, he growled, slid his hands from her breasts to her back, and yanked her against his chest. He took what he wanted, conquered her mouth, her senses, yet it wasn't enough. She craved more. Her body ached to know him better, closer, harder.

He broke the kiss and pinned his cheek to hers, his rasps hot over her ear.

Her cheeks flushed at what she had to admit. "Oyaz, I'm not sure I can take more."

He leaned back to smile. "You lack patience, *ensa*."

Since the opportunity presented itself, she peeled his robe's magnetic clasp apart and rubbed her breasts against his chest, fluttering her eyes shut on a whimper. The heat of him, the velvet of his muscles teasing her nipples, stole her ability to think.

On his rumble, her world tilted as he flipped her. He sprawled on top of her. Even though he kept his weight off in a push-up, the warmth of his body saturated her. She spread her thighs wide and hooked her legs around his hips, tugging him. As his hard-on pressed at her sex through her skirt, she writhed, searching for a specific position. It wasn't enough.

"Next time, I'll wait for you naked." She clawed his biceps, urging him closer. Twisting and stretching, she tried to reach his lips.

"Izabelle..." He moaned, his muscles twitching under her fingertips.

Shifting his weight to one hand, he gripped her knee with the other and slipped his hand under her skirt. His hot touch along the sensitive skin of her inner thigh seized her lungs. Her core twanged and cried out in silence for release. Another rip registered as if far off, and air cooled her legs. A tug followed, and his fingers slipped, unhindered, into her folds.

She cried out, arching into his gentle touch, gyrating her hips until he brushed something infinitely sensitive. Then she gasped and held herself still, digging her nails into his arms as waves of bliss flowed outward, up to her nipples to her voice lodged in her throat.

He kissed her, and she latched onto his lips, needing them against her own, longing for the swipe of his dominating tongue.

Ending the kiss, he dipped his head and glanced at his hand between her thighs.

Fear was swift to cast its darkness, and she looped her arms around his neck and hung on. "Don't stop."

"Oh, *ensa*," he smiled, "I have no intention of stopping. But I must learn what pleases you." Pulling out of her embrace, he shifted onto his knees without breaking contact. "If I do this?" He flicked his finger to the side, and she whimpered when he stroked neglected nerves. "Or this?" Circling her nub, he strummed back and forth, and she cried out, coming off the bed when burning pleasure hit her.

Her world exploded. She didn't care what she looked like writhing and thrashing. Colors trickled across her vision, her senses slammed into a pinnacle, every nerve ending tingled, reporting for duty, and the sweetest, purest joy saturated her body.

"Oyaz," she hummed, ignoring the tug and pull when he shifted between her thighs.

"Guide me, Izabelle, my Dar Eth." At his guttural request, she wrapped her fingers around the girth of his hard-on. She took a moment to gape at his bronzed length, then nudged it lower until he pressed into her.

"There." Running her palm over the head, she released him, looped her legs around his hips, and angled her pelvis.

He supported his weight in a push-up again as he dipped into her. How he stretched her, how he stimulated the sensitive flesh of her channel, she couldn't describe. She whimpered, needing each stroke, aching for that complete moment of peace that would fill her when he buried himself to the hilt.

They were not there yet, and he trembled, his eyes closed, his jaw clenched.

She feathered kisses along his chin, to his lips, and when he focused on her, she smiled. "Nice and slow, you can do this."

He chuckled. "That is a given. Not harming you is not."

"Then roll over."

"Why?" Frowning, he pulled out with a groan.

She scrambled to her knees, and with her palm on his chest, shoved him onto his back. "If you're scared of hurting me, let me do the impaling. You can flip me over once you're in me."

He folded his arms behind his head and watched as she climbed over him. Rumbles traveled through him when she spread her legs wide, exposing herself to him. Crushing her breasts to his chest, she twirled her hips, searching for the head of his cock, and once it stroked across her entrance, she lowered herself.

Sitting up took him deeper into her, but the sensations were wonderful, as he stretched her, rubbed along the walls, and reached her core. He gripped her hips and held her still while he raised his pelvis to meet her descent, but she was selfish and wallowed in the sensations of him deep within her.

Then her world tilted again when he flipped them. She laughed, stealing a kiss.

"Maker, Izabelle, you feel so good…Like nothing I have experienced before. So beautiful, I must be dying." His eyelids fluttered as he withdrew and thrust in again.

Tears prickled her eyes, and her laughter caught in her throat. A breathless groan took over, and her mind blurred, as he 'claimed' her. There was no other word to describe him pounding into her, hitting her G-spot, shattering who she was, and reforming her as his. The colors left blinding spots on her retinae, and she clung to him, relishing the texture of his skin beneath her hands.

His roar reverberated off the walls, and he froze, while his gaze snagged hers. Something swirled in the ice blue depths, as intense as him buried in her. He cupped her cheek, traced the line of her nose, and pinched her chin, holding her still for a gentle kiss, one filling her with the ultimate hope.

That he would one day love her.

Chapter Fourteen

Izabelle sprawled across Oyaz. Her breasts were crushed against his chest, and the swing of her raised foot rocked her body along his. Not by much, but it was enough to renew the desire he'd just spent. *Maker.* Her sweet smile, the way her gray eyes turned smoky, and when she nibbled her lip like she did now, he wanted to kiss her. His malehood tingled, hardened, and drove lust through his mind.

After sweeping curls off her cheek, he draped an arm over her, pulling her closer and tighter against him. Her fulfillment had driven him wild, and the compulsion to bury himself within her had stripped his control. Had she not taken him in hand—he shuddered at the memory—he might have harmed her.

She was small, yet all female, in her curves, scent, nature, petite hands stroking his skin, and in the tightness of her sex when he plundered her. *Alodon's balls, she is perfect for me.*

"I...have to explain, Oyaz, the earlier scene. My sister..." She sucked in a jagged breath.

The air in the room thickened. He froze, cupped her shoulder, and listened.

"That day she irritated me more than normal, with her bossiness and lecturing me on how to improve my studies so I wouldn't fail. Always better than me, doing well in her classes, the apple of my parents' eye. I wasn't. The epic failure, setting fire to the kitchen when I tried to bake, splattering paint across Mom's cow-leather couch. No matter what I touched, I destroyed."

She wiped a stray tear, and he hurried to help her, catching the droplets on his fingers. This was sorrow, the dark gray of her eyes, the faraway gaze, the downturn of her lips as she spoke, and the strangled tone in her sweet voice.

"Dad thought a picnic would be a treat, in a conserved park an hour's drive from home. Simmy and I quibbled the ride there. I threw hateful glances at her, as if my failures were her fault. I know now she tried to help me. In the end, it was I who nudged her off the path. I hadn't anticipated her tripping. The snap of her ankle echoed in my ears, muting Mom's cry of alarm. But when Simmy smacked into the tree…" Izabelle paled. "Oh, Oyaz, I'll never forget the sound."

Tears flowed over his fingers, but he didn't pull away. Lady Simmy was right. Izabelle had to release her self-hatred. They'd been *damu* when it happened. He didn't blame her, neither did her sister. And yet, the helplessness in her voice was something he understood all too well. When Madyx had ignored wise counsel, Oyaz hadn't known what to do. In the end, he'd lost his battle-bond to a shuttle crash. All his life, Oyaz hadn't been able to shake the thought that had he been on Fuyra, Madyx wouldn't have died.

"Dad's expression haunts me. Worse when we learned she'd never see again. I withdrew. And every time I tried to help, I was my usual failure. Knocking things over, leading Simmy into objects, dropping cups of coffee on her... I retreated deeper within me, keeping to my room, to myself, not sharing my favorite pastimes, not joining the family. But when I was forced to interact, I covered it well, hiding it all behind a bubbly façade."

She sniffed, then nuzzled his palm.

"Little did I know there was more to come. We were returning from yet another dismal medical assessment when Mom lost control of the car. The impact crushed the front, killing her. But Dad lived long enough to make me promise to look after Simmy." Izabelle met Oyaz's gaze and splayed her fingers across his chest. "I tried my best, y'know. Did everything I could, sacrificed all that I am. But still, I'm the failure, the useless excuse for a sister. She's better off without me, Oyaz." Her bottom lip trembled, even as she squared her shoulders. "It will take every ounce of me to let her go, but if we leave Earth, she stays behind."

Oyaz stiffened. Was that not too drastic? "You will never be at peace if you abandon her, Izabelle."

She shook her head. "Simmy's fought me every step of the way. Trust me, a life without me is all she wants."

At the idea of a life without Izabelle, cold engulfed his soul. "It is not what I want." He gathered her close and tugged her up, leveling her lips with his.

Her smile before he kissed her heated the air in his lungs. The nuances of her, the pendulum swing of her emotions, her boundless energy fascinated him. And the sweet softness of her lips lured him to dive deeper, to learn everything that made up his Dar Eth. He feathered his lips along her cheek to her ear. The taste of her skin on his tongue was more addictive than hot chocolate, regardless of the saltiness of her tears.

"Okay, a quickie, but then we have to discuss my farewell gift to my sister," she said.

"Quickie?" His eyelids fluttered as the O.D.I educated him. One image snagged, and he growled, sliding out from under her so fast she lay there on her stomach, her face in the bed.

Laughing, she rolled onto her side and raised a brow at him. With a firm grasp of her hips, he lifted her onto her knees.

"Oh." She wiggled her backside, her folds glistening as in his vision.

He ran a finger along her delicate flesh. Her breathless moan bolstered his confidence. She arched her back the more he stroked her, her curls flying everywhere when she tossed her head and clawed the bed.

She wriggled before peeking over her shoulder at him. "Oyaz, please," she gasped, her gray eyes hooded, and her lips parted.

He looped an arm around her pelvis and lifted her backside higher, positioning the head of his malehood at her entrance. With a hand splayed over her belly, he inched in, stretching her. Pushing forward, he hissed when she gripped him in her tight sheath—so hot and silken that each inch conquered was with a victorious explosion of color and pleasure.

She curled her body, rubbing something along the ridged denit of his length that stole his thoughts. *Maker.*

"Move. Faster. Now."

Her command was one he willingly obeyed. He withdrew and slammed into her. She screamed his name, begged for more while her channel pulsed, released, and worked him deeper.

Using him as leverage, she matched the rhythm of his thrusts, shoving her backside back until she stilled, her hips tilted, and a whimper escaped her kiss-swollen lips. Waves of heat gushed over him, throwing him over the crest of his fulfillment. Unable to halt his twitching hips as lightning skittered along his malehood, he roared.

He struggled to calm his erratic heartbeat, he a trained warrior, battle-ready, conditioned. Collapsing, he held her to him, layered his chest to her back, and fell, landing on his side but keeping himself inside her. With a tug, he pinned her to his body, relishing her tiny explosions squeezing him.

She sighed, holding his arm around her, and snuggled deeper against his chest.

With a kiss to her temple, he inhaled the combined scents of their mating, letting it expand his lungs, along with the sense of peace that saturated his body.

"Your gift to Lady Simmy?"

Izabelle twisted in his embrace to meet his gaze. "Her clay. She has to finish sculptures for a gallery. I was hoping you and I could fetch her tools and materials. Please."

"Of course, *ensa*." With no word from Garix, Oyaz assumed the housing unit was secure. And perhaps, the journey would reveal more of the dynamics of her relationship with her sister.

She squeezed his arm and offered him a wide smile that warmed her eyes. "Thank you, Oyaz."

Her stomach gurgled, and as her Eth, he was duty-bound to care for her.

"Hungry?"

"A little." She rubbed her backside against him, a sigh slipping past her lips. "Are you hungry? I can make a salad?" Rolling within his arms, she faced him, her eyes wide and her smile bright.

He grinned. "I have not tried your salad." Images flickered across his mind. The ingredients' bold colors and variety intrigued him. "Please."

She bounced off the bed, jogging to the rehydrator. He didn't dare blink and miss the jiggle of her backside and the wild mass of curls brushing along the curve of her waist. *Maker, I am a blessed male.*

"Garix loves my—" She gasped, punched something in the replicator, and pulled on a colorful dress that reached her toes. Her jogging to him was as mesmerizing as her leaving him. "I meet you and neglect my friend. Oyaz, please...where's Garix?"

"I had him relocated to the barracks. He is well, *ensa*."

Her shoulders slumped, and she offered him another smile. "Good. Do you think he's hungry?" She slapped her thigh. "Duh, of course he is. Call him, Oyaz. I'll make enough for him too." Darting to the rehydrator, she missed his growl.

Leaping from the bed, he yanked on his breeches and strode barefoot to her. "I would prefer not to."

She froze and faced him, her brow furrowing. "Why? Is it a rank thing?"

"A what?" He frowned.

"You know, Garix being a warrior and you a supreme commander?" She clasped her hands in front of her, wringing them.

Oyaz shook his head. "I want you to myself, Izabelle."

"Oh." Pink splashed her cheeks. "I'll make him a salad and have it delivered. Is that all right?"

"Yes." Oyaz circled her waist with his arms and rested his chin on her shoulder as she browsed the rehydrator. Objects appeared as vibrant as the O.D.I's images. She set those aside before ordering a dagger from the replicator. Then with admirable skill, she sliced the colorful food on the Fuyra-stone counter.

She fed him pieces as she worked, and each flavor was sharp, sweet, and earthy. The red balls popped in his mouth. Cherry tomatoes, she called them. The purple vegetable with white center was too pungent. Red onion when it was purple? But the yellow slivers were his favorite.

"What are those?" he asked. Contentment settled where his impatience had been that morning. Warmth, joy, and hope engulfed his chest until it expanded to a snapping point.

"Yellow sweet peppers."

He pressed a kiss to her throat, tasting her skin, while she tossed the ingredients and drizzled a sweet-smelling yellow sauce over it. Honey mustard? Two massive bowls sat to one side with a smaller bowl closer to her.

"Sit. I'll bring it to you."

He obeyed, eager to share this meal with her. She placed the bowl in his hands and held out a fork.

Once he accepted both, she skipped to the display vid. "Garix et Orix."

Garix's face appeared. He rubbed his eyes with his posture stiffening. "What is it, *minus susa*?"

"I made you a salad. Thought you could collect."

Oyaz clutched the bowl to his chest, his fork bending in his grip

Garix frowned. "You are with your Eth, Izzy."

She grinned, bouncing on her toes. "So, get it and get out."

He chuckled. "Fair enough, *ensa*. On my way."

The screen flickered to black, and she smiled at Oyaz as if fire didn't course through his veins. Minus susa? How dare Garix have an endearment for Oyaz's Dar Eth? *Little Joy* was not one of deep emotion, still, their familiarity irked Oyaz. She treated Garix as a brother, a friend, he got that. But he would never let his friendship with Macy come between her and Xeus. Garix should agree to step aside.

Oyaz unclenched his jaw and forced a stiff smile when Izabelle sank into the comfy beside him.

"Don't you like it?" She stared at his untouched meal while nibbling on her bottom lip. "Shit. I'm sorry, Oyaz." She placed her bowl on the table and crossed to the rehydrator. "I forgot you eat more than me."

Two brown wedges formed on the rehydrator, and the rich aroma of meat twitched his nose. She removed his bowl cradled on his lap, and minutes later, he held a plate with a massive strip of meat on one side and the pile of salad on the other.

"Try that."

With an eating dagger she'd ordered for him, he sliced a piece of the succulent meat and popped it into his mouth. The savory flavor coated his mouth, stronger than Macy's hamburger. Along with the yellow sauce, his tastebuds leaped and dance. He groaned, closing his eyes as he chewed.

Garix arrived and left with the same meal in his hands.

This time, Oyaz didn't let it bother him. It showed that his Dar Eth had a soft heart, and he was a brute for thinking otherwise.

Chapter Fifteen

Oyaz rubbed his bare stomach. A satisfied sigh escaped him, and he settled his gaze on her, sparking a familiar burn in Izzy's core.

"That was delicious, Izabelle. My gratitude for sharing it with me."

Heat burned her cheeks, and she dipped her chin, stopped her foot from swinging back and forth, and shrugged.

"Shall we visit Lady Simmy's housing unit?"

She gasped. "It's just called a house," she stuttered. "Let me change."

Not waiting for him to answer, she leaped to her feet and rushed to the room to strip. Whipping off the dress, she jumped up and down to yank on each leg of her jeans. Voices rumbled from the living room. She hurried. After she snapped on a bra and wrestled with a T-shirt, she sat on the edge of the bed to pull on sneakers. Lastly, she slid her dying phone into the back pocket of her jeans.

While she flicked her hair out of the collar, she skipped to Oyaz and faltered. He wore a white T-shirt. It molded to his bronzed chest, so bright against his dark skin that her mouth watered. Flaming nipples, who did she have to thank for this delicious eye candy? He looked like a biker from old, in black camo pants, thick boots, and that T-shirt. Hot jam and buttered toast.

Oyaz closed his eyes on a groan, and when he settled his gaze on her, the intensity in their blue depths snatched her breath.

"Congratulations, Lady Izzy." Their guest was an Etterian she'd never seen. His relaxed posture and lack of staring said he'd been around human women.

"Thank you." She flashed a smile.

When Oyaz held out his arm, inviting her to hug him, she didn't hesitate. She had the Eth she wanted, she just didn't know him well enough yet. Did he tolerate, or better, like public displays of affection?

She pressed her body to his and slipped her arm as far around his waist as she could reach. He rumbled and kissed her forehead, cradling her close to his chest. Humming, she nuzzled a pec with her nose.

His voice was hoarse when he said, "This is my Sub-Commander Aaro."

The new male's eyes widened, and his shoulders stiffened. "Truly?" He shook his head. "I serve Etteria, and my thanks for your faith in me."

Oyaz laughed. "Prince Enyl recommended you, Aaro. I studied your file and agree with his assessment. Izabelle and I will relocate to the *Valiant* once we return from Earth." He lowered his gaze to her upturned face. "I promised my Dar Eth a quick visit."

Hiding the knot of dread twisting in her stomach, she gave his waist a squeeze. They were moving to another battleship, and she couldn't hold this bold decision against him. He was a Supreme Commander with duties. Besides, she'd said she was done babysitting Simmy. Still, to test her resolve sent a tremor of fear through her.

Aaro spread his legs and clasped his hands behind his back. "Shall I gather a few males?"

Oyaz grinned. "It will not be necessary, Aaro. I cleared the housing...*house* when we collected Lady Simmy. Garix has also scanned for additional threats. I do not anticipate any."

Aaro pursed his lips. "As you wish, Supreme Commander."

"Once Danic is well, return to the *Valiant* and attend to tasks in my absence." As soon as Aaro left, Oyaz cupped her cheek. "Does this alarm you?"

She shrugged. "I go where you go."

A magnificent smile swept across his lips and took a one-way ticket to her puckered nipples. *Wow, with just a smile?*

"Izabelle, I cannot wait to return to our quarters, to the pleasure between your thighs. You please me." With one arm, he dragged her up until her face aligned with his. As if she weighed nothing, he held her there while he buried his fingers in her hair. A gentle tug pulled her head back. Through hooded eyes, she watched him dip his head and brush his mouth across hers. He groaned, and a slight tremble rippled through him. "I want you, *ensa.*"

She wrenched her trapped arms free and looped them around his neck. "You have me."

His breath caught, and the ice-blue in his eyes swirled. He raised his gaze to the ceiling. A pulse ticked at the base of his jaw. She feathered a kiss across it—the flutter of the pulse like a butterfly's wings against her lips.

He rumbled, squeezed her, then slid her down his body. "Let us hurry."

She struggled to focus. Potent, addictive, that's what he was, and the idea of spending the rest of her life on her back didn't bother her. After selling the Cheery Cherry, she had no plans to fill her time. When she had a moment, she would list all the things she wanted to do, like pottery or oil painting. Hell, a woven rug would prettify their quarters.

He typed on his O.D.I. then drew her into his arms again. Frowning, she opened her mouth to ask him what he planned, but he silenced her with another kiss. No more tentative forays, just a bold expedition around her mouth, dueling with her tongue, and nipping her lips. Her body flooded with tingles, and she wrapped her legs around his waist, seeking a closer connection. She throbbed between her thighs, and her breasts grew heavy. Her nipples ached for his touch. He broke the kiss to run his lips along her jaw to her earlobe.

She cried out when he nibbled on it while he massaged her butt cheek.

When he released her, his face contorted with harsh desire, and the blue in his eyes glowed. "Come, get what you need."

She blinked at him, struggling to string her thoughts together. "What—?"

"We are here, *cnsa.*"

She gasped and spun, facing her sister's house. The cool breeze, the fading sunlight, and the sweetness of the air should have registered. But all she had wanted was the spiciness of Oyaz's skin.

"You zapped me?" She raised her face to Oyaz's, trying not to gape. No nausea lingered, no urge to gag, just a desperation to climb him like a tree.

He laced his fingers through hers and ushered her up the stone steps onto the porch. There he froze and listened, then opened the front door.

Things were out of place.

She frowned. "You said you cleared the house. What did you mean?" Picking up a strewn paintbrush, she rubbed the soft bristles across her palm.

"Two Yithians—"

"Sharkmen."

"Yes, they do resemble your shark sea creatures." With quick strides, he opened the kitchen door. "I found them here."

She peeked around him and grimaced. The kitchen had also been ransacked. "Oh, no. This might take longer than I thought." She grabbed what brushes and pallet knives she recognized and hurried to the front of the house where the studio dominated most of the living room. There, she found bags of clay and a crate. Dumping the tools in the crate, she tried to pick up a bag. Oyaz nudged her aside and lifted it with one hand, stacking it and three others into the crate.

Complete statues and busts lined a wall. And a half-carved face dominated one workbench. An old woman formed, with grooves in her craggy cheeks, and somehow, in her eyes, was the passing of time and the accumulation of knowledge.

Izzy's breath stilled. *Damn.* She'd known Simmy was good, but this...? How had she managed to capture so much emotion without seeing it in the model's eyes?

"It is beautiful, *ensa.*" Oyaz stood beside her.

Izzy wiped away a tear and forced a smile. "This needs to go, Oyaz. Maybe if I hold it when you zap us?" Smothering a shiver, she squared her shoulders, instead. For Simmy, she was willing to have a little clay in her DNA.

"I shall tag them, and Pilot Vyar will port them to Lady Simmy." He tugged out of a pocket a white disc the size of a thumbnail. "Tap the center of the tag to activate. You have three seconds to pin it to the object."

"What about a workbench?" Ice drenched her, and she gasped. "I'm so sorry, Oyaz, to ask so much of you. Perhaps just zapping it there is enough. Let Simmy decide what she wants."

"You are my priority, *ensa*. Whatever you need, you have but to ask. Whatever you want, it will be my pleasure to provide."

Her heart fluttered as she absorbed the sincerity carved across his indomitable face. "Samesies. Now bend so I can kiss you."

He did without hesitation, and she grasped his cheeks to plant a wet one on his lips.

Stepping away lest she rubbed herself against him like a cat in heat, she held out her palm. "Give me the tags. I'll move around and choose what has to go."

He dug into his pocket and dumped small, white circles in her hand. "That is all I carry. Should we need more, we can return."

She danced around the room while he typed on his holographic letters. Whenever his gaze returned to her, something fuzzy and warm ran along her skin. One by one, the items she chose zapped away.

Along with the art supplies and statues, she'd tagged Simmy's cactus. Who knew if it would grow or survive on a battleship, but if it died during her time away, Simmy would be devastated. How long she'd stay onboard hadn't been discussed yet.

"I'm done." Izzy studied the room and nodded.

"Good." Oyaz's lips across her neck snatched her breath.

She faced him. "Fun time?" She wiggled her eyebrows while splaying herself across the front of him. "Let's get naked and see where that leads." Despite the twinge of soreness from their previous sessions, she was eager to go again. If need be, she would ask for pain meds to be added to the shower.

"Here?" He scanned the living room, where only a double couch occupied the space. It was big enough for them if she straddled him.

She grinned. "Yes." Trailing her fingers down his T-shirt-covered chest, she hooked on the waistband of his pants and tugged. "Strip."

Releasing him, she toed off her sneakers, whipped her shirt over her head, and unzipped her jeans, shimmying out of them.

He watched her, his focus intense.

In her bra, panties, and socks, she sashayed to the couch. Rewarding her efforts with a rumble, he bolted forward and swept her into his arms.

"Oh, no, you don't." She laughed, wriggled out of his embrace and patted the couch cushion. "Strip and sit."

He grinned and pulled his shirt off. With a tap at his belly, his pants opened, exposing the V of smooth, bronze skin to his large bulge. He unsnapped his boots and wrenched those off, before he lowered his pants down his sculpted thighs, past his knees to his rock-hard calves. Her core throbbed, and she pinched her thighs together to ease the ache. Him naked before her, she'd never seen anyone so beautiful. All those edges, those rippling muscles, shimmered in the fading sunlight, along with his hard-on, proud, erect, and bobbing with eagerness.

"Izabelle?"

She snapped out of her daze to point at the couch. When he settled his ass with his cock resting on his flat stomach, she unclipped her bra and let it fall from her fingers. She cupped her breasts and massaged them. His gaze was riveted on everything she did, and her inner slut toyed with the idea of playing stripper for him. She shook her head. Knowing herself, she would snag her bra in her hair or pull a muscle. Hooking her thumbs in her panties, she lowered them to the floor then pushed them aside with her toes.

Climbing across his lap, she spread her thighs wide to cradle his cock where she ached for it most. She moaned as a frisson of pleasure bolted from her core to her breasts.

He gripped her hips with a grunt, guiding her as she rubbed herself along the length of him, driven mad with lust and unable to stop herself. His gaze didn't drop from hers, and compelled by an unknown force, she couldn't break the connection. She rose, angled her hips, and impale herself. His eyelashes fluttered, but he maintained eye contact. His teeth dimpled his bottom lip, and his nostrils flared.

Cool air brushed across her, tossing her hair and puckering her nipples. A shiver assailed her. With each gyrate, as she withdrew and plunged, a burning need grew until breathing was inconsequential, and only the staccato beat of her heart filled her ears. Digging her nails in his shoulders, she increased the pace, climbing a mountain peppered with mini-bursts of joy to the pinnacle of pleasure. Her gasps merged with his grunts, and he thrust upward, meeting her downward strokes. Tingles—cold, hot, intense—swept across and through her until white explosions of light blinded her.

His shoulders tensed, his grip tightened, and his eyes widened. A pained expression crossed his face. He roared her name. By then, she didn't care, riding her wave of divine bliss, bucking and thrashing as new bolts of heat shot through her.

She slumped. Her energy drained from her limbs, and a lassitude melded her to him.

He caught her, crushed her to his chest, and pressed his hot mouth to the pulse in her neck. "Maker, Izabelle, you are perfect."

She winced, and pain pierced her ecstatic heart. Her spectacular orgasm broke her control, and a flood of tears barreled up her throat. She wasn't perfect. Far from it.

Scrambling off him, she tried not to ogle him as she dressed. Even though, she knew full well how his gaze didn't shift from her while he pulled on his pants with efficient movements.

But when he froze, forming a statue, she frowned and tilted her head to listen. Her senses heightened, and every hair on her body rose. Tingles of another kind rippled over her skin. In one swift move, he shoved her behind him.

His body was that of a coiled snake. Anger hardened his face. He dipped his head to whisper, "Come, we must port now." Yanking her into his arms without bothering to put on shoes or his T-shirt, he touched his O.D.I. "Pilot Vyar?"

The front door swung open in slow motion. Two sharkmen sidled in. They raised their black guns. Oyaz twisted and wrapped his body around her, offering the aliens his back. They fired yellow bolts of lightning without hesitation.

Oyaz slumped, hitting the floor, almost dragging her down with him.

She gaped. Had they killed her Eth? She narrowed her focus on the rise and fall of his chest. Relief, like a dunking of hot water, hit her shoulders, and her breath whooshed out.

With wide eyes, she paused as realization dawned. She was alone and unarmed, but self-preservation wasn't in her thoughts. Fire burned along her veins where moments ago euphoria had resided.

She was pissed.

Chapter Sixteen

What the fuck? When the hissing shark approached, she leaped over Oyaz's body, ready to defend him with her life. She had no weapons but her wits, and after an epic orgasm, even those had abandoned her. She struggled to form a plan.

"Don't you fucking touch him." She spread her legs, ready to tackle the alien.

The alien's backward swing took her by surprise. She landed with a cry. Fire spread across her jaw, and the familiar metallic tang of blood pooled in her mouth. Her shoulder and hip throbbed, and the back of her head ached like it had bounced off the floor.

Before she could scramble to her feet, the shark used his booted foot to pin Oyaz's arm to the floor. A bolt of yellow shot out the gun and hit Oyaz's wrist. She screamed when another bolt hit him. Electric sparks dissolved into his skin. He twitched and jerked. She crawled across to cradle his head.

Despite the tears blurring her vision, she glared at the alien. "I hate you. He was unconscious. You didn't have to shoot him over and over. Are you such a coward that a harmless male threatens you?" Since the tremors had subsided, she set Oyaz's head down and jumped to her feet.

"I am no coward, Earthian female."

She jerked, and like with Vorn, fury slammed into her and stole her tongue for a second. "You fucking understand me?"

"Your voice irritates, puny female." The other sharkman hiss-laughed, and since her gaze was on him, she didn't sense the other's movement until he swung an arm around her collarbone.

Screaming, she squirmed, trying to break free, then froze, her limbs numbing.

There on his arm was a bitemark. No fucking way.

She had nothing to hurt him with, no weapons, no random sporting equipment, and no spade. And she didn't have Oyaz's arm thingy to zap or to call Pilot Vyar. On the verge of giving up, she spotted an unused tag on the table.

Keeping her gaze on the laughing shark watching his friend struggle, she dug into her pocket, tapped the front of the tag, and stuck it to the bitemark. When Vyar zapped him, she would go with and get Oyaz help. Argh, shark DNA. She shivered, swallowing a gag.

But the stupid alien dropped her. She fell, landing on her arm. Gritting her teeth, she rolled over onto her stomach, huffing the hair out of her face.

He was gone.

His friend released a war cry that drenched her with ice from scalp to toes. Panic was swift to strike, and she activated the last tag and threw it at his lunging body. It stuck to his shoulder. He rasped something, flung his black gun aside, and tried to swipe the tag off. Bam. He too was gone.

"Sorry, Vyar. Hope you zapped them to storage."

Realization struck, and the horror of it froze her veins. *Shit.* Had she just sent two sharkmen to Simmy's room? Izzy whimpered, collapsed to her knees, and let the sobs rack her. Her tears flowed unhindered, and she only moved to swipe a wrist across her runny nose. Everything she touched turned to disaster. And there was nothing she could do to fix it this time.

Oyaz was unconscious, and who knew for how long. She couldn't operate her sister's tech since it was set to her voice. Nor could they stay here or hide in the tunnel. More aliens might search for their friends. Leaping across to Oyaz's sprawled body, she climbed over him to pat his cheek.

Nothing happened. She might as well have been touching a cyborg.

Swinging her hand back, she slapped him hard. He didn't flinch.

As fresh tears rose, she clung to his chest and sobbed again. She needed him, now more than ever. They had to return to the battleship to save Simmy.

Her head whipped up mid-sniffle. With their sensitive noses, would smelling salts work? Or vinegar? Scrambling to her feet, she sprinted to the kitchen, skidded on the floor, and slammed into the doorframe while she passed through. Rubbing her burning arm, she scrounged through the cupboards and was victorious when she emerged with a small bottle of vinegar. Holding it uncapped under his nose drew a twitch but not enough to wake him. Right, what was worse than vinegar? Bleach? Back to the kitchen she darted. Under the sink was a bottle of turpentine. That would do.

She was careful, though, not to let the rim of the bottle touch his skin. He jerked, his eyes flew open, and a shudder tore through him.

She squealed. Relief washed over her. There was still time, but they had to hurry. Yanking the bottle back, she capped it, put it aside, and threw herself against him.

He held her away, muttering something.

She frowned, not understanding his words. Was he injured? Why couldn't she hug him? When she stared at him, her world tilted, her hope and joy drained from her.

His eyes were dark blue.

Her chest cinched on a whimper. "What's wrong?"

Pushing her aside, he used the coffee table to stumble to his feet. One side of him dragged as if numb, useless, and confusion twisted his features when he scanned the living room. His gaze settled on her, and her worst fears were realized. He didn't recognize her. His tone and words confused her.

Again with the strange language, but as lyrical as it sounded, she didn't understand him. "Don't you speak English?"

He frowned and stroked his forearm, over a black burn on his wrist. No holographic lettering formed, and no response was forthcoming when he spoke to Vyar. At least, she recognized one word out of his gibberish.

"Oyaz." He touched his chest, his gaze pleading for help.

"Izzy." She bit her lip, hoping the sharp pain of her teeth tearing into her flesh would stem the fresh flow of tears. Crying wouldn't solve anything.

His rattled-off words, though beautiful and foreign, were drenched in a confused tone, with the sentences ending on high notes.

Assuming he was asking about his injury, she hiss-laughed, unable to think of another way to indicate that sharkmen had attacked.

Twisting, she hefted the black gun and showed it to him. After he took it from her with one hand, she pointed to it, then double-tapped her wrist.

Capturing his injured hand in hers, she used her forefinger to touch his chest.

"They did this to you. We must leave... Hide somewhere safe and think of a plan, maybe—" her voice cracked, "—buy you time to heal."

He tilted his head, listened to her but didn't respond, just blinked.

She looped an arm through his on his sagging side and urged him to sit on the couch. Memories assaulted her, and she raised her chin toward the ceiling, fighting the sting of tears. He settled back and sniffed the air. His gaze flicked to her and widened. He studied her, lingering on her breasts.

Yes, her Oyaz was there deep inside. She just...had to get her shit together. Brynr or another medic could heal Oyaz, could bring back her Eth. As long they survived, then she could fix this. Throwing out her palms, she urged him to stay seated.

She dived into the deep chest set in the corner where her camping gear was stashed. She dumped the tent, the sleeping bag, and a medkit on the coffee table before climbing the stairs to her childhood room. One of her old jackets would keep her warm and dry. She didn't pause to travel down memory lane, not when more sharkmen could arrive. Throwing her closet open, she yanked out a drymac and put it on while clambering down the stairs. All they needed was sustenance.

Grabbing a hiking backpack from where she propped it against the hall closet's door, she threw bottles of water inside and what snacks she could find. Simmy wasn't good at cooking, so she stocked instant meals like nuts, dried fruit, energy bars, snack packs, and dried meat.

Izzy filled the bag. The more she had, the better because staying for longer than a night was possible. As she searched the kitchen, she told Oyaz her plan, talking to him from all over the house. Without much effort or her assistance, he was trapped to the couch for now. His arm-thingy must have acted as a translator because with it gone, he didn't understand her. But she had to voice her thoughts, as if doing so tested the validity of the plan.

"I know these woods. My neighbor Miri and I would spend summers camping. We'll hide there for the night while we think of a way to get you to the battleship. Maybe if we're gone long enough, one of your men will come looking. Hopefully Aaro or Garix will miss us." She pulled out her phone and waved it at him. "It's dying. I don't know who to call for help. It's not the same as your display vids. I must have their number first."

She knelt before him, cupping his knees. "Oh, Oyaz, why did this have to happen? You...you're my Eth." Tears trickled free. Grabbing his boots, she helped him clip them on. "You were my one chance at happiness, at meaning something to someone."

Scrambling to her feet, she laughed at her silliness. He didn't understand her, and the sadness in his eyes only mimicked her mood. As she stuffed the sleeping bag into the backpack's compartment and strapped the tent to the bottom of it, she snuck peeks at him. He rested his injured hand on his thigh and curled his fingers, as if he tried to form a fist. When he failed, he'd grunt and try again. She bit her lip, wanting to cry at how helpless she was. Hoisting the backpack onto her back, she snapped the hip belts in place.

"Come, Oyaz, let's leave before more sharks arrive." Fear slithered down her spine as if Death trailed his cold, boney finger. More sharkmen meant two things. They'd be pissed she did something to their buddies. And she had no more tags, leaving her and Oyaz at their mercy. When he didn't budge, she whimpered as the full impact of the situation hit her. Sucking in calming breaths, she fought a rising wave of fear leaking into her limbs, threatening to numb her. Tugging on his good arm, she tried to show he needed to follow her.

He frowned and assessed her backpack. Just like that, with one awkward push off the couch, he stood. Gathering his T-shirt, the only cover he had, she left him to pull it on, even one-handed. She was too short to be anything but a hindrance. Instead of watching all that gorgeous skin disappear behind the white fabric, she closed the front door and latched all the locks. If they tried to get in again, they would have to blast the door off its hinges.

When she faced Oyaz, his shirt was on. Relief slumped her shoulders. But when he shuffled to her with his left side dragging, her hope fizzled. A pulse ticked at his jaw, and his eyes darkened. Vibrating with fury, he spewed words, but since she didn't speak Etterian, she went with what it sounded like, which was cursing.

He waved the gun then tapped his leg with it. She assumed he wanted help to strap it to his thigh. Kneeling with a backpack on wasn't easy, but gripping his thigh helped her balance. He growled, and her heart leaped, recognizing the rumble from their quickie. But a glance showed his stoic gaze. With one hand, he held the gun in place. She had to peel the holster's magnetic straps apart before she could wrap them around leg and gun. They snapped closed.

Rising, she lifted his left arm and slipped under it, supporting as much of his weight as she could. "We're going out the back door."

Pointing toward the kitchen propelled him in the right direction. It was slow going. A fine sweat coated his brow by the time they limped across the kitchen. He must be in pain, but except for the tremor running through his body and the occasional groan, he said nothing. Her thighs burned, not used to carrying this much weight. She kept a steady, cheerful chatter on what she and Miri would get up to in the forest. The best place to camp would be at Flat Face, a wall of rock they had painted stick figures on. One side of the hill was off-limits. It had a cave entrance where, a century ago, a hiker had plummeted to his death. The forest was denser on that side too. She and Miri had snuck as close as they dared before they hit the boundary markers. Those had flickered red, still active and monitored by law enforcement.

"If you weren't injured, you might ask me where Miri is." Izzy flashed him a cheeky grin, as she slid from under his arm to hurry down a step, offering her hands to guide him. He stared at her, at her palms, and frowned. She captured his massive mitts in hers and pulled gently. With each step they managed, she bubbled with encouragement. Perhaps if she urged him on, his anger might ease.

When they reached the worn path leading into the forest, she danced around him to lock the back door. She pocketed the key. Under his arm again, she gripped his waist and chatted on, sharing her life with Caro and what happened at the club. His silence dampened her spirits. The falser the hope sapping her energy, the more she called forth from within her. He could never know how worried she was, how fear churned her stomach.

The sun had set by the time they breached the forest's outskirts. The moonlight illuminated the way, painting the trees in silver. An owl hooted from the northeast, another responded from the west.

Various insects serenaded each other—a low buzz, a trill, and somewhere in the middle was a tweet-tweet. A few night birds added their calls, and nothing strange pierced the noise. Any movement would be marked by silence.

If she wasn't familiar, they would've been lost ten minutes into the dark interior. But trees had personalities, and as teenagers exploring the peace and joy of the forest, she and Miri had named them. Old Man Carn was the first she and Oyaz would come across, with his scarred bark and moss growing like a mustache around a coiled branch.

She veered west. Two more trees lay in their path. The Dandy with his limbs extended as if he offered a handkerchief, Next would be Lady Artwell with her knotty 'nose' tilted to the air and her roots like a draped gown. Both trees pointed in the direction Izzy had to go.

Her voice grew hoarse, but Oyaz's breathing labored more. She couldn't give up now. In another hour or so, they'd reach Flat Face. Still, a little break wouldn't go amiss. But then, if she couldn't get him moving again, it would strand them in an indefensible spot.

She stopped and rested him against The Dandy's chest—half a pec molded in coarse bark—to dig a bottle of water out of the backpack. Uncapping it, she handed it to Oyaz, before opening one for herself. Taking a long pull, a moan tore from her as the tepid water soothed her raw throat. Flashing him a smile, she capped the bottle and tossed it into the backpack along with his empty one.

"Ready?" She faced him while snapping the hip belts in place.

He didn't move, except to extend his right hand and cup her cheek, brushing his thumb across her skin. Pain fired in its wake. Her breath caught. She'd forgotten about the sharkman's backhand.

Since all she had heard was her inane chatter after they'd left the house, his deep rumble sparked joy within her. Still, she wished she spoke Etterian. He could be asking her anything.

She frowned at him. "I don't understand, Oyaz. If you're asking me about my sore cheek, a sharkman...um...a hiss slapped me."

Whipping her head to the side to mimic a backhand summoned a yelp as fresh agony stiffened her neck muscles. Concern furrowed his brow, then he drew back as if he hurt her. There wasn't a way for her to explain he hadn't, so she grinned to show she was fine and slipped under his arm.

Westward at Lady Artwell and around Snot Rock they continued until Flat Face loomed, casting its long shadow. A jagged wall of sandstone lay at the back of a small clearing that had overgrown since she and Miri had last camped. She shrugged. It would form a softer bed to sleep on. After helping Oyaz slide down Flat Face and lean against its solid surface, she set up the tent. She hadn't planned for a fire, not wanting to shine a beacon if the sharkmen trailed them. Unwrapping a snack bar, she offered it to Oyaz. He took it, sniffed it, then bit off half. Sighing, he chewed then paused, gesturing to her to share his.

She laughed and dug one out for herself as well as dried meat for him. Then she placed the meat and another water by his knee. While chewing on the snack bar, she unrolled the sleeping bag and flattened it. Pausing on her haunches, she admired the tiny confines of the tent. He could climb in and sleep. Keeping warm was another issue unless he slept on the bottom of the tent and used the sleeping bag as a blanket. Huffing, she stuffed the empty snack bar wrapper in her pocket, whipped out the sleeping bag, and dropped it at the entrance.

After reversing out butt first, she hurried over to him. "Oyaz, rest."

Pressing her palms together, she pretended to sleep, then opened the tent flap and showed him the 'bed.' He popped the last piece of the dried meat into his mouth and shoved off the wall. He grunted, stopped to gain his balance, then limped to the tent. With each limb trembling, he lowered himself to his knees and crawled into the tent. His legs stuck out from his calves to his boots, but she followed, clambering over him like a spider monkey. Unstrapping his gun, she draped the sleeping bag over him.

He watched her, his gaze unwavering. Dark circles under his eyes and the slight sheen to his skin said he suffered.

He ended his words with an arched a brow.

She frowned. "Okay, I get you're asking me something."

He patted the tent floor beside him.

She shook her head. "I'll guard. You sleep, heal, then help me. I tagged those sharkmen, and Vyar zapped them. I don't know where, Oyaz. Simmy might be in danger." Biting her lip silenced a sob and clamped down on the rising panic bubbling up her throat. "So, please, don't give me shit about this." She cupped his cheek. "Sleep, my Eth."

Dragging the gun behind her, she left the tent, hoisted the heavy thing into her arms, and leaned against Flat Face in the same spot he'd sat. A little of his warmth lingered. She balanced the gun on her lap and stared at a row of black buttons with the yellow one glowing. Playing with the settings was beyond stupid when one could mean self-destruct, so yellow it stayed.

While she stared at the night sky, the repetitive cacophony of the forest didn't soothe her. Tears leaked free, and with Oyaz asleep, she let them drip off her chin. As long as she made no sound, she could mourn alone.

Chapter Seventeen

Oyaz awoke with the sense that something was wrong. Calls, cries, and twitters bombarded his hearing, organic fragrances assaulted his nose, and a warm feminine body nestled against his side. When he dipped his chin, rubbing it across the female's temple, his first thought was Macy. But when he pressed his lips to the female's hair, her scent dominated, drowned out others, and summoned a peace he couldn't describe.

Izzy.

She claimed she was his Dar Eth, and despite knowing it possible, he couldn't recall falling to a knee for her. His last vivid memory was when he'd first commed Garix and Izzy.

Heat burned down one side of his body to inflame his groin. Shifting images flickered across his mind, the same as when they were in the housing unit: the darkness of her nipples, the curve of her breast, the indent of her waist, her feminine folds sliding along his hard malehood. Had the Ethera chosen her as his gifting, or had he tossed his soul into the void for a blissful moment between her thighs? Or was his imagination playing with him with what he wanted to do to her?

He tightened his fingers around her waist, crushing her curves against his chest. She moaned and snuggled closer, throwing a leg over his.

Maker.

Lust pulsed, and he hardened. He had to take care of his morning chore.

In the middle of the night, tingles along his numb side had awoken him. His nerves healing were a good sign. It was a matter of time before he had the full use of his limbs again. And yes, not having access to his battleship worried him. Where was his unit? How foolish could he have been to come alone without a weapon and a medgun? And without a sub-commander, Oyaz couldn't expect assistance soon. Perhaps Garix would raise the alarm? By now, he must realize something was wrong. Failure to reach any warrior planetside was an instant alert."

Oyaz shook his head, sparking a dull throbbing. His memories were clouded.

Desperate to relieve himself, he'd crawled from the odd structure Izzy had erected. He stumbled into the darkness. As he relieved the pressure on his bladder, his gaze rested on her slumped against the wall, the blaster across her lap. She would guard him—the determined tilt of her chin, the seriousness in her eyes. Yet, here she sat, asleep and shivering.

His chest exploded in a wealth of emotion he couldn't explain. He paused and assessed the void. Had it grown closer? No, it sat there, like a dormant black hole, not growing but not fading either.

Little did she know he understood her, though how that was possible with his destroyed O.D.I., he couldn't say. Nor could he explain it to her with hand gestures, so he let her ramble on. Her stories were amusing and revealing. She was a bundle of contradictory emotions, swinging from bouncing elation to dragging sadness. What slammed into him the hardest was her hope for an Eth, someone to *love*.

Love. And she claimed to be his.

Visions of her curves against his, her hair brushing his shoulder, her breasts bouncing, altered his breathing patterns and set his heart pounding. He liked the look of her.

And having carried her into the tiny shelter, shared his warmth with her shivering body, he liked the feel of her too.

Rustling nearby jerked her awake. She paused, stretched, then lifted her gray eyes to his face. "Morning." She smiled, and oh, did his heart leap at the sight of it. She was breathtaking even with the blue and purple mottling her cheek. Furious fire swept through him, and he trembled with the urge to kill the Yithians responsible.

Her eyes widened, and she scrambled to her feet, shifting the blanket to let in the cool morning air. "Flaming nipples, Oyaz. How did I get here? Oh, shit and corruption, I didn't guard us."

Crawling to the entrance, she blessed him with a view of her backside. An image of her bare, of her wiggling and urging him on tore a growl from him. He was Fuyra hard. No wonder he risked his soul for her.

She peeked out, then, with a smile, glanced over her shoulder. "Nothing there, thank goodness. Just going to pee." And she left him alone.

As trembles raked his body, he lay there, unable to regulate the bottom half of his armor, to comm or port, or to claim a human woman. He groaned, wanting to pin her beneath him, to plunge into her soft, heated depths he had faded memories of.

If she was his Dar Eth, if half of what she said was true, then he had to heal, had to remember, had to reclaim her.

Crawling out of the shelter was easier than before. Prickly sensations had begun to ripple from his fingertips to his neck, burning along his nerve endings. His body was attempting to heal the damage done. His numb limbs worked despite the tingles affecting his motor coordination and touch. Rising to his full height, he shivered against the pale sunlight offering no warmth.

The bushes parted, and Izzy skipped toward him, her mass of hair bouncing with her. He waited for the Ethera to strike him down. It didn't.

"Hungry?" She arched a brow then frowned. "Oyaz?" After rubbing her stomach, she pretended to eat.

Finding her communication signals amusing, he grinned.

She pointed to the wall of rock. He shuffled across and lowered himself palm under palm until he could rest his back against it. As she dug in the bag, he watched, waited. She jogged toward him with a pile of prepackaged food. Handing him a bottle of water, she stacked the items beside him, then disappeared into the structure. She stumbled back to him, hidden beneath the blanket in her arms.

Nudging him to lean forward, she wrapped it around him and tucked the edges under his sprawled legs, then placed the pile of food on his lap. Again, she left him and returned with a bottle pinned under her arm. She carried the blaster, as if she was ready to lay down her life for him, his little warrior. After lowering it to the floor in front of him, she sat beside him with her back against the wall and snatched a food pack.

"It's not much. Garix eats like a mountain, so if you're hungry, just say so. I can dash to Simmy's house and grab more." She opened a bag and handed it to him. "Might do that anyway to charge my phone." A frown furrowed her forehead. "Shit, I should have done that last night. Didn't think of it, but to be honest, I liked the comfort of the phone in my pocket. If only I could call for help."

Her voice snagged at the end, and she dipped her chin, but not before he caught the shimmer of tears. "I'm sorry you got stuck with me, Oyaz. I don't know much about surviving. I used to own an ice cream parlor."

He tried to tell her something, but whatever it was, it was lost on her.

Offering him a smile, she patted his leg. "I don't know what you said, but I hope it means I'm not an idiot, or a rescue is on its way." She groaned, and the sound of it shot heat to his groin. He pinched his lip and shifted, trying to ease the growing agony. "I'm desperate to ask you where the tags sent the art materials and sharkmen." A tear slid down her cheek. "Did I zap those aliens to Simmy's quarters? Is my sister a hostage, or worse, dead?"

"We just have to wait for someone to send a search team."

He patted her knee as she had done to him, hoping to convey the same emotion. She had nothing to worry about. If she was referring to porting tags, the goods would be sent to storage. From there, they'd distribute as needed.

"I hope that means all is well, Oyaz. But pats can also mean 'I'm sorry, you're screwed.'" She bit off the compressed bar of fruit and chewed, watching his face with hope and sadness on hers.

He opened the blanket and wrapped it around her, pulling her against his body. They ate in companionable silence, the sunlight warming him as much as her body did. She closed her eyes and sighed, tilting her face to catch the warmth.

"Mom would bring food parcels since Miri and I spent so much time here. We had books to read, board games to play, and only when we stank like dead rats did we go home for a quick shower." Izzy pointed east. "That way is the caves, and yes, we did sneak closer to see what all the fuss was about." She laughed. "I remember how we scurried from tree to tree, hands raised as if we held guns."

Breaking off, she scanned their sleeping structure and the surrounding forest. "We returned, exhausted and giggling like the girls we were. Carefree days, Oyaz. And this was after I blinded my sister."

Blind? As in without sight? He frowned. He knew the word but could not recall learning it. So, he asked her, "How did you blind her, *ensa*?"

Izzy raised her face to his, then shrugged. "I miss talking to you." She wiped her cheek, staring at the teardrop on her fingertip. "For a little while, you were mine. I wasn't alone." Her laughter was cold, sad, nothing like her usual joy. "What shall we do? E.A.F. will ask too many questions, but at least, they could reach Director Reyes." She grimaced. "We might spend a few days in custody." Tapping her chin, she settled her focus on him. "I could call Miri. She's on a hike, but she could reach Reyes or fetch us herself. Either way, I must charge my phone." She scrambled to her feet. "I'll leave the gun with you."

He growled, shaking his head, not knowing who Reyes was. But no way would he let her leave him here or head to the housing unit alone. Hand over hand, he lifted himself to his feet.

She pushed on his shoulders, but the pressure she applied was so slight, it did not hinder his movements. In the end, she plastered herself against his chest. "Stay here, Oyaz. It's safe."

"Safe?" he roared. Did she not know as a female, he had to protect her? Whether she was his Dar Eth or not.

She pulled away to rest her hands on her hips and glare at him, a challenge in her gray eyes. His chest swelled. Need slammed into him. She was pure emotion, fire and sweetness, innocence and sensuality.

"Stay. Here." She pointed to the blanket, her chin rising.

Gathering his thoughts, his concentration, working past the pain lancing through his skull as he forced himself to focus, he uttered one word she would understand. "N...No."

Her mouth fell open, revealing the pink depths tormenting him. He imagined burying his fingers in her wild curls and dipping to capture her lips. Her flavor, summoned from fleeting memory, exploded across his tongue. His nostrils flared, but her addictive arousal scent wasn't present. *Thank the Maker*. He wasn't a weak male, but scenting her need might've destroyed his control.

"You understand me?"

He waved his hand to say somewhat, lest she stop revealing her thoughts, emotions, and sharing her wonderful stories.

She studied his face, her breasts quivering as she sucked in ragged breaths. "Fine. But at the slightest trouble, you're to hide in the tunnel." Holding his gaze, she waited, as if she had all day.

He shook his head. Etterian warriors did not hide.

She gritted her teeth. "You're so stubborn." With a huff, she stomped off. Five paces ahead, she faced him. "And if the house is fine, I'm taking a shower."

He chuckled, planning to guard her. But at the thought of watching her cleanse, images flickered of water running rivulets over her curves. When he trailed her, he was no longer smiling.

The return trip to the housing unit was easier with his limbs no longer numb. Still, he let her help him when he shouldn't have. Her body against his inspired a wealth of emotion he cherished. Guilt pinched his lips. Touching another male's Dar Eth was forbidden, and despite Izzy claiming to be his, he had to act as if she wasn't until Brynr healed him.

With a piece of metal, she unlocked the door, then pushed it open. Unstrapping the blaster from his thigh, he followed her. Nothing had changed, which meant no intruders, or they'd been careful not to disturb anything. When he re-strapped the blaster to his thigh, she clasped her hands and bounced on her toes.

"I'm all for a shower. You?"

His breath caught, and he ran his gaze over her.

She didn't wait for him to respond but placed her communication device on a dark-gray circle, then bounded up the stairs.

"You can stay in the bedroom while I shower. I'll leave the door ajar, so if you need anything, I'll hear you."

Sitting on the edge of the bed, he watched as she darted around the room, stacking thick, folded cloths next to him before disappearing into the cleansing room. The spray of water preceded the shifting shadows on the patterned floor as she undressed.

He gripped his knees, his left hand weak, but the action served to keep him seated. The urge to rise, to open the door, to watch her cleanse, bombarded his mind until he could think of nothing else.

"I won't be long. I'll leave enough hot water for you."

The torture continued, with the shifting shadows and splashes teasing his mind with possible scenarios. He gritted his teeth, willing his Fuyra-hard malehood to subside. Attending to the chore was first on his list.

True to her word, she emerged minutes later with a cloth around her head and body. Water droplets clung to her skin, and a fruity, exotic scent circled her.

"Your turn. White bottle to wash your hair."

He pushed himself off the bed, took a wide step around her lest he buried his nose in the curve of her neck and inhaled the unique fragrance of her skin. He angled the door as she had, then stripped off his boots, tunic, and pants. She had left the water running, so he stepped under it. His shoulders brushed the walls, but the hot water eased the tension in his muscles. He groaned, raised his face to the spray, and splayed his hands on the cream-colored wall.

His arousal bobbed, but he hesitated. Washing his hair first would be wise. The few minutes delay would mean a longer time before he hardened again. He released his hair and placed the clip on the shelf provided. As his braid unraveled, he studied the white bottle, learning how to open it. A sniff revealed the source of her exotic scent. He drew it in deep, savoring the fragrance even as it burned his nose. Pouring a dollop onto his palm, he slapped it on his head and waited.

His hair shot out in spikes, unhappy with this. In the mirror embedded in the wall, the potion trickled down his head, trickled to his eyebrows, and dripped off. Maybe he needed more? Pouring and slapping on another dollop had the same results. Growling, he rubbed his face.

An itchy fire burned his eyes, and he roared. Wiping it off worsened the agony. Blinded, he could do nothing but bump into the wall and the glass panel.

"What is it, Oyaz?"

He stilled, wishing he could look at her, but he'd squeezed his eyes shut.

"You're not supposed to get it in your eyes, silly." She chuckled. "Kneel. Let me help you."

Desperate, he obeyed.

Softness engulfed his face when she wiped him with a cloth. Parts of her touched his body as she worked. For balance, he threw out his hands and found her thighs. Sliding his hands up her smooth skin, he skimmed his fingers over thin straps to grip her hips. As she washed, rinsed, wiped, dried, the burning in his eyes lessened. He chanced it and peeked.

A rumble slipped free, having risen from the depths of his belly, traveled along his chest to his throat.

She wore a small undergarment instead of pants. Her tunic was white, tight, and ended above her hips. And the spray had drenched parts of her, molding the fabric to the curve of a breast and its pebbled nipple. He stopped breathing, wishing he could capture it in his mouth. The memory of its taste coated his tongue, and he grunted, tugging her closer.

He flicked his gaze to her face and found her focused on his hair. She massaged the white cream into his long strands, and despite not liking the potion, his hair curled around her fingers.

When she rinsed, shifting from one side to the other, her nipple stroked his cheek.

Alodon's balls. His years spent training on Gikaet hadn't prepared him for this. The true test of a male was how he persevered through trials, how he maintained his honor. Oyaz was failing. Groaning, he tilted his head and captured the peak with his lips.

She gasped and dropped her fingers to his shoulders.

Emboldened, he ran his hands from her hips, along her waist, and under her damp tunic while he suckled her taut nipple into his mouth, tasting the cloth with flicks of his tongue. She cried out, arching into him. Breaking away summoned a whimper from her. He shoved her tunic up, exposing her breasts to his hungry gaze. Swooping in, he swept his tongue across the other nipple. His malehood bobbed, making demands he was eager to fulfill.

Bursting forward, he pinned her to the wall and spread her thighs for his hips to nestle. He stared into her dark and hooded gray eyes. *Maker, she is beautiful.*

"Oyaz?" She parted her lips for her ragged gasps.

Growling, he splayed his hands on the wall on either side of her and claimed a kiss. Tilting his head, he plundered the pink depths of her mouth like he'd longed to do. The taste of her trembled his body, pinging weakness through his healed limbs. His hair stroked her cheeks, her arms, and wrapped around them, forming a cocoon.

"Izzy."

She jerked back, her face paled, and she turned away. "I want you. You can't know how much. But I want my Oyaz, my Eth." Cupping his cheeks, she blessed his lips with a light kiss. "When you can remember who I am, you and I won't leave a bed for days."

He sucked in a sharp breath. This tiny human woman was stronger than he was.

She offered him a tremulous smile. "Now, rinse. The towels are on the bed. I'll wash your T-shirt, and I ordered pizza."

His stomach gurgled, but he hesitated, gliding his hands along the outside of her bare thighs. He kept his gaze locked on hers, for if he lowered it, the sight of her heaving breasts would shatter what control she'd returned to him.

Cursing, he dropped her feet to the floor and stepped back.

She righted her tunic and scurried out the cleansing room, closing the door with a definitive click. Grunting, he dipped under the spray and waited, then before he thought twice about it, he took care of his chore. One, two pumps and bombarding images of Izzy riding him spent his seed.

He smothered his moan and ignored the mini-shivers while he washed. Fiddling with the strange silver handles taught him how to adjust the temperature, and to switch off the water. The cloths barely wrapped around him, but he managed to dry himself. He tugged his pants on over damp legs, then taking a fresh towel and pocketing his clip, he rubbed his hair while strolling down to the lower floor of the housing unit.

Izzy waited for him with a bright smile curling kiss-swollen lips. "Pizza's here."

She bounced around him, settled him in the big chair, and placed an opened box on his lap.

"I called Miri too." Izzy scooped a slice from him and bit into it. "Left a message." As she chewed, she tapped buttons on her communication device and held it to her ear. "Hello, please put me through to E.S.A." She took another bite. "Director Reyes, please."

While tearing into his slice, Oyaz listened to the conversation on the other side.

"Who may I say is calling?" a female asked.

Izzy sat up, excitement twitched her limbs and tightened her posture. "This is Izzy Reeves. He knows who I am."

"I'm sorry, Ms. Reeves. I've been instructed not to patch anyone through. Since the shooting incident, security has been stricter."

"I need his help, miss. I can't reach the battleship *Gladio* and Sub-Commander Vorn." She huffed, revealing her opinion of the male.

"Thank you for calling E.S.A. I will be sure to leave a message for Director Reyes."

Izzy jumped up, tossing her half-eaten slice into the box. "Listen here. I have an injured Etterian warrior sitting on my couch. If I don't reach someone, preferably my friend, Garix, also an Etterian, we can't return to the battleship."

The female on the other end sighed. "If you persist with this nonsense, I will have security trace this call. Have a *lovely* day."

"Do you want proof?" Izzy punched a button on her phone and climbed over the couch to press her cheek to Oyaz's. "Now do you believe me?"

On the small display vid, the female gasped, and her dark eyebrows shot to her hairline. "Oh, dear. Yes. I'll leave a message for Director Reyes, marked urgent. He's unfortunately out of town at the ESACon in Geneva."

"Are you kidding me?" Izzy threw her hands in the air. "My warrior's injured. I need help. More of those damn gray sharks could arrive any minute, and Reyes's at a conference having tea with the powers-that-be?" With a scream, she ended the comm and threw the device at the chair. "We're on our own, Oyaz." She wrapped her arms around her trembling body. "Flaming nipples, how I wish Garix was here. He'd know what to do."

Oyaz gritted his teeth. She would be in more trouble had Garix been here instead of him. There was no way she could support Garix's weight when she struggled with Oyaz's.

He patted the chair beside him and held out her half-eaten slice.

Sighing, she squeezed in beside him and rested her temple on his arm. "I'm sorry. I can't say it enough. This is all my fault. When we get you back to your ship, and if Brynr can't heal you, I'll leave, get as far away from all this as possible." She raised sad, gray eyes to meet his gaze. "You're better off without me too, Oyaz."

Burying her face against his arm, she cried, the tears hot where they landed on his skin.

Handling a weeping female was far beyond Oyaz's skill sets. But he did know one thing, he wouldn't let Izzy leave him.

Chapter Eighteen

With Izzy tucked under his arm, 'helping' him along the path toward the forest, his health was much improved. The shower, despite the detour, and a full belly of pizza had bolstered his energy. She was quiet, her lips pursed, with her gaze far away. Returning to the shelter made sense since it was an unknown factor. It was also defensible if their backs were to the rock wall.

She stumbled and slumped. Frowning, he dipped to catch her.

"Izzy?" He fell to his knees and gathered her unconscious body close to him. The salty stench of her blood seeped into his nose, dominating his thoughts. Like a tidal wave, a wealth of unknown emotions bombarded him. Intense heat and pain pierced his chest. The keening sound that ripped from his throat was unrecognizable as his voice.

Cradling her on his thighs, he brushed the hair off her face and ran his finger down her cheek to the red stain on her tunic. When he lifted the fabric, the shape of the wound was unmistakable.

He whipped his head up and scanned the forest wall, trying to find the source of the blast. No approaching footsteps, rustling of the green vegetation, or other disturbing noises had reached him.

He curled his arm around Izzy and cradled her. "Show yourself," he roared. He darted his gaze from side-to-side, peering into the shadows.

The lone figure who stepped out seized every muscle in Oyaz's body. The Etterian warrior leaned against a brown tree and crossed his legs at the ankles. The smirk was one Oyaz would never forget and had longed to see again. Madyx. How was this possible?

Oyaz tightened his arm around Izzy, pulling her snug against him. He gaped at the male, at his dark blue jeans, black tunic, and Etterian boots. Shaking his head, Oyaz tried to clear his vision.

"Well, what do we have here?" That was Madyx's voice.

He is not an illusion? "Madyx?" Warmth burst through Oyaz, with darkness drenching his joy a moment later. "You died."

"Died?" Madyx laughed, his unbound shoulder-length hair swirling around him. "No, I escaped Fuyra in an explosion. Father would have been proud."

Oyaz sprawled Izzy on the ground and stumbled toward Madyx. "Maker, you are a sight. You look well, my battle-bond."

"Battle-bond?" Madyx pinched his lips. "That was decades ago, Oyaz. We are strangers now."

He patted his blaster against his thigh in a rhythmic beat. The yellow blinking light on the side flooded Oyaz with relief. Like someone drenching him with hot water, his shoulders drooped in relief. Tears prickled his eyes. Izzy wouldn't die. Madyx had only stunned her. Still, set for an Etterian's muscle mass and weight, such a shot had drawn her blood.

"Why, Madyx?" Emotion rose like a crescendo, bombarding his thoughts. Fury he recognized. Red tainted his vision. His nostrils flared, and the blood rushing through his veins increased his heart rate.

"Do not bore me with questions, Oyaz. The buzz wants me to believe Etterians find Earth fascinating." He pushed off the tree and circled Oyaz, forcing him to turn to maintain eye contact. "Imagine my joy at stumbling upon Xeus tasking you to protect this pathetic blue orb. From that, it was easy to trace your comms and roll out a plan to entice you into my trap. You could never resist playing the honorable one." He smacked the red button on his blaster, setting it to kill. "My time for revenge is at hand."

"Revenge?" Oyaz frowned at the male he had once considered his dearest bond.

Madyx's face contorted into a snarl. "You knew I did not touch Azian, yet you said nothing."

Oyaz flinched at the pain in Madyx's voice. "I did defend you."

Madyx snorted. "Weak attempts made by you and my father."

"His hands were tied, Madyx." Oyaz glanced at Izzy, not in the mood to discuss this.

"And like the pathetic king he is, Xeus sided with the female."

That snapped Oyaz's focus back to Madyx. "He did not. Azian was as punished—"

Madyx laughed. "Regardless, I mined rock while you became a commander. How is that fair?" He nudged the blaster at Izzy. "Enough nostalgia. You will follow me freely, or I will terminate your pet."

Oyaz frowned at the odd command. Go with him where? And no way in Alodon's hell would he abandon Izzy. "I do not understand. Why did you not come find me?"

"Why, he asks? You do not know, *Supreme Commander*?" Madyx smirked.

Oyaz bristled. "Where have you been all this time?"

Two Yithians and a Maloidian flanked Madyx. Oyaz gritted his teeth, having not heard them approach. Frowning, he studied the males, not in armor and sporting no allegiances.

"Why did you harm her?" He knelt beside Izzy to gather her into his arms, cupping her cheek to feel her lifeforce. Her skin's warmth lessened the pain cinching his chest. He sucked in a deep breath, hoping to calm his deafening heartbeat. "She posed no threat." Anger tore through him, clenching his jaw and his arms. He pressed his temple to hers, missing her sad gray eyes and her effervescent chatter.

"I could kill her." Madyx waved the blaster. "Would you prefer that?"

Oyaz struggled to his feet, bringing Izzy with him. He clasped her to his chest and kissed her cheek, hoping she could feel it in her unconscious state.

"How touching."

Oyaz glared at Madyx. "She is...precious to me."

"The way you are acting, I could almost believe her your Dar Eth." When Madyx stepped closer, his males followed. "Your eyes..."

Oyaz's breath hitched. Ice blue eyes meant Izzy was his. Of all the things he wanted in life, she was his greatest desire. "What color are my eyes?"

"Blue." Madyx chuckled.

Oyaz growled. "Alodon's balls, Madyx, give me your medgun." He had to heal her. Everything within him compelled him to care for her. She may not be his Dar Eth, but she was his...friend.

"Such a soft heart. Regardless, she will have to seek her own healing." Madyx twitched his fingers, and three blasters leveled on Oyaz then at her. "She is a nuisance, costing me two males so far and thwarting my plans."

Oyaz frowned. Was he talking about the two Yithians Izzy ported? "What is the meaning of this?"

"So straight and narrow. Oh, ignorant Oyaz, the universe is shades of gray with many twists and turns. King Xeus," Madyx spat, "has you well-trained, like obedient soldiers, never questioning his methods or decisions."

"Our king serves Etteria, as we all do," Oyaz snapped.

Madyx snorted. "Come along, Oyaz, or I will have my males stun you again."

"Again?" He squared his shoulders. "None of this makes sense. Why are you behaving this way?"

"Fine then. If you are unconcerned for your life, what about your pet?"

Oyaz's gaze dipped to Izzy's pale face. Peace covered her, and her chest rose and fell as if she slept well. He had to protect her at all costs. "I will come with you."

"A wise choice," Madyx said. The Maloidian approached, yellow skin and spots fading into his swaying tentacled hair. "Allow Balllio to slip on restraints."

Oyaz frowned. "Why? You have injured me, harmed my...Izzy, and now this? Afraid I am no longer an honorable male?"

"Honor?" Madyx laughed. "You are entertaining. No, the restraints are for my protection."

"What? Why would I harm you? I thought you dead, Madyx. I grieved." Oyaz glanced at Izzy, and that compulsion surged through him, demanding he carry her pain and ensure she was well-cared for. As she had done for him since this adventure started.

"Leave her," Madyx growled, leveling his blaster on her.

"No, I will not abandon her." Oyaz raised his chin.

Four blasters turned on him. If he left her, at least she was not in the line of fire. Sighing, he marched to the housing unit.

"Where do you think you are going?" Madyx bolted, leaping in front of Oyaz.

"I will not leave her in the open." Circumventing Madyx, Oyaz shouldered his way into the housing unit and draped Izzy on the big chair. He unstrapped his blaster, checked the activated button was yellow, and left the weapon on the table. With a jog, he was through the back door just as Madyx opened it.

Oyaz held out his arms to Balllio. The click of the Maloidian steel shackles made him wince. "At least, tell me why?"

"In due course, Supreme Commander."

Oyaz trailed Madyx into the forest. He threw backward glances at the housing unit, skimmed over the Yithians and Maloidian before resting his gaze on Madyx.

Hours passed, the one sun tracked its path across the sky, and still, Madyx didn't answer, didn't speak, except to nudge Oyaz onward. Rounding a copse of trees, a cave appeared in the distance, gaping like the ravenous mouth of an omeika. The jagged rock dripped like fangs. Izzy had mentioned this cave, said someone died here over a century ago. As they ventured into its depths, the shiver rippling down his spine had nothing to do with the cooler temperature.

Agonizing fire woke Izzy, and she kept herself immobile while she assessed her body. Why did her shoulder hurt so much? Exhaustion drained her limbs. That was understandable after the last two days of stress.

Flicking her eyes open, she squeaked at the bloodstain on her white button-up shirt. Well, Simmy's shirt. A minor detail, but blood was a nightmare to clean.

The house was too silent.

"Oyaz?" she whispered, expecting him to hear her with his preternatural hearing. There was no response. The last time she'd seen him, they were on the path to the tent. Fire had exploded across her chest, and darkness had claimed her. She snorted. Fainted, that's what she she'd done. Right?

She peeled her shirt back. Or had someone stunned her? Flaming aliens and their weird guns. Maybe she should call Earth Armed Forces and ask for assistance. Her gaze rested on the blaster. She winced. Endangering more lives didn't make sense, not when she didn't know what they'd be up against.

Ice slithered between the cracks of her volcanic fury. Where was Oyaz? Leaping to her feet, she sprinted out the back door. Many footprints led into the forest but east. Hurrying into the house, she grabbed her phone off the couch and dialed Miri. She didn't answer again.

"Dammit, woman, I need you. They, whoever they are, took Oyaz. I think they're going to the cave. You know the one." Izzy paced, then paused to blink at the blaster Oyaz had left her, like he was giving her a signal. She could rescue him. "Get in touch with Reyes. I need Garix. Hell, I'll even take Vorn. Or some guy named Arrow." Slumping, she tapped the phone on her temple before pinning it to her ear again. "All right, this might sound stupid, but I'm going after him."

She pocketed her phone, popped two of Simmy's pain caps, hefted the gun, and hiked along the path. The forest's shadows were cool against her bare arms. She turned east when she hit Old Man Carn. The terrain dipped, rose, and dipped again, the trees growing closer together as if to stop her. She clenched her jaw and rested the gun on her right shoulder, trying to ease her cramping arms and the weight on her wound.

The afternoon sunlight didn't pierce the canopy, but like it was yesterday, she knew where to go. She had no way of leaving breadcrumbs for Miri to follow, other than firing the gun at the tree trunks. Since she didn't understand how the gun worked, or whether it could fire indefinitely, she preferred to save its battery, just in case it had one.

Besides, Miri was a park ranger. If anyone knew how to track, it was her. Peering from behind a tree, Izzy studied the cave's opening about twelve meters long and five meters high. Something kept the boundary markers' sensors active, despite them grouped and propped against a tree. There'd be no interference from the local E.A.F. precinct.

Crates were stacked to the right of the entrance. If she sprinted, she could dive for cover. With a quick prayer, she burst into a run, skidding the last meter to slow her approach. She threw herself into the gap between the crates and the rocky wall. Holding her ragged breath, she listened past her thumping heartbeat. No alarm sounded, no cries, and no footsteps drew near. That had been too easy. Now, the hard part. With the sunset at her back, if she hovered in the entrance, anyone inside could see her.

A metallic bridge lined the cave's entrance to even the jagged rock bed beneath it. She could slide around the side and into the gap between bridge and rock. From there, she might see more. As tiny as she was, it shouldn't be difficult unless a crevice lay beneath the bridge. She sagged. Thoughts of Oyaz alone with someone evil rushed renewed energy and determination through her. Or it could be the pain caps talking. Her shoulder no longer throbbed. Placing a hand on the top of the crates, she vaulted over them and darted through the cave's mouth. She slammed into the rock wall and threw herself onto her stomach, hoisting the gun even as she grazed the hell out of her elbows. No twinges of fire reached her mind, and no burning agony pierced her shoulder when she collided with the wall.

Ice cream parlors were so much safer than this bullshit.

The cavern stretched before her. Tall poles lit great circles on the ground, casting the walls of the cave in darkness. A row of tents lined one side, and crates peppered the space. In the center of the clearing was Oyaz on his ass with his hands tied behind him to a metal pole driven into the rock bed. She twitched with the urge to sprint to him and throw her arms around him. But that was foolish unless she wanted to be caught, as well.

Seventeen sharkmen and five yellow squidheads loitered, some carrying crates crisscrossed the clearing. Alien guns were strapped to their thighs. Though, she doubted that was all of them. If she could take care of the aliens first, then she could free Oyaz. Darting across the bridge, she ducked behind a crate. She vaulted over it, dived behind the next stack, leaped over those, until she was near enough to Oyaz to see the blood dripping from his wrists.

Her face burst with a tingling heat, and she bit her tongue to swallow a sob. How dare they hurt him. She hunched, sank onto her backside, and leaned against the crate. Placing the gun beside her, she rested her elbows on her knees and shoved her fingers into her hair. A plan would help. All she had was the gun. As she peered over the top of the crate, an Etterian stepped from the large tent at the end of the row.

Hope blossomed in her chest like a burst of sunlight, and she opened her mouth to call out. But when he kicked Oyaz's boot and laughed, she pinched her lips. What the flaming nipples was this? An evil Etterian? He was gorgeous, though, but they all were. Long legs in blue denim, a black T-shirt molded to an impressive chest, and his hair brushed his shoulders. He had a biker vibe of old.

Still, she'd receive no help from that quarter.

His head whipped up, and he scanned the crates. She crouched, praying he hadn't seen her. What kind of rescuer was she if she didn't even make it to Oyaz? A shitty one.

"Well, this is indeed a surprise."

She squeaked and raised her gaze.

The evil biker palmed his gun and fired.

Chapter Nineteen

When Madyx carried Izzy's limp body from behind a crate, fire shot through Oyaz. He burned with fury, yanking on his chains to reach her. Part of his anger he directed at her for following, for endangering herself. The other part was furious that fear—the cold, seductive, dark slither—fixed his gaze on Madyx. Once he had known this male, now his actions were unpredictable.

"She is persistent." Madyx draped her on the ground, close but too far for Oyaz to offer comfort. With his arms shackled to the pole behind him, he couldn't hold her anyway. Still, the whisper of her breath against his skin would be sweet to his ears.

"She is loyal to you, Oyaz." Madyx circled her. "I shall let her live for now." He strode off, disappearing inside his shelter.

Two hours passed, and her skin had taken on a paleness Oyaz didn't like.

"Izzy." He stretched out his leg until he could nudge her with the tip of his boot. "Silly female. I left you in the housing unit to be safe." He grunted.

She moaned.

With another nudge, she rolled over and faced him. Her eyelids fluttered open. She stilled, blinking at Oyaz as if dazed. Gasping, she scrambled to her feet and threw her arms around him. Peace engulfed his soul, dragging a sigh from him.

He nuzzled her hair and kissed her forehead. As soon as his lips touched her skin, the urge to taste her bombarded him. It was so potent, he shifted to her lips before he could stop himself.

"Oyaz?" she whispered when he was an inch from his mouth touching hers—the loss of opportunity hovered between them. She peered into his eyes before scanning the cavern around them.

"You are wounded," he grumbled, hating scenting her blood when he was unable to heal her.

"Still can't understand you", she sang. "We have to escape, Oyaz. Got any plans?" She giggled, then pinched her lips. "Try telepathy, aliens are supposed to have that power. Telekinesis would be better, though." She assessed him. "How do you feel? How's your arm?"

Her gaze was like a caress, making him harden with need.

He scowled. "I am well," he ground out. "It is your injury I worry about." He nudged his chin at her shoulder.

"Did the evil-biker stun me?" Her fingers fluttered to his chest, and words escaped him at her touch—so trusting, so soft. *Maker help me.*

"Which time? When we headed toward the forest or now?" He sniffed. The scent of her blood sparked a primitive reaction in him to kill, to protect. He jerked on the shackles. "I cannot heal you, Izzy."

Twisting around him, she pressed her body to his chest as she bent over his shoulder. Her touch along his fingers revealed what she was doing. He froze, his face inches from her backside.

"Flaming nipples, Oyaz, those look…bad. We're doomed, aren't we, Oyaz?" She leaned back and closed her eyes as pain twisted her brow. Curling onto his lap, she burrowed into him.

Madyx leaving his shelter raised her head off Oyaz's chest.

"Is he with them?" She clung to Oyaz, as if he could shield her. At his nod, her eyes widened, and the gray in their depths darkened. "An evil Etterian?"

He shook his head, stifling a laugh. "He is not evil."

"Laugh all you want, my Etterian. I choose to think the shark-men are evil, and if the yellow squidheads and your Etterian friend are with the sharks, then ipso facto, they're evil too." She harumphed. "By association."

"Yithians are not evil. Greedy, short-sighted, desperate, perhaps. I am learning they are cunning, as well."

Her brow dipped while she stared at him. "That's a long sentence to agree with me, Oyaz. Evil." When she raised her stubborn chin, she was adorable. "No one will find us now," she whispered, and her shoulders slumped. "First chance you get, Oyaz, you escape. Don't worry about me. You get free, and bring the reinforcements."

He growled. "I will not leave you."

"It's my fault you're here. My fault you were injured." She glared at him. "You are so stubborn."

"As touching as this is, it is all my fault." Madyx chuckled. "So, you can save your theatrics."

She squeaked. "You can speak English?" Her body stiffened, and a tremor swept through her. She faced Madyx, turning away from Oyaz. Something in his battle-bond's words had angered her.

"She is entertaining, Oyaz." Madyx pinched his chin. "I see why she is your pet."

She huffed. "So rude. I'm kind of done with you people switching between English and Etterian. How do you know each other, Oyaz?"

Madyx's laughter lacked humor. "Know each other?" he said in English. "Why, yes, pet, we do *know* each other. Oyaz betrayed then abandoned me."

"Liar." She waved a fist at Madyx. "How dare you accuse noble Oyaz of such a thing."

A silly smile split Oyaz's lips. Her defense of him for whatever reason was breathtaking. He nuzzled the crown of her head, and when she tilted her head to meet his gaze, he brushed his lips across hers.

She gasped.

Madyx's eyes widened before they narrowed before he said in Etterian, "She defends you... How sweet."

Oyaz grinned. *She is sweet and so precious.*

"Listen, talking in another language is rude. R.U.D.E." She folded her arms across her chest, crinkling her shirt and blessing Oyaz with a glimpse of her cleavage. "Since you're being a dick, why don't you just get on with it? Or is it your intention to be irritating *and* an asshat?"

Madyx froze, his shoulders stiffened, and his cheeks darkened. He opened and closed his mouth, then growled, "Call me names again, and I will harm your Oyaz."

"Hah. There you're wrong, asshat. He's not mine..." Izzy mumbled, then offering Madyx her back, she dismissed him to cling to Oyaz's tunic.

A YELLOW SQUIDHEAD GRABBED her hand and shackled her wrist above Oyaz's. She didn't bother tugging on it when even super-strong Oyaz couldn't break free. Part of her wanted to stare. So close, the markings on the man's face were beautiful, his thick hair like an octopus's tentacles. No way would past-self believe she'd find herself in this situation.

While wearing his signature smirk, Asshat spoke in lyrical language.

She abhorred it when he spoke so she wouldn't understand. Her anger fired her blood, and she dug her nails into her palm to resist punching him...if she could reach him. But she couldn't look past the blood smeared around Oyaz's wrists.

"Heal him, dammit." She raised her chin to glare at Asshat. "Why let him bleed? Have you no honor?"

Asshat jerked back as if she'd slapped him. He grabbed her, yanked her to her feet, and dragged her across to him, snapping the shackle tight. Fire shot outward from her wrist. She gritted her teeth, not wanting to give him the satisfaction of knowing he hurt her. He wrapped his long fingers over her shoulder to embed in her wound. She cried out, the pain excruciating and making her squirm to free herself. Her vision tilted as agony barreled through her. She swallowed her whimpers and froze, praying he'd grow bored and stop.

"What about you has earned Oyaz's loyalty?" Asshat mused, his breath feathering across her ear. Without warning, he released her, spun her to face him, and ripped her shirt open.

Oyaz roared, pulling on his shackles, his face mottled. He bellowed in Etterian.

Asshat laughed. He had partially broken the front clasp of her bra, but it held firm, keeping her breasts covered. She shivered, the cool air in the cave sweeping goosebumps along her skin. If she rushed to cover herself, Asshat might take it as encouragement. She tapped a foot, hoping to appear unfazed.

He trawled a finger from her jaw, down her neck, into the dip of her collarbone to a heaving breast. Everything within her wanted to jerk away from his touch. Instead, she smothered a gag and held herself still. With deliberate slowness, he stroked her, his focus on Oyaz when he spoke.

She frowned, not liking his gentler tone, whatever he'd said to Oyaz. There was admiration and longing in his voice.

When he stepped closer, she stiffened. Pressing his nose to her neck wasn't what she expected. Was he sniffing her? The urge to knee him in the groin or bite him took all her strength to tamp down. Any rebellion on her part, Oyaz would pay for. She had no doubts Asshat would follow through on his threats.

Madyx crooned, his voice liquid silk. But he ruined the sinful visage with a wicked grin, unconcerned with the fury and hatred pouring from Oyaz's swirling eyes.

"Are you done?" She stood tall but was desperate to cover herself.

"For now." Asshat grunted without looking at her.

She straddled Oyaz's lap and looped her arm around his neck. He calmed enough to rest his cheek on her forehead.

"I am sorry, Izzy," he mumbled.

That sounded like an apology, though what he had to be sorry for, she didn't know. Sorry he didn't remember her? Sorry he had blessed her with the best orgasms of her life? Sorry he couldn't save them? And calling her Izzy instead of Izabelle proved he wasn't her Eth anymore.

"How you react gives him leverage, Oyaz. Let him strip me naked, it doesn't matter. If he beats me, don't fight it. Don't give him the satisfaction. Don't let him win."

He shook his head and gritted out words that dripped with fury.

She huffed. "I assume you're not listening to me." Pinning her body to his, she cupped his cheek, forcing him to meet her gaze. "Simmy's not my problem anymore. Caro has Malo. If I can save you, Oyaz, then I'll die happy."

"Izzy—"

She held a finger to his lips. "I don't want to talk anymore." And she didn't. If he could speak English, she suspected he'd tell her she was special, that her life had meaning, but they were lies. If she fell off the face of Earth, no one would feel the loss. Had Oyaz remained her Eth, she would've fought to live. He would've been something worth fighting for. He was someone worth dying for.

As he leaned against the pole, his hands pinned behind him, she snuggled against his chest, needing his warmth. Now that she'd made it inside the cave, been caught, faced an evil Etterian, adrenaline no longer flowed through her veins. The chilliness seeped into her skin, making her shiver. She sighed, wishing Oyaz could hug her, but she was content to breathe in his cologne and fall asleep to the steady beat of his heart.

"Izzy..."

Izzy twitched awake, groaning when her stiff shoulder throbbed. The blood had caked the shirt to it, and touching the fabric pulled on the wound. The pain caps had worn off, and her body broadcasted every bump, scrape, and graze. Rubbing her face, she gazed at Oyaz. He pointed with his chin to behind her.

"Izzy Reeves."

At the harsh whisper, Izzy scanned the crates, yanking on the cuff pinning her in place. She yelped as the metal sliced into her wrist.

Miri cowered behind a crate, popping her head above the tops before sinking again. Ice coated Izzy's scalp. Panicking, she pinned a finger to her lips to silence her.

Oyaz's flicked a gaze at the tent and said something before glancing at Miri and the cave entrance.

Izzy slumped, wishing she understood him. "Miri, go, please. Asshat will see you."

Not one to listen to reason, Miri crouch-walked over to Izzy. "What? When I went to all this effort? You left such a message, Izzy, what did you expect me to do?" She gestured to her ranger uniform. "I abandoned my clients in a ravine."

"Do as I asked you to. Contact Director Reyes, get him to comm Vorn or Garix. We need reinforcements." Izzy massaged her temple, having forgotten how stubborn Miri could be. "No one has seen you yet. Leave. Hurry."

Miri hesitated, whipping her gaze around the cavern. "But—"

"Oyaz and I will wait. We're having a marvelous time, right, sweetheart?" She winked at him. "Best date ever."

Miri snorted. "Nice try, Izzy. Did you forget who you're talking to? Oh, ye of little faith. I reached Director Reyes, he commed your Garix, and reinforcements are on their way." A wicked smile curled Miri's lips. "But *I* know the forest." Her gaze dipped to Izzy's gaping shirt and scowled. "Asshat?"

"Yeah," Izzy muttered. "Go before he captures you too."

"At the cave entrance, I left an open-ended call on my mobile. Garix's tracing it. Just stay calm. Help's coming." Scurrying to her hideout, Miri emerged carrying the gun Izzy had left there. "Which one?" she showed Oyaz.

He arched a brow.

Izzy sliced her attention between the cave entrance in the distance. It was solid black, with night having set in. Behind her sat the partially lit cavern, aliens loitered around a meal-prep station. Something savory twitched her nose and her stomach gurgled. Oyaz pressed a kiss to her temple. She snuggled against him, using his warmth to barely hold back the chill.

Garix was on the way. That thought circled her mind and did much to ease the tension knotting her back muscles. "He doesn't understand us, Miri. You have to act out your question."

Miri gagged, twitched, then fell to the floor, playing dead.

Oyaz chuckled.

Izzy's breath caught, and a flutter consumed her chest. She loved his smile, the way it warmed his eyes and tilted the corners. His dimples were sexy as hell.

Miri pointed to each button until she reached the red one.

He nudged his jaw.

"Okay, see you in a bit." She took off, slinking into the shadows, sneaking deeper into the cave. Cries of alarm filtered to where Izzy clung to Oyaz, having climbed him to see better. Bodies littered the clearing. Gunfire flashed like exploding fireworks. Shit. When had Miri learned to do that?

"Stubborn, insane, crazy, stupid." Despite the warmth creeping up her throat from having shoved her breasts in Oyaz's face, she scrambled around and over him, trying to peer into the dark.

Darkness reigned, and a few men had spread out, no doubt searching for Miri. The silence was deafening, and every time a gun was fired, Izzy jerked, half expecting Miri to scream as she died.

"I'm going to kill her." She paused, then gaped. "Oh, no, Oyaz, I killed her by calling her here. Her death is my fault." She bit her lip as self-directed anger gripped her, heating her chilled body. She had endangered yet another person she cared for. Stilling, she raised her gaze to Oyaz. When had she started to care for him?

He shook his head, though what that was supposed to mean, she couldn't say.

Dropping into his lap, she straddled his thighs, ignoring his moan. Her weight was negligible, so he shouldn't complain. "I'll get off you in a minute," she whispered, rising on her knees to level her gaze with his. "Oyaz, if we get out of this...I want you to know I...care for you. I want you to be happy." Her cheeks trembled, and she winced. "To find your Dar Eth."

Asshat gestured to her and grinned as he strode into the clearing.

She slipped off Oyaz to glare at Asshat, hating his smirk. Miri had yet to return after the cries of surprise or agony had ended. Izzy tried not to glance behind them, to draw attention to her childhood friend and whatever she was up to.

Rasping, Asshat asked something as he captured one of Izzy's curls, released it then ran a finger along her cheek.

Oyaz roared, rising to his knees and shoving Izzy aside. If it wasn't for her shackled hand, she would have fallen onto her ass. As it was, her knees took the brunt of it.

"Speak English, dammit. What are you saying?" She splayed her fingers across Oyaz's chest, hoping to calm him.

"I will take a taste of you." Asshat unstrapped his blaster, hit the blue button, then fired at her cuff. It unclipped and fell onto the rock. He gripped her upper arm and jerked her to her feet. Oyaz thundered what sounded like curses, yanking on his shackles with enough force to tremble the thick metal pole.

But Asshat had stopped, tilted his head to listen then stared into the direction Miri had disappeared. His grip loosened. Oh, no. He'd see the bodies and know something was up.

Izzy tugged free, dusted her ass, and clasped her shirt closed. Distraction, that's what she needed. "Sure. What sort of taste were you thinking? Toe jam? My ass crack? My blood?"

His focus snapped to her, and his lips thinned. "I will cut your tongue from your mouth, female." He dragged her to the largest tent.

"Remember my words. Be happy, Oyaz." Casting a last glance at Oyaz and the pain twisting his face, she dipped her head to hide her tears. Maybe if she went willingly? It would buy Garix and Miri some time. She drew in a slow breath and shrugged off Asshat's hand. "I can walk." Squaring her shoulders and ignoring the fire of her wound, she strolled into the tent.

Soft unfamiliar furs were spread in one corner. A table and chair sat to the rear. A few trunks in the same metal as Oyaz's pole lined one side. Smaller boxes gaped, holding glowing stones sharing their intimate and inviting light.

"Undress," Asshat barked, then chuckled at Oyaz's roars and pleading.

"You're an evil bastard," she spat.

Asshat clenched his jaw. "I will let that insult slide since I have you here. I will, however, not ask again."

Huffing, she toed off her sneakers and socks. She shimmied out of her jeans. Peeling off the blouse drew a hiss as it tore off dried blood. Her wound oozed fresh crimson droplets. Shivering in her bikini briefs and broken bra, she met his gaze. "All of it?"

He waited, his gaze unblinking.

She unclipped her bra and looped it off her, tossing it on her discarded jeans. Hooking her fingers in her panties, she slipped it off, and with her toes, swept it closer to the clothing pile.

"You are not a pet, are you?" he whispered, his gaze on her body.

Desire heated his dark blue eyes, making her skin crawl. She struggled to swallow past the lump in her throat. Goosebumps rippled across her skin, sparked fresh shivers along her limbs, and worst, pebbled her nipples.

His breath hitched.

Her fingers twitched with the urge to cover herself, but she dug her nails into her thighs, fighting for calm.

"Your males are finding Dar Eths among us." She hoped by telling him this, he might think twice about...doing something to her.

"You lie," he growled, but she held his gaze, uncaring whether he believed her or not. He caught one of her curls and toyed with it. "Oyaz is your Eth?"

Her heart cracked, and despite the sting of tears, she shook her head. "He was, but you changed that. He has no memory of the Ethera."

Asshat stumbled back and slumped into the chair. "I have a Dar Eth?" A slow smile spread, changing him from a glowering enemy to a handsome man.

"I hope she's the sweetest, kindest, most loyal woman on this planet. You need every drop of goodness you can get."

His glazed eyes said he hadn't heard her. "How many Earthian females are there?"

"Billions." Another shiver tore through her, reminding her she was naked. "May I dress?"

"You may lay on the furs." He rose to his feet, stalking across to her.

She glanced at the 'bed' and grimaced. Wanting her there meant one thing. "You will force me?" Furious with how weak she sounded, she dug her nails into her thighs again.

He gestured to the bed while placing his gun on the table. She crept to the furs and stood in the center of them, unwilling to kneel or sprawl. He lunged, scooped her off her feet, and lowered her but with unexpected gentleness. The softness and warmth at her back drew a sigh.

When he stretched alongside her, she froze, resisting the urge to pull away from him. He brushed his lips along her throat to cup a breast, his touch hot. She whimpered, wanting to curl into the heat pouring off him. His masculine scent itched her nose, and she sneezed, bouncing her bruised temple off his chin. She moaned while wiggling away from him, trying to create distance between them.

He wasn't Oyaz with his addictive cologne. Nor did Asshat have that intensity in his eyes that Oyaz did when he looked at her. In Oyaz's arms, she was alive, sensitive, aroused, and when he kissed her... Heat flooded her core at the thought of Oyaz kissing her. Just the sweeping of his lips across hers was enough to draw a reaction from her.

Asshat's nostrils flared. He growled, and the pressure of his hand intensified.

Oyaz roared in his beautiful language, begging, then yelling again.

Izzy layered Asshat's hand with hers. "Please... Don't do this. Don't let revenge consume your soul."

He paused to stare into her eyes, his fingers caressing her cheek before diving into her hair. "Revenge? I desire you, *minus cesu*."

She glared. Angry heat rushed through her. How dare he? A pair of partially concealed breasts was enough of an enticement? And he had the nerve to call her by an endearment. Rolling onto her side to face him, she waited until he aligned his body with hers, and ran his hand down her back to cup her ass. Then leaning in as if to kiss him, she raised her knee with all the strength she could muster. At his gut-wrenching groan, she shoved him off her, scrambled to her feet, and lunged for his gun. She couldn't take the time to dress, not knowing how long an aching groin would hold him. Hefting the damn gun, she slapped the yellow button and fired.

Chapter Twenty

Oyaz clambered to his feet the moment the cloth shelter closed. Blood slicked his wrists where the shackles dug into his skin. The sting was negligible. He honed his ears, listening for a whisper, a groan, anything to reveal what was happening inside the shelter.

Their conversation aside, her moans and pleas ripped his control from him. He yanked, tugged, lunged, trying to tear the pole from the rock. His roars and threats went unheard and unanswered.

I desire you, minus cesu.

At Madyx's *'little cat'* endearment and the truth in his voice, Oyaz's vision tainted red. Every sense focused on the male he would kill, old battle-bond or not. "Do not touch her, Madyx. I will kill you for this." He roared a battle cry, one Madyx would understand.

If he harmed a hair on her head, left a bruise, no matter how small...

If he kissed her...

Claimed her...

Images assailed Oyaz, of her sweet smile, her laughter, of the taste of her lips, the sweep of her tongue. Izzy pinned beneath him, on top of him, against the wall. His malehood hardened, and he grunted, unable to deal with his arousal when her body and life were in danger.

He would never have believed Madyx could behave this dishonorably. For the first time since his sentencing, Oyaz doubted his confession, how Azian had seduced him, then claimed he'd forced her. Doing the same to Izzy implied he might have done so with Azian. Had Oyaz been blinded by their bond? No, he wasn't a fool.

Ceasing fighting the restraints, he attempted to calm down, to appease the insatiable burn of anger tensing every muscle. Helpless to stop Madyx when he ripped Izzy's shirt, baring her beautiful breasts. Helpless when he trailed a finger along skin Oyaz longed to kiss and had memories of doing so. Oyaz's heartbeat thundered in his ears, and if he didn't slow it, he wouldn't hear Izzy above it.

"Where's Izzy?" Miri crouched beside him. Blood trickled down the side of her face, her thick braid had begun to unravel, and blood stained her garments in blue, black, and red.

He nudged his head at the shelter.

Miri rose, checked the red on the blaster, and squared her shoulders.

"Wait." Oyaz jangled his shackles. "Release me."

"What do you want me to do?" Miri frowned, her brown eyes darkening.

Oyaz clenched his jaw, wanting to rail at her. He pointed with his chin at the blaster.

She jerked and raised it. "This will free you?"

He flashed a grateful smile. Izzy's friend was intelligent, brave, and capable.

"Which button?" She pointed to each one until he grunted. Hitting the blue button, she twisted around him and fired at the shackles. They unclicked and fell, the noise loud in the silence of the cavern.

Stumbling to his feet, he took the blaster from her and charged into the shelter. He jerked to a halt, not expecting to find a naked Izzy aiming a blaster at Madyx. The image would remain with Oyaz for an eternity. His breath caught. He had never seen anyone so beautiful.

"Oyaz." She smiled, placed the blaster on the table, and threw herself at him.

He caught her with one arm and crushed her to him, relishing her softness against his body. Burying his nose in the curve of her neck, he inhaled her scent. A shudder tore through him when she wrapped her legs around his hips. "You're free."

She lowered her feet to the ground and pulled away. Pink stained her skin from her breasts to her cheeks. "Oh."

Spinning, she offered her back and the delectable curves of her backside. She lunged for her pants and yanked them on, ignoring her tiny undergarment. When she slipped on her tunic and faced him, the torn fabric gaped over her. He hovered his fingers over the rise and fall of a breast, the heat of her skin discernible. She was tempting him without even trying. Not that she noticed. *Maker.* He wanted her to be his. Gripping the blaster between his thighs, he ripped off his tunic, and with trembling fingers, offered it to her.

She blessed him with a bright smile. The joy on her face tugged on his heartstrings, whispering that he had seen her this happy before. When she raised her arms to pull on his tunic, her breasts lifted. His heartbeat pounded in his ears, and he sucked in a breath. Brynr would heal him, and soon, Oyaz could claim her.

Leaning over Madyx's unconscious body, Oyaz activated the O.D .I. in his limp wrist. "Pilot Krist, this is Supreme Commander Oyaz."

"Supreme Commander, the ground unit from the *Gladio* has landed and is almost at your position."

Oyaz flicked a glance at Izzy. Miri had slipped into the shelter, and the two whispered to each other. "Can you not port us?" The need to be done with this adventure drove him to be a little reckless.

"The rock striations are interfering with accurate porting. Sub-Commander Vorn and Aaro opted for a hands-on approach."

Oyaz grunted. "Expected arrival of the unit?"

"Two minutes, Supreme Commander."

So, not long. Oyaz forced his jaw to relax. "Very well, Pilot Krist, we shall await the unit."

"Do you require medical?"

"Affirmative." Izzy's shoulder needed healing, and Oyaz wanted his O.D.I. re-implanted. The stun button glowed yellow from the blaster Izzy had tossed on the table. Madyx would sleep for perhaps ten minutes, maybe longer. They would be gone by then. Typing on Madyx's holographic buttons, he chose the translator and faced Izzy. "How are you feeling, *ensa*?"

She raised her gaze, and her mouth parted, revealing the dark pink depths he craved. "You speak English?"

"Only through Madyx's translator."

"Is that his name?" She huffed. "He tried to convince me you were a mean bastard. I was having none of that, Oyaz."

He chuckled, offering his hand. She slid her delicate one into his without hesitation. "A rescue is en route. Let us wait outside this cave."

Izzy grabbed the blaster and allowed him to escort her out of the structure. Clutching her blaster to her chest, Miri followed. They strolled along the bridge to the entrance.

"Oyaz." Madyx raced toward them, pumping his arms while gripping another blaster. Oyaz shoved Izzy behind him. Miri ducked behind a crate.

"What now? You are determined to pursue this idiotic vendetta? Revenge for what, Madyx? For remaining true to my principles? For declining Azian's offer? For being your battle-bond even when you betrayed the code? For mourning your death as if you were my blood-bond?" Oyaz shook his head. "Azian served one month on the omeika farms and the rest of the year attending classes we all suffered through as *damu*. I have not heard of her since."

Madyx lowered his blaster. "She did?" He raised it again. "I do not believe you."

"I have no reason to lie. That you imply so means you have fallen beneath your honor. Your males are dead, and a ground unit is here. You have lost, Madyx."

Indecision twitched his eyebrows. His eyes darkened, and a pulse ticked at his jaw. He slapped the red button on his blaster and aimed at Oyaz.

A rock bounced off the side of his head. He roared, spun, and fired in Miri's direction. Oyaz tackled him, grunting when he hit the ground hard. They grappled, but Oyaz was a heavier male and pinned Madyx. Using a sharp knee and a foot thrust, Madyx threw Oyaz back. Before he could scramble into the fray again, Miri fired a blaster at Madyx.

"Miri." Izzy pressed four fingers to her parted lips. "You didn't just kill him, did you?"

"Of course not. Yellow for stun, red for kill, blue to unlock. Oyaz, what's the white button?"

Sitting on his ass, Oyaz's laughter barreled up from his stomach, consumed his chest, and tumbled free.

"Izzy?" Garix's voice penetrated the quiet.

She squealed, dropped the blaster, and yanked her comm device out of her back pocket. "Garix? Please... We need help. Those bastard sharks stunned Oyaz's O.D.I." Her voice caught on a hitch. She raised her sad gaze to Oyaz.

"Lady Miri said Supreme Commander Oyaz was wounded. I am tracking this device, as well. We are en route."

"Oh, good Lord. Thank you." Izzy slumped beside Oyaz, leaning her shoulder against him.

He looped his arm around her, pulling her into the curve of his body.

Miri joined them, balancing the blaster across her thighs. "How does Garix fit into this?"

Oyaz closed his eyes to calm his breathing. Exhaustion drained him, and a rescue was imminent.

"He's my Etterian friend." With tear-stained cheeks, Izzy met Miri's gaze.

Since Madyx sprawled nearby, his translator continued to work.

"You like friends?" Oyaz wouldn't admit he hated that she had male friends. Not that he had a right to an opinion when she wasn't his. And by that thinking, he couldn't be Macy's friend, for it would displease the king. He rolled his bottom lip. When things had settled, he would comm Macy and ask.

"Yes, life is lonely without them. Garix's huge where I'm tiny. It gives us a connection."

Ah. A commonality. What did Oyaz have with Izzy? This misadventure? "But if you have an Eth?"

"What's an Eth?" Miri frowned.

"Friends don't come between...lovers," Izzy whispered, then smiled at Miri. "An Eth is your Etterian soulmate."

Miri froze then rocked on her backside. "Are you serious?"

"And if Garix is your Eth, Izzy?" Oyaz frowned, not liking that he couldn't let this subject go. Why did it bother him that Garix might be hers?

Izzy's smile faltered, and she dipped her chin to her chest. "He's not. Neither is Ronin. I thought I had found my..." She glanced at Oyaz, then shrugged, wincing at the same time. "I'll just keep looking." She straightened her back, as if drawing on inner strength.

"Izzy." The roar came from outside the cave.

"Garix." She leaped to her feet and burst into a run.

Oyaz trudged behind her, taking each step as if he faced Adviser Cales. Miri strolled alongside him, the blaster clutched to her chest.

Izzy threw herself into Garix's arms, laughing and crying as she clung to him.

"You, *minus susa*, are a pain in my backside," Garix mumbled, but he didn't release her.

She chuckled. "You have a big ass, Garix, what's one more pain?" She gestured to Miri. "This's Miri."

"Lady Miri, I am pleased to meet you." Garix held out his hand and pumped Miri's three times.

She gaped at the huge male. Her dark gaze darted between him and the arriving warriors falling into formation behind him.

With a cry, Izzy tugged on Garix's arm. "Sharks attacked, please ...help Oyaz." She rushed to Oyaz and gathered his wrist in her hand to show Garix. "See. Two shots here and his memories were gone."

Oyaz glaring at Garix was lost on Izzy, whose attention had shifted from Oyaz's wrist to his shoulders.

"Supreme Commander," Garix greeted.

"Elite Warrior Garix, clear out the cave, port any Yithians or Maloidians alive, and capture Madyx et Todyx. Hand him over to Sub-Commander Vorn for questioning. Return the cave to its natural state with no sign of our presence."

Garix barked out orders, then placed a hand on Oyaz's shoulder. He gestured with a sideways gaze at Izzy. Oyaz laced his fingers through hers, then held out his hand to Miri. Frowning, she grasped it. "Four to port to medical," Garix spoke into his O.D.I.

They phased in at medical with Medic Brynr rushing around them.

"Place Lady Izzy on that bed," he instructed Garix.

Oyaz jerked back and held onto Izzy's hand, keeping her close. She was his to care for.

Garix frowned.

Brynr crowded Oyaz, gestured to the central bed, and activated the med-E.D., forcing Oyaz to release her.

Oyaz stared at Garix's hands on Izzy's waist to lift her onto the fold-down bed. He didn't like the male touching her. She was talking a mile a minute, to which Garix would grumble or shake his head. Their easy comradery Oyaz didn't like either.

"Where the hell are we?" Miri asked the room in general.

"Oh." Color exploded across Izzy's cheeks. "They teleport. We're on a battleship."

Miri paled under her darker skin tone. "What?" she squeaked. "Izzy Reeves, you start talking."

Brynr blocked Oyaz's view. "I will induce sleep to heal your neural connections."

His gaze shot to Brynr in alarm. Oyaz didn't want to lose sight of Izzy. "No," he said, but the medic ignored his command.

Sleep claimed him with immediate effect.

Chapter Twenty-One

"And that's how I came to know Garix." Izzy grinned, then shoveled strawberry ice cream into her mouth. It wasn't the same as Cheery Cherry's, but it would do. She tried not to slice glances at medical with Oyaz still in some sort of pod. Hence the ice cream. Once, she'd told Caro she didn't eat the stuff, and that wasn't a lie. But under the circumstances, she needed it. Things were bad. Sure, they were on board the battleship again, but she was without an Eth, and now Miri's life was as disrupted.

"When were you going to tell me?" Miri tapped a spoon on the bowl, her salted caramel ice cream, for the most part, untouched. Garix was on his fourth bowl and as many flavors.

Men lingered, tossing their gazes at Miri. With her black hair and dark skin, she could pass for an Etterian. Except her eyes were a deep brown, and she had the most gorgeous plump lips.

"Tell you which part?" Izzy shrugged. "With Caro kidnapped, Simmy in danger, I haven't had the chance to breathe."

"But you sold the Cheery Cherry. You loved that shop."

"It meant nothing without Caro there, and I was hoping to find my Eth. What would I do with the shop when that happened?" Izzy spun on Garix. "I zapped two sharkmen. Where did they go?"

"They suffocated in storage. It is without oxygen," he said in a monotone as if their deaths meant nothing.

She squeaked. Nausea churned in her stomach, and she shoved the ice cream aside. "I killed them?"

Miri flicked a dismissive wrist. "What are you complaining about? How many did I kill, Garix?"

He stilled with his spoon in his mouth. "Thirteen Yithians and three Maloidians."

Izzy tilted her head. "Maloidians? Are they the yellow squidheads?"

After his eyelids fluttered, his shoulders shook when he laughed. "Yes." He nudged his chin at the gathered men in the common. "Lady Miri, you are revered for your courage and determination."

She dipped her gaze while spooning ice cream into her mouth.

"They're hoping you're their Dar Eth, their mate," Izzy teased. "Hot jam and buttered toast, Miri, you can have a sexy man today." She sounded like a digi-ad. Step right up, get your free alien today. But wait, that's not all, if you hurry, mind-blowing sex awaits. Memories of Oyaz drained the humor from her, and she slumped. Maybe her next lover or Eth might... No, she couldn't think about spreading her legs for another man or male. Not for a while.

"Well, as fun as this has been, I came to rescue you, not commit my life to a man, no matter how sexy he is."

Izzy pressed a hand to her stomach, willing the ice cream to stay down. "I'm thinking of touring Europe, might even visit Lunar Base and Mars. I'll get an O.D.I., though. Would love to be able to speak

French or German when I get there." She activated Garix's wrist to show Miri.

"Ah, the translator." Miri dropped the spoon in the bowl and sighed. "I heard that Madyx dude is onboard. I'd love a chat with him."

Izzy winced, images of him touching her breast inflamed her cheeks with a mixture of anger and embarrassment. She curled her shoulders, tucking her hands between her thighs.

"I'm curious as to his motivations. Also," Miri grinned," I want to rub it in his face that I kicked his ass."

Izzy forced a chuckle. "That's not very sporting."

Miri shrugged. "Sue me. Besides, when I get home, you know Darius. My brother always wants to know what happened. I need all the details." She scratched her scalp. "And I could do with a shower." Blood still matted her hair after Brynr had healed the gash.

"Okay." Izzy rubbed her palms together with pseudo-glee. "How about the bestest shower ever, a change of clothes, we pop in to visit Simmy, then you zap home?"

Miri arched a dark eyebrow. "After I visit Madyx?"

"Sure." Izzy rose, patted Garix on the shoulder, and led Miri to her quarters. She palmed the panel, and it opened with a gentle whoosh. "Wait till you try the water. No soap's necessary. The shower senses your core temperature and sets the water a few degrees hotter. Just rinse your hair and gargle. That's it." She flicked her matted hair. "I'll shower too." She pointed to the buttons on the wall. "Blue to dry, white for a toweling robe."

As soon as the bathroom door closed, Izzy collapsed in a chair. A sob echoed off the metallic walls, so she sucked it in. She hadn't lied when she said she'd tour Europe. Having sold her ice cream parlor, she had no other purpose in life. What she would do after she'd seen the sights she didn't know.

She pulled Oyaz's T-shirt over her nose and sniffed. The scent of his skin still lingered. Her heart fluttered, and her arms ached to hold him. Although, the muscle twinges might be from carrying that stupid gun. The damn thing should be lighter. She rose and ordered clothes from the replicator and a bottle of water from the rehydrator.

She paced the confines of her quarters, listening for the dryer. When it came on, she stopped, flicked her fingers, and rolled her shoulders. "Paste on that smile, Izzy. Remember. Happy people attract good things."

Pain lanced across her chest and seized her lungs. How many more years did she have to smile, skip, laugh, dance, as if nothing in the world bothered her? How many more times did she have to swallow her pain? When would the good things start happening to her?

When she'd been with Oyaz, she'd hoped this meant a brighter future, a place she was meant to be, with someone who might end up loving her. Instead, she was alone, having lost her best friend, given up on Simmy, and broken the promise she made Dad. But she had also met Garix. She smiled through the tears. And Oyaz. The time spent with him, despite the Asshat-ordeal, had been wonderful.

"That was amazing. Not sure about the blow-my-body-dry thing, though." Miri strolled through the door, gripping her robe closed. "And this robe's useless. Where's the sash?"

Wiping her cheeks, Izzy leaped to her feet with her signature smile in place and activated the magnets. "Come, let's choose your clothes. You can change while I shower."

Miri shrugged and trailed Izzy to the replicator. It took a few minutes for Izzy to explain how it worked with her limited knowledge. Miri ordered black leggings, a baggy camo T-shirt, and fresh socks. She loved her thick boots and wouldn't budge on ordering a new pair.

Gathering her clothes, Izzy disappeared into the bathroom. As the water flowed over her, she succumbed to a good cry, blessing the water spray with silent wails. When she couldn't wallow any longer, she stepped out and activated the dryer. As it worked, it gave her a few moments to gather herself. Miri knew her too well, but Izzy didn't want to burden her with her sad life. Besides, what could Miri do except pat Izzy on the hand?

After she emerged in a colorful skirt and plain pink T-shirt, Miri gripped her shoulders and ushered her into a chair. "First, why the hell didn't you warn me that this thing moves? I lost ten years off my life. And second, spill. I haven't seen you this down since Danny said your hair looked like a troll doll."

"Ah, come on, Miri, I just got my shit together. Flaming nipples, if I spill, I'll be a sobbing mess again." As it was, her eyes burned and a tickle had taken up residence in her throat.

"So give me the short and sweet."

"Fine. I had an Eth, and I lost him." Izzy controlled her breathing, hoping to hold back an influx of tears. "Best sex of my life."

"You slept with him?" Miri squeaked.

"He was my mate, as in my forever. Why play coy?" And now she had memories to sustain her for the rest of her miserable, lonely life.

"And how did you know he was your...Eth?"

"They kneel when the Ethera strikes them. And by the looks of things, it's painful." Izzy jumped up to pace, folding her arms across her chest only to throw them out wide. "And their eyes change color to this spectacular cerulean blue. They're honorable men, for the most part. Not like Madyx."

"He must have had his reasons."

Izzy shrugged, not caring how or why Madyx lost his honor. "Come, let's comm Simmy." Facing the display vid, she said, "Simone Elora Reeves."

It took a second to flicker. An image of replica quarters formed. A male dominated the display. His cheekbones were wider than his jaw and forehead. He had a lovely nose leading to his wide oversized upper lip. Straight eyebrows that could've been drawn with a ruler knitted above his ice blue almond-shaped eyes.

Izzy frowned. Had she dialed... No, wait, she'd spoken her sister's name perfectly. "Um, hello, I'm looking for Simmy."

"Simone? You have a comm." He blessed Izzy and Miri with a side-profile, as handsome as his portrait.

"Who is it, Danic?"

He arched a brow at Izzy, but she couldn't look past his swirling blue eyes. Did Simmy have an Eth? One side of Izzy's heart wrenched with jealousy, and the other side was pure joy. Her sister would be protected. This discovery solidified Izzy's decision to leave. Now was as good a time as any. They said she could find herself in Paris.

"Her sister, and if she doesn't get her ass here, I'll find her quarters and serenade her."

"I'm coming, dammit." Simmy came into view, her eyes still white.

Izzy shrugged. Remaining blind was Simmy's stupid decision. Horse to trough and all that. "Good to *see* you too, sis."

"Ha ha, like I haven't heard that one before."

Izzy chuckled. "Just checking in. Letting you know I'm off to tour Europe, and I'll see you when I see you. If ever."

Miri's eyebrows shot to her hairline.

Simmy rolled her eyes. "Right, like I can believe that."

"What you believe is up to you. I had some of your art supplies brought up." No way on this massive battleship would Izzy reveal to Simmy what it had cost her. "Consider it my farewell gift."

A frown furrowed Simmy's delicate brow. "But you promised Dad—"

"I did. Still, here you are, choosing to stay blind after Mom and Dad *wasted* their savings on specialists. What you decide is on you. I'm done. I'm tired of pretending to be something I'm not. I'm me, the sister who braided your hair with earthworms and put paint in your shampoo bottle. I love you, but I don't like you. So, this is it. Have a nice life."

She ended the comm and slithered into a nearby chair. Her limbs twitched as if she had run a marathon. But the heavy weight that had dampened her soul for decades lifted.

"What was that about?" Miri crouched beside Izzy and clasped her forearm.

"Simmy can see if she undergoes healing. She chooses not to."

"What?" Miri gasped. "But your parents—"

"I know. I've finally forgiven myself for whacking her on the ass with an umbrella." Izzy smiled.

"That's what you did?" Miri frowned. "But I thought you shoved her down the hill."

Izzy waved a hand. "Close enough. Now, let's get you access to Madyx." Climbing to her feet, she faced the display vid again. "Garix et Orix."

"Minus susa." He smiled. Sweat dripped down his face, and by the looks of things, he was sparring with a greatsword. Pity she'd missed that.

"I need a favor, teddy bear. Can you sneak Miri in to speak to Madyx?"

"Sneak, no." He harumphed. "I have spoken to Sub-Commander Vorn, and he has agreed to the visit. Since Lady Miri had a hand in securing the male, and since he is behind a shielding, she should be safe. Let me cleanse, then I will escort you."

"Meet us in the common. I want to ask Brynr to fit an O.D.I."

Garix grinned. "This pleases me, Izzy."

The comm ended, and after tugging on her slippers, Izzy led Miri to the common. Oyaz was still in his pod. Izzy paused alongside it to place her palm on the glass. In the bright light, every valley and curve of his naked chest was a visual delight. She sighed and pressed her temple to the glass.

"Miladies," Brynr greeted while punching on his holographic buttons.

Izzy dragged her gaze from Oyaz, trying not to remember where her fingers had stroked, her lips had kissed, how he'd blown her mind with his sexual prowess. She faced the medic and cleared her throat. "Brynr, how do I get an O.D.I.?"

His head whipped up. "You ask for it."

She smiled. "Just like that?"

"It is good that you have one, Lady Izzy. It will make it easier to track and communicate with you should you be in danger again."

Miri laughed. "Danger is her middle name."

Brynr's eyes widened. "It is?"

Izzy glared at Miri. "She's teasing, Brynr. Where do you want me?"

He unfolded a bed, and she climbed onto it. While she watched Oyaz's chest rise and fall, Brynr gathered the tools he'd need, including the shaver from last time. Miri shuffled closer, with furtive glances behind her indicating she found the constant attention unnerving.

"What would you do if you sparked the Ethera, Miri?" Izzy traced a pattern on her skirt before glancing up.

"Run?" Miri wiggled her brows and chuckled. "I don't know, Izzy. I love my life. I enjoy the long hikes and spending nights under the stars. I like the cold winters in front of a fire." She twirled a forefinger. "I'd hate to be stuck in a metal box traveling through dark, unemotional space."

"Your male must remain with you," Brynr said as he slid something under Izzy's skin. She hadn't felt him make an incision, and no blood trickled from the cut.

"What? He'll leave this and live with me?" Miri scanned the men watching her.

Izzy didn't bother telling her that the Ethera would've happened when they first saw her. But then, what did Izzy know? Oyaz had spoken to her on the screen first, but his eyes hadn't changed color. Only when she met him face-to-face did he kneel. And look how that turned out.

"Flaming nipples, Miri, you almost sound like you're interested."

Miri shrugged. "To share my love of our planet with someone other than my brother Darius would be wonderful. Regardless, after Madyx, I'll go home, and this'll be a mute discussion."

Garix strolled in wearing fresh armor. He munched on an apple, his pockets bulging with more. "Lady Miri, are you ready?"

"Thank you, Garix."

Izzy gestured to Oyaz's prone form. "I'll stay here. Find me when you're done."

Miri rocked on her toes while chewing on her lip.

Izzy sighed, knowing her childhood friend's expression all too well. "Fine. I'll come with." She swallowed hard. Everything in her wanted to *not* visit Madyx.

"Done." Brynr tapped her left wrist. Holographic buttons in English flickered an inch above her skin. He scanned his wrist overs hers, and tingles rippled to her elbow. His name appeared with his contact details.

"Thank you, Brynr." Izzy flashed him a smile.

She leaped off the bed and followed Garix and Miri along meandering corridors to a wider one. It spiraled into a large room with cells leading off it. In the center sat a circular desk with flickering buttons on the counter. One cell hummed. Its lighting glowed a bright cool-white, and a man sprawled on the bunk fitted to a wall.

"Lady Izzy and Lady Miri, this is Elite Warrior Karg," Garix introduced them to the man typing behind the desk.

"Thank you for allowing this." Izzy offered her hand.

Karg hesitated, then shook it three times but didn't release her. With his thumb, he stroked her knuckles. "It is honorable to serve." Pulling away, he faced the cell. "Madyx et Todyx, you have visitors."

Miri stopped an inch from the shimmering shield. Izzy and Garix lingered farther back.

Madyx grunted. "I do not want visitors." He folded his arm behind his head and didn't look at Miri.

"Not even the woman who hit you with a rock and stunned the shit out of you?"

Karg arched a brow at Miri's taunting.

"Long story," Izzy whispered.

Madyx grunted and swung his legs over the side of the bunk. Gripping the edges, he stared at Miri, running his gaze over her. "You?"

She grinned.

With a grunt, he fell, landing with his hands splayed on the metallic flooring. Garix lunged forward, stepping between the cell and Izzy. She huffed, gripped his hips, and peered around him.

"Do not touch the shield, milady." Karg vaulted over the counter to stand beside Miri.

"Is he ill?" Miri's fingers twitched as if she wanted to help.

Pain rippled beneath Madyx's skin, and a layer of sweat gleamed under the bright lights. He groaned, his body shuddering. If Izzy didn't know any better, she would think... She cupped her mouth and flicked a gaze at Miri's face then Garix's. He looked pissed, his eyes darkened, and his jaw clenched, jutting out his chin.

"Flaming nipples," Izzy muttered. Of all the males to fall for Miri, why did it have to be Madyx?

"Leave," Madyx growled at Miri.

"Why?" She dropped to her ass and crossed her legs. "I came here for a reason."

"Female." Madyx raised his head to glare at her. His eyes were ice blue.

Izzy grasped Garix's arm and tugged, gesturing to him that they should go. Garix pursed his lips but let her lead him away. As they strolled to her quarters, she couldn't decide between laughing or crying.

"I wished her upon him, y'know." Maybe she had supernatural powers? Just by speaking things, they happened. Hysteria bubbled up her throat like too much champagne.

"What do you mean, *minus susa*?"

"I told Madyx I hoped he got the sweetest, most loyal woman on Earth."

Garix scoffed. "You cannot determine between whom the Ethera will burn, *ensa*." He swept her into a hug, leaving her feet dangling inches above the floor. "I have missed your silliness."

She pressed her temple to his chin. If only Garix was her Eth... She did love the teddy bear. Alas, as a brother.

He left her in her quarters, but she didn't stay, choosing to head for the viewing deck for a last glimpse of space before she planted her feet on terra firma for a while. As she settled her ass in the built-in chair she'd been in when Oyaz had first hugged her, tears burned behind her eyes. With no one to judge her, she let them slip free.

Splaying her fingers on the screen, she waved goodbye.

Chapter Twenty-Two

Oyaz's eyes fluttered open. Along with awareness, came the memories. He had kneeled for his Dar Eth and lost her, as simple as that. The color of his eyes in the nearest reflective surface didn't lie. The urge to cherish her had gone as swiftly as the Ethera had struck him down. His breath caught on the throbbing pain in his chest at the mere thought of leaving Izzy unprotected. Perhaps the Ethera was returning? Or was it residual concern? He was uncertain, but he did *need* to know she was well.

"Supreme Commander Oyaz, you are awake." Vorn's cheeks darkened. "I must apologize for not sending aid. I assumed you wanted privacy with your Dar Eth."

Oyaz winced as he swung his legs over the side of the bed. "For days?"

"What readings we had of your O.D.I. registered as you disconnecting from your side." Vorn rubbed his temple. "To discover you were assaulted, your O.D.I. destroyed in such a manner as to impact your...mind, this does not bode well, Supreme Commander. It is a weakness we must mitigate."

"According to Lady Izzy, two stuns from the blaster disabled your O.D.I., removed your memories of the previous day, and numbed the left side of your body." Brynr tapped on his O.D.I, the holographic lettering flickering as he sifted through information. "Until your neural pathways are fully restored, it will be at least three days before a new one can be inserted."

"Three?" Oyaz roared, leaning forward with clenched fists. "I cannot communicate with my...Lady Izabelle." He grimaced.

"She requested an O.D.I. We inserted one into Lady Simmy as a precaution. I have instructed the annals to add it as procedure for any Earthian female on board a battleship." Vorn clasped his hands behind his back and spread his legs. "I will accept whatever punishment you deem necessary for my negligence."

Oyaz pinched the bridge of his nose. "The mistake was mine, Vorn. Believing the housing unit secure, I did not plan for the worst scenario."

Vorn's shoulders relaxed an inch before he squared them. "You could not have known Madyx et Todyx would lie in wait for you, Supreme Commander. May I also suggest all males receive a second O.D.I.?"

Had he had another, the cave adventure wouldn't have happened. "Would not a blaster shot destroy the secondary O.D.I?"

"If we maintain secrecy. By the damage done to your nerves, it impacted the one side of your body only." Brynr gestured to his side. "To incapacitate you, both wrists would need to be stunned."

Oyaz rose to his feet, testing his balance. "Lady Izzy?"

"Her wound is fully healed, and the synthetic skin applied."

Oyaz nodded his thanks. "Where is Elite Warrior Garix?" He waited on Vorn, who activated his O.D.I. "Send him to the comm room."

After ordering and donning fresh armor, Oyaz strode through the common to the comm room, channeling his energy into his limbs and stride. A compulsion took hold of him, demanding he find Izzy, to see for himself she was well. He shoved the urge aside. Not his Dar Eth meant not his problem. His heart twanged, and he swallowed hard. He wanted her to be with every molecule of his being.

A minute after he entered the comm, Garix strode in. "You summoned me, Supreme Commander?"

"How is she?" Oyaz's voice was hoarse, but there was nothing he could do about it. Worse, that wasn't what he meant to ask. Garix had been in charge of ensuring the housing unit was secure.

Garix stilled, clasped his hands behind his back, and spread his legs. He pursed his lips on a sigh. "Sad."

Oyaz halted his pacing to raise his gaze. "Why?"

"According to Elite Warrior Danic, she severed ties with her sister. Izzy also insists on returning to her housing unit. I do not think she will remain there. She talks of visiting places, some off-world."

Tingles traveled from Oyaz's hairline down his face and stopped at the back of his neck. She was leaving, as she'd said. He lunged across the room to grip Garix's shoulders. "Where is she?"

"Viewing deck, Supreme Commander."

He bolted, sprinting along the passages, uncaring that his boots announced his path. At the door to the viewing deck, he halted. There, he tested his muscles, mind, and memories as he watched her. Her teasing him when he'd kneeled for her almost summoned a smile. Her pleading with him to be happy, to find...another Dar Eth stripped him of joy.

Against the glass display vids, she rested her flushed face. *Maker, she is beautiful.* She must have sensed him. Twisting to face the door, she settled her gaze on him.

"Oyaz? How are you feeling?" She rushed toward him then stopped short of touching him, as if she remembered she had no right. He craved her caresses, her hand against his chest, the sense of peace her proximity brought him. He longed for her joyful chatter, her way of talking, her strange curses. He ached to hold her, to eradicate the sadness darkening her gray eyes and tugging at her lips.

"Good, and you?" He grimaced.

"Fine," she mumbled and turned away from him, dragging her feet until she settled on the seat again. In the reflection of the display vid, a tear trailed down her cheek. She didn't wipe it away, choosing to ignore it instead. "I'm sorry," she whispered. "I wanted someone to love. Someone who would love me." She gave a self-deprecating smile, one he didn't like.

He crossed with weakened knees to the closest seat and sank into it.

"I guess I screw up everything I touch." Her breath caught on a moan, and she rubbed her face. Her voice faltered. "I hope you find your soulmate, Oyaz. You didn't deserve this." She abandoned him. The sight of her leaving was haunting. A cold, penetrating ache spread across his chest.

"Supreme Commander Oyaz to security." Pilot Vyar broadcasted the instruction since Oyaz didn't have an O.D.I. yet.

He gritted his teeth, wanting to chase after Izzy. But what would he say, what could he do, she wasn't his. Grunting, he stomped to security, suspecting Madyx of foul play.

Striding into security, he paused at finding Miri sitting cross-legged in front of the shielding. Madyx kneeled on the other side, a smile breaking through his glower.

"What is the meaning of this, Elite Warrior Karg?" Oyaz halted beside the console.

"A complication." The male beamed. "A pairing. I never thought I would witness—"

Oyaz growled. "Alodon's balls, I must release Madyx for Etteria's sake."

Something coated his heart, sinister, greedy, and he gaped. He was...he winced, jealous? Allowing the fury to barrel along his veins, he circled the console and faced Madyx, his intentions clear.

Madyx raised his gaze and scowled.

Oyaz glanced at Miri. "Milady, please excuse—"

"She can stay." Madyx gazed at Miri. "What I am, what I have done, cannot remain secret between mates."

Oyaz pursed his lips. "Lower the shield, Karg."

As soon as its humming died, Madyx lunged across and yanked Miri into his arms. His sigh carried across the room. Miri squeaked but wrapped her arms around him. The male sucked in a sharp breath and shuddered.

Oyaz spread his legs and clasped his hands behind his back. If he had to release Madyx from all crimes, Oyaz needed the full detail. King Xeus would demand it. "All right. Start from the beginning."

"I was a week on Fuyra when I met a Maloidian. He claimed he could sneak us both out. I refused. I was determined to see my month through." Madyx smirked, harkening to their *damu* days. "You were waiting for me, Oyaz, and that alone, kept me honorable. I was there when Azian lost two feet of her hair, but after what she had done, it was not enough for me. I felt...cheated. I did not know of her omeika punishment or her extended education." He laughed while running a hand up and down Miri's back. "The following year, Azian gave birth to a daughter with a kreso farmer. I had Karg research her."

Madyx lifted Miri into his arms, stepped into the cell, and sat on the bed, tugging her across his lap. She snuggled into his embrace. "It was the eighth day when I learned you were...*rewarded* for your part in this."

Oyaz pinched his lips. "I should have told you."

"You tried to refuse. Karg showed me the judgment recordings. A little too late." Madyx slumped against the bulkhead and buried his face in Miri's hair. "You asked to serve alongside me, Oyaz. You were always a better male than me." He shook his head. "I did not know and assumed the worst. Betrayed by Azian, who I thought I loved, and by my battle-bond, the male I held in the highest regard. It was an easy leap to believe you two conspired against me. So, I waited, I watched, noting when the supply and cargo ships arrived, who was on board, how long they docked. Setting the explosion was easy, stealing a Maloidian junket easier. It helped that I had an accomplice." Sadness hardened his face. "Balllio."

"I'm sorry, Madyx." Miri rubbed her nose along his throat.

"I do not blame you, *ensa*. You did not know, and it was I who placed Balllio in harm's way." He kissed her temple and faced Oyaz.

"And when we stumbled on news of your imminent arrival, I wanted revenge. Malo planetside posed a problem. I needed him distracted. We planned to kill his Dar Eth and kidnap the other female...Izzy."

Madyx grimaced. "But she turned out to be resourceful. Her image on Earth's buzz feed brought us here, to this cave behind her housing unit. It was a matter of time before Etterians or Izzy would come for her sister. Failing your involvement, I hoped to bargain. Her for you." He cupped Miri's face, his touch gentle. "My deepest apologies, *ensa.*"

She layered her hands over his. "There is much we must deal with, Madyx. You almost raped my friend. And you had no problems hurting her." She rested her temple on his chin. "We will need to learn to trust each other. I get that me not staying with you means your death, but after what you did... My father believed in giving people second chances. This is yours. Hurt me in any way and I will shoot you."

He crushed her against him, his smile reminiscent of his charming old self. 'The Ethera will not allow me to harm you, *ensa.*" Keeping his arm around her, he faced Oyaz. "I cannot make amends for all I have done, but I can share what I know. Karg, please, record this. A civil war is coming, not for Etteria or Maloid but Yithia. By now, a Yithian male named Kbal and his commander Pyo should have reached out to the members of the Global Council. They are looking to overthrow King Urio." Madyx bumped the back of his head against the bulkhead. "Do not be deceived, Oyaz. Urio is aware of this...faction and has allowed certain leeway. He tests his allegiances, his standing within Yithia, and has plans to crush Kbal and his followers."

"And you know this how?" Like Oyaz was supposed to believe a male who had cost him so much?

"Balllio was Queen Alllero's nephew. She hoped a trip to Fuyra would make him...stronger. In a way, it did. He became desperate and cunning. He bargained our way onto the junket, and the explosion was a diversion, a reason for Etteria not to search for us."

"Maker." Oyaz hunched over the console. "Are you saying the only heir to the Maloidian throne is dead?"

Miri squeaked and pushed off Madyx. Her cheeks had paled. "I killed a prince?"

Madyx drew her onto his lap. "He was a prince no longer and wanted no part of the throne."

"Maloid will fall into chaos when Alllero dies, Madyx. As the only supplier of Maloidian steel, we are at their mercy." Oyaz scanned the surrounding cells, all empty, then settled on Karg. "Are there any prisoners ported from the cave?"

Karg typed on the console before meeting Oyaz's gaze. "A few were taken to a separate medical and are being treated by medics in training, Supreme Commander."

"Are any of them Maloidian?" Madyx's voice was faint, yet hope brightened his ice blue eyes.

"One moment." Karg's brow furrowed as he searched. "Two are. They have not disclosed their names and have been scheduled for interrogation."

"Lead the way, Elite Warrior Karg." Oyaz gestured to the passage. "Perhaps if they saw Madyx alive and well, they would be more forthcoming."

Karg clipped a blaster to his thigh and strode out of security. He turned left and hurried along a passage. Oyaz trailed Lady Miri and Madyx walking arm-in-arm. Through a sealed door and along another corridor they strolled until they entered a common in an unused barracks. Beds filled the room as medics worked from one patient to the next.

"Madyx?" A whisper was the catalyst to a susurration of 'Madyx' as his males rose onto their elbows to smile at him.

"I am well, my battle-bonds." He laced his fingers through Lady Miri's and tugged her from male to male, introducing her. Laughter echoed across the metallic bulkheads. Karg guarded the door along with other warriors.

Oyaz sought the closest medic. "How many?"

"A dozen, Supreme Commander. All are well. Two need new eyes. We have begun the growth process."

"Lady Miri blinded them?" Oyaz gaped.

"One yes, the other no, a birth defect weakened his cornea."

Releasing Madyx but not those under his lead was illogical. Their actions rested solely on his shoulders. Oyaz glared at Miri as if it was her fault she'd triggered the Ethera. For the betterment of Etteria and the possibility of daughters, Oyaz had no choice. "Well done, medic. In your rounds, discover where they would like to be released. After Vorn and his males have questioned them, we will ensure they find their homes." He settled his gaze on two Maloidians tucked in the corner.

The medic pursed his lips. "As commanded."

Oyaz weaved between the beds and paused alongside the first Maloidian. "Name?" He studied the male's markings where they faded from his temple into his tentacled hair. For once, it did not sway but twitched.

"None of your bus—"

"This is Zammar, Oyaz. That's Balllio." A grinning Madyx released Miri's hand and bounded over to his battle-bond. He'd once worn the same happiness when he'd greeted Oyaz. Decades had passed between them, and they had lost much. Oyaz didn't believe their relationship could be restored. "I thought you dead, Balllio."

"I am sturdier than I look," the male grumbled, struggling to sit up.

"It is good to see you alive. This…" Madyx held out his hand to Lady Miri.

Balllio lunged out of the bed and wrapped his long yellow fingers around her throat.

Madyx roared, yanked the Maloidian off her, and threw him against a bulkhead. "My Dar Eth."

The male sprawled on the floor, raising an accusing finger. "She killed—"

"To save Lady Izzy, as you would do to save me. As you have done." Madyx crouched beside him. "I cannot blame her. The Ethera demands I forgive and forget." He flicked a gaze at Lady Miri, and his expression softened. "Here we part ways, my battle-bond. I go where she goes."

"And I go where you go." Balllio rested his hand on Madyx's shoulder.

"If you vow not to harm my Dar Eth, then you are most welcome."

"I must notify King Xeus of your survival." Oyaz faced Madyx. "Queen Alllero's health is deteriorating, and your father, Madyx, has mourned you all these years."

Both males dipped their heads.

"Please stay with us for as long as you want to, Balllio." Lady Miri squeezed Madyx's shoulder. "We'll leave as soon as you are well." Her eyes shimmered as she offered a tremulous smile. "And I'm sorry I shot you. Had I known to use the yellow button, all your men would be alive."

Madyx rose and pulled her into his arms.

"May I suggest you receive an O.D.I. before you port? Should anything befall Madyx, you can reach me." At her nod, Oyaz waved the medic over and instructed him, then left for his quarters, needing somewhere private to comm the king.

Chapter Twenty-Three

The moment Garix told Izzy via her O.D.I. that Malo had found Caro, she leaped out of the chair to face the screen. She choked on saying Caro's full name, as undulant waves of emotions crashed through her. Swiping away a tear, she bounced on her toes and waited for the call to connect.

"Caro?"

Seeing her beloved friend's face was glorious, a crescendo of joy rose within her, and she beamed.

"Izzy? Where the monkey's bananas have you been?"

"You're one to talk after traveling the galaxy. I merely had an incident and just returned. When Garix said Malo found you, I had to call you. I need you, babe. The shit's hitting the fan, and I don't know how to handle it." Izzy winced at the truth in her words.

Caro folded her arms across her belly. "That doesn't sound like you. Your solutions are usually too creative for me."

That was so not helpful. Izzy leveled a glare on her.

Caro chuckled and held up her palms. "Okay, start from the beginning."

"When those bastards took you, I was so scared, but not once did I think it was me they were after. A second attempt to take me changed things. I was shafted from stick-up-his-ass Vorn to some guy named Oyaz. I didn't care who, as long as they rescued Simmy first. Can you imagine her alone?" Izzy shook her head. Simmy was no longer her problem. "Regardless, after Oyaz and his team brought her to the battleship, I met him." She clasped her hands together, recalling how he'd hugged her. "My own Eth, Caro. At last." And the joyful wave plummeted Izzy into the depths of despair. She sniffed, twitching her nose to hold back another round of tears. "But on a mission to collect Simmy's art supplies, Yithians ambushed us and blasted Oyaz's O.D .I." She sobbed behind her cupped hands. "He awoke not knowing who I was, and while I tried to drag his huge ass into the forest to hide, his memory didn't return. I couldn't get in touch with Garix or Reyes, stranding us."

"Holy noodles, Izzy. Does he remember you now?"

Oh, if it were that easy. Healed and still, nothing, no recollection in his eyes. And by calling her Izzy proved this. She'd loved the way Izabelle had rolled off his tongue, in that baritone and accent. Tears dripped off her chin. "I found my alien only to lose him." Shaking her arms to rid herself of energy, she fell into pacing. "No other male has claimed me, so I assume it's Oyaz or no one." She raised her gaze to Caro, praying her genius friend had a solution. Hit him with a baseball bat, a shovel, a brick? Stun him with one of their guns? Something had to trigger his memory, or else, she was doomed. "I don't want anyone else. What do I do?"

"Be patient? Granny's nipples, I don't know what to tell you, Izzy. What does the medic say?"

"There's no medical reason for his memory not to return." She paced again. "Maybe he doesn't want a soulmate? Maybe he doesn't want me as his Dar Eth?"

"They can't choose, babe. It happens once in their lives. If he dropped to a knee for you, I'm afraid the poor bastard's stuck with you." Caro chuckled. "Now be patient. Yeah, I know it's a curse word for you, but let nature heal him. He'll kneel for you again."

Days loomed ahead with Izzy doing nothing but waiting. No, she'd leave as planned. Seeing Paris would be a start, and distance would help her gain perspective. In the middle of her soul was a darkness she didn't understand. "Patient? That's worse than a rash on my lady bits." She pouted. "You look good though, Caro. Are you glowing?"

Her dark hair draped over one shoulder, no doubt from the many Etterian showers she must have had. And it looked as if she had lost weight but in a good way.

Caro drew in a shuddering breath, with a smile lingering then fully forming. "As expected of a mom-to-be, Aunt Izzy."

Lights exploded in Izzy's chest, and she gaped. "I'm an aunt?" She squealed, throwing her hands in the air as she danced. "Way to go, Malo. He has super swimmers, he does." She stilled and flipped her hair out of her eyes, her joy lingering. "But how are you doing, babe? You seem off. Are you unhappy about the baby?"

"No, never that." Tears shimmered in Caro's eyes. "Malo doesn't love me, Izzy. I'm not even sure they know what love is. The sex is amazing, and he's attentive, even affectionate."

Ice cloaked Izzy's heart. They didn't love? Maybe what happened was for the best? No, she couldn't think like that. "I can't believe that, babe. I mean, once they feel, they *feel*. They have no idea how to hold back emotions. Maybe he does love you but doesn't know what he's feeling is love?"

Caro snorted. "Getting a human man to admit love is like pulling teeth. How the hell am I going to teach an Etterian how to recognize it, Izzy?" She slumped, dipping her chin to her chest. "It's impossible."

"Let me know if you figure out how. Once Oyaz returns to his senses," she winced, "I might need that info."

Caro jerked back, and her cheeks flushed. Malo's face filled the display vid.

"Hi, Malo." Izzy waved. She'd give a kidney for Oyaz to look at her like that. Something intense warmed his eyes when he gazed at Caro.

"It is good to see you, female. Your disappearance would have delayed heading home. Now you are well, I may show my Dar Eth Etteria sooner."

Izzy blinked. Caro wasn't coming home? Darkness engulfed Izzy, and she curled into herself. She was alone, as she'd expected.

"What?" Caro squeaked. "We're not going to Earth?" She waved at Izzy, and the vid faded, as black as Izzy's soul.

A sob escaped, and she whimpered, throwing out a hand to slow her descent. Crumpled on the floor, she wailed, allowing the pain, loneliness, and lost love a voice. The cold metallic flooring burned her flushed cheek, and she sniffed, not wanting to pull herself together, to pretend she was fine.

"Just one more time, Izzy. Go find Garix, have lunch with him for old time's sake, then leave." She wiped her nose on her T-shirt. "You can do this."

She rolled onto her hands and knees and crawled until she could stumble to her feet. Activating the shower, she stuck her hand in the spray to dab her cheeks. Then ordered a clean T-shirt without the snot streaks. She studied her reflection above the vanity. Her pale face, her almost-tamed hair, but two red spots glowed on her cheeks, and her eyes shimmered with fresh tears. Pinching her lips, she rolled her eyes. *Right, I am so fine. Nothing wrong here.* Forcing a weak-assed smile, she cursed at failing, then she forced another smile. This one lasted longer. Splaying her fingers, she ran them down her skirt.

Faking a laugh, she bounced on her toes, hoping to appear happy. Then with a flounce, she marched out of her quarters to the common. Seven-foot Garix was easy to spot, biting into a salami stick. She took a calming breath then skipped across to Brynr, dancing around the males crowding the common.

"Medic Brynr, how do I move my tokens from my paychip to my O.D.I? And how do I activate languages?"

The older male smiled, pushed off his chair, and strode toward her. "I have activated Etterian for you, Lady Izzy."

"I'd like German, French, Italian..." She tapped her chin. Technically, English was the global language chosen in 2110. Still, smaller towns clung to their cultural languages, and she hoped to wander through a few of them. Real pasta sauce with authentic cheese? Her stomach gurgled, and she yearned to share the experience with Garix. He'd love the food. She slumped. This adventure was by choice, and a desperate chance for her to forget Etterians existed. Having Garix along would defeat the purpose.

"Why would you want these?" Brynr frowned as he typed on her O.D.I., syncing her bank accounts. He patted the bed and helped her climb up. "Let me remove the old chip."

She offered him her wrist. "I'm off on an adventure, Brynr, to visit Paris, Berlin, and Rome. I want to see it all. Well, as many as I can. They had to dome the Colosseum, the Berlin Wall, the Eiffel Tower due to our corrosive air, but still, to see them, to be in their presence."

"Alone?" He held the medgun to her wrist, healing the sliced skin.

That one word was a dagger to her heart. "Garix can't come with. He's a warrior with obligations. His Dar Eth awaits him somewhere, and babysitting me will prevent him from finding her." She squeezed Brynr's forearm. "I'll be fine." It was sweet of him to worry. At least, someone did.

"May I suggest you take a blaster with?"

She laughed. "Where would I put it?" On a whim, she threw her arms around the male and hugged him. "Thanks for worrying, Brynr."

He patted her back, and when he pulled away, his cheeks had darkened. "Still, a weapon of some sort—"

"Wouldn't make it through the airport checkpoints." She leaped off the bed while he packed away his gadgets, including the massive shaver she now knew was their medgun. "I plan to go without luggage and no travel route in mind. If I love a place, I'll stay longer. I have the funds to buy whatever I need, go wherever I want."

"Sounds wonderful, to be that free." Brynr smiled. "I might join you, Lady Izzy."

She treated his offer as a joke and chuckled in the hopes of not offending him. "You are needed here, and your Dar Eth awaits you too." Patting his chest, she tilted her head to maintain eye contact. "But my eternal gratitude for offering, Brynr."

"I—"

"You'd stop at the first medical clinic, lose your shit over how we're struggling to cure cancer, and abandon me to my adventure."

"Cancer?" His eyelids fluttered, and he gasped. "Truly?"

"See. You can make more of a difference on Earth than touring with me."

He grinned. "Lady Izzy, you are a marvel. I will convene with the medics onboard the orbiting battleships and plan how to eradicate this cancer."

"Promise me, Brynr, you'll start with the children."

He jerked back, and his cheeks trembled. "This I vow." He tapped his O.D.I.

She sighed and plastered on a smile. Drawing from the bottom of the barrel, she gathered her energy and skipped to where Garix had almost finished the salami stick. She draped an arm across his shoulders and smacked a wet kiss on his cheek. He brushed her aside with a grunt.

As if it rained outside, she ordered a plate of cinnamon sugar crepes and slid the plate in front of him. "Try these, babe. Perfect rainy weather food."

He unraveled his legs so she could sit next to him. Gathering the plate closer, he sniffed and closed his eyes on a hum. "What is this?"

"Just try it. Flaming nipples, Garix, you'd swear I'm poisoning you." She laughed and ignored it cracking at the end. "Let me tell you, my grizzly, it would take a shit load of crepes to kill you." Leaping to her feet, she ordered two forks and offered him one. "Have I led you astray before?"

His gaze whipped up. "Pineapple? Olives? Oysters? Tequila?"

"So, who's counting?" She dug her fork in and held it for him to bite.

He wrapped his lips around the fork and groaned. "This is so good."

"It's better with ice cream, fruit, whipped cream, chocolate. Some eat it without sugar but with a chicken or minced beef sauce."

She dug her fork in again, but he smacked it with his.

"Mine."

She gaped. "What?" Trying again got the same result. She huffed. "You're being silly."

"No. You share with me and eat most of it." He pinched his lips while she scoffed at the accusation. But he was serious, pushing the plate out of her reach.

Fury burned her hairline, and she narrowed her eyes on him. "Are you saying little me eats more than you?" She gestured to his size, and a pang shot through her at his wince. That was mean of her. "More than any Etterian male?" She scrambled to ease the pain she'd inflicted.

Yes, whatever she touched, she corrupted. Garix was better off without her. "I thought we shared everything, my friend. Who knew crepes would be a no-go." She tried again to stab the last crepe. "If you don't learn to share, I'll stop introducing you to our delicious foods." She grinned. "Fair's fair."

"You can order your own. Why must I share this time, *ensa*?"

"Because I don't want a stack. I just want a bite. Garix, it's just a crepe. You're acting as if I asked you to share your last iced coffee." Fuck it. "That's it, Garix. I'm done with this...bullshit." She threw down her fork and punched her O.D.I. "Pilot Vyar, zap me to my housing unit, please."

The male's voice vibrated up her arm. "Zap, Lady Izzy?"

How she heard and felt his voice, she wasn't going to understand, ever. She gritted her teeth. "Port, teleport, zap, dematerialize, play with my DNA. Just get me home."

Garix leaped to his feet. "Ensa—"

And bam, she stood in her living room. She patted herself to make sure her ass wasn't on backward, then drew in a shaky breath. Maybe she'd spend one night here, then head out? Running to her room, she threw herself onto her bed and yanked her pillow into a crushing hug. And maybe a last meal at Papa and Milly's. A friendly non-Etterian face was just what she needed.

"Izzy?"

She groaned and threw the pillow at Garix just as he filled her bedroom door. "What? Go away, Garix. I don't need protection any-more."

He hesitated. His furrowed brow and sad eyes tugged at her resolve.

"Flaming nipples, Garix. Go find your Dar Eth. I'll be fine. Madyx was behind the attempts to take me. Which means no more sharkmen and squidheads."

"But—"

She squealed, thrashing her legs and arms like a toddler throwing a tantrum. "What?"

"Is it because I would not share?"

She stilled and mumbled, "No." Her voice was small. How could she explain her emotions to the big hulk? Rolling over, she sat up and faced him. "For once in my life, I have no responsibilities, Garix. I'm free to choose my life and path." She scooted off the bed to sit on the edge. She dug her nails into her thighs and persevered. "I want no reminders of this...adventure." She winced. "So, no Etterians, Garix, please."

"You want to forget about me?" His eyebrows shot to his hairline.

"Oh, big teddy bear, I could never forget you, and I don't want to." She pushed off the bed to rest her hands on his stomach. "I want time to heal my...heart." *So cliché.*

"Your heart?" He jerked back to type on his O.D.I. "Medic Brynr—"

"Can't mend a broken heart. No one can...well, except time." She waved a hand and slipped around him. Explaining her emotions to him was futile. "How about burgers at Papa and Milly's?"

He huffed and stomped after her.

At the front door, she paused and arched a brow. "Coming?"

He grunted. "Fine, but this discussion is not over, *minus susa.*"

She snorted as she headed downstairs to call a cab. When she walked out of her apartment for the last time, boarded a plane for Europe, then he would realize, there was nothing he could say to make her stay.

Chapter Twenty-Four

THE HOUR WAS EARLY with Oyaz's sleep elusive. His bed was cold and his arms empty. His thoughts were far away, replaying every moment with Izabelle he could recall. Her sweet smile, her energy, her sassiness, and kindness vibrated outward, announcing her presence. Her resilience and determination jutting out her jaw. Her inner strength surpassed his. As he cycled through the play of emotions on her face, he couldn't avoid her sadness, her belief that life had cursed her.

"Supreme Commander Oyaz, what are you doing?" Brynr slid onto a seat in front of Oyaz, who nursed a cup of coffee.

"Drinking coffee?" He flashed a smile, but it lacked warmth. Because *he* lacked warmth.

"Why are you not with Lady Izzy?"

"She is not mine," Oyaz released a long-drawn-out sigh.

"I saw the Ethera take you down, Oyaz, and the latest med scans showed your body still experiencing the effects."

Oyaz frowned. "But my eyes—"

"Fluctuate as I look at you." Brynr drew in a deep breath. "She is human, Oyaz."

Oyaz's head shot up to look at Brynr, his eyes widening at his words.

He spun his head, searching for her or Garix in the morning crowd. He'd seen her earlier, seated next to Garix and attempting to stab his food with a fork. Oyaz closed his eyes and focused his senses, hoping to scent or hear her. Yet silence reigned with no *damu*-like arguing. The last time she'd gazed at him when he'd entered the common, her face had paled, and she'd curled into herself before giving Garix a small smile.

"Supreme Commander Oyaz." Pilot Vyar's voice echoed through the common. "Queen Macera is on comm. Patching it through to your quarters."

Oyaz bolted, abandoning his coffee on the table. He skidded into his quarters and touched the display vid. When Macy's face formed, his shoulders dipped. How he missed her, needed her joy, her sweetness.

She smiled. "Oyaz, so glad I caught you."

Happiness warmed her brown eyes where once sorrow had lingered. Her cheeks were pink, and as she peered at him across the many comm stations between them, she glowed as if the magnus sun kissed her face.

"It is good to see you, my queen."

She peered at him. "You're not angry that I only called now?"

He chuckled, but it ended too swiftly. His ability to laugh had abandoned him days ago. "No."

"Then what's the problem? Your brow's furrowed, your lips are pursed, and—"

He shuddered, wishing he could convey the turmoil he endured. "I had a Dar Eth for a morning." One glorious, memorable morning.

"What?" she squeaked, and her eyebrows rose.

He spilled the story, revealing far more than he wanted to but unable to halt the words. If anyone could understand what he was going through, it was Macy.

"Oh, shit, Oyaz. You had her, and those effing Yithians stole her from you." She raised her hand, halting him mid-gape. "Losing memories of someone is worse. Thankfully, you have those back, sort of. Can't you fight for her anyway? Don't you want to?"

"Without the Ethera, claiming Izabelle would be akin to stealing another male's salvation. I could not live with that on my conscience."

She flicked her fingers. "Step closer to the screen."

He did so but frowned at the command. Had she not been his queen, he might not have obeyed.

"Your eyes swirl from blue to ice blue, Oyaz. That has to mean something."

Brynr said the same thing. "I am overly emotional. That is to be expected."

She tapped her chin. "And would the Ethera bend your knee twice? Surely, it would assume the connection made? So, not chasing after Izabelle might mean dooming yourself and her to a life of celibacy?"

A life of celibacy for them both and him circling the void until he died?

I wanted someone to love. Someone who'd love me. Izabelle's words slammed into him, and he grimaced.

"She's not Etterian, Oyaz. She chose you. Do you think your eye color matters to her?"

Hope struck and exploded in his chest like a supernova. "You mean, I can choose her, and the Ethera will follow?" He'd never considered that. Could it be that simple? *Maker, I hope so.* He ached for her. Memories tormented him. Sleep was elusive, peace more so, and yet his void remained dormant.

"All I'm saying is try, if you love her."

"Love?" Was love this intense sadness and extreme elation merging to press on his soul?

"Your eyes could be healing, and once enough time has passed, the ice blue color of the Ethera may return." Her eyes twinkled with mischief. "Tell me, how do you *feel* if I say another male has claimed her?"

Red burst across Oyaz's vision, and the urge to rip things apart twitched his arms. He gritted his teeth to swallow a growl.

Macy laughed. "I rest my case. Go get her, Tiger." The screen faded to black.

"Mirror," he commanded the bulkheads and waited for them to alter into reflective surfaces. His eyes did swirl, flashing between dark and ice blue. "Pilot Vyar?" He didn't have an O.D.I. And porting anywhere without one wasn't wise. Never did he want to be so vulnerable again, but he was if he thought long and hard about it. Without Izabelle, he was raw, like an open wound that would never heal. "Where is Izabelle?"

"She ported to her housing unit yesterday. Elite Warrior Garix did so as well and requested permission to follow Lady Izzy on her travels," Vyar said. "The request is urgent, Supreme Commander. Lady Izzy leaves this morning."

Oyaz clenched his jaw, then forced himself to relax. "Port me now."

"Yes, Supreme Commander."

He appeared on an enclosed balcony and paused to listen, praying she was home.

"This is insane, Izzy. Come back."

"You know I love you, Garix, but this is best for everyone. My place's yours for as long as you want to stay."

She *was* leaving like she said she would. And the promise Oyaz made himself flashed across his thoughts. He ran, nudging Garix through the door he blocked. Oyaz jerked to a halt, stunned at her strolling along the corridor. Determination squared her shoulders. Her leggings clung to thighs he knew well. Her tunic was white, triggering memories of her damp breasts and sucking a nipple through the thin fabric.

"Izabelle." His voice hoarsened with need.

She stilled, her posture drooped, and she shook her head. "Goodbye, Oyaz."

He lunged forward but stopped an inch from touching her. The darkness crushing his chest, the void expanding said it all. She *was* his. And if she left him, he'd die.

"Where you go, I go." He prayed she remembered she had once said those words to him.

She turned on a heel to face him. Tears shimmered on her lashes, and the gray of her eyes shone like Maloidian steel. "You're better off not knowing me, Oyaz. Go, find your Dar Eth." Her breath shuddered out, and pain twisted her delicate features.

"I have found her."

Her cheeks paled, and a tear slipped free. "Good." She pasted on a smile, one that didn't touch her eyes except to crinkle the edges. "I wish you all the happiness."

He swallowed past the lump in his throat, aching to hold her. "She will not have me."

"What?" She jerked back, and her cheeks flushed. "Why not? You're perf—" She bit her lip, lowered her gaze, then offered a stiff shrug. "Send my love to Simmy." Her curls bounced as she stomped off. A whisper of a sob reached his sensitive ears.

"Why will you not send your love to me?" Could she not see how much he longed for her? How much she meant to him? "Do you not...*love* me?" Ice engulfed his body, his blood, freezing each muscle, the air in his lungs, and time around him. He waited.

A sob jerked her shoulders. "Of course..." She sniffed. "I love you, just as I love Garix."

Oyaz growled, not liking that every tactic he tried failed. "Why do you not ask if I love you?"

She laughed and flashed him a smile despite her tear-stained cheeks. "Etterians can't love. I told Caro you bottle it all inside and feel things intensely. I lied." She closed her eyes while she drew in long breaths.

He pounced, taking the opportunity to approach her. Inches from her, he cupped her cheeks, catching her tears on his thumbs. "I love you, Izabelle."

She opened her eyes to meet his. Joy curled her lips and pinkened her cheeks, then darkness prevailed. "You don't. I'm just a foolish female you accidentally fucked." Yanking out of his arms, she stormed off, her shoes slapping the patterned floor.

He hesitated, gritted his teeth, then trailed her. She hadn't given up on him in all the time he was injured or captured. "So, where are we going?"

She swung on him with fire in her eyes. "*You* aren't going anywhere."

"Where my Dar Eth goes, so must I." He activated her O.D.I. while admiring her upturned face and the heat in her gaze. "Sub-Commander Aaro, I resign from my command—"

"What are you doing?" She slapped her hand over her wrist. "Belay that order, Aaro. I'm not your Dar Eth, Oyaz. Remember?" She stretched onto her toes to touch his temple. "Are you ill?"

He laughed. She cared, his Izabelle. "No, just an Etterian male in love."

She lowered her arm and stepped back. "Stop it. You don't say such things unless you mean it, Oyaz."

"Oh, heart of my heart, Etterians do not lie. It is dishonorable."

"Well," she huffed. "You're deceiving yourself. Your eyes are dark blue."

"My eyes can be green, purple, orange, the color does not matter."

"Yes, it does, and you damn well know it." She darted her gaze everywhere but on him. "Now, I'm going, so quit following me. I didn't get an O.D.I. for nothing."

He trailed her down the stairs, and at the first landing, she paused with a hand on the railing. Her pleading gaze wrenched his heart. "Why are you doing this?"

"I love you. I cannot survive another moment without you."

Her chuckle was self-deprecating. "Right. Out of the blue, you love me."

"Yes. Macy made me see my eye color does not matter to you. Only the state of my heart."

Izabelle studied him, and her gaze softened, despite her leaping heartbeat. "You're serious? You want me?" She gripped the railing with both hands. "I'm trouble, Oyaz. Bad things happen around me."

"Good things too. And Madyx was not on you, Izabelle." He skipped the steps to her, then swept her into his arms, relishing her warm softness. "Besides, my heart is yours. I cannot take it back and cannot live without it." He pressed a kiss to her nose. "You are stuck with me, beloved."

Color bloomed across her cheeks, and she snatched a kiss. "Want to zap me to your quarters?"

He grinned and buried his nose into the curve of her neck for a deep inhale. "Not yet. You have not said how you feel, and do not dare compare me to Garix again."

She laughed, the joy bouncing off the walls of the stairwell. "I do love Garix. But..." She licked her lips. "I love you more, and I would never let Garix pin me to a bathroom wall."

Oyaz growled. "He better not." Lifting and throwing her over his shoulder, he tapped her O.D.I. "Pilot Krist, two to port to my quarters."

"Congratulations, Supreme Commander."

"Oyaz, let me down." She wiggled, then slapped his backside, drawing a grunt as heat shot to his groin. "Who's Krist?"

"He pilots the *Valiant*—my battleship." When Oyaz lowered her, they were in his quarters on board the *Valiant*.

As soon as her toes touched the floor, he claimed her mouth. Her lips parted in readiness. Unable to deny himself this craving to taste her, he plunged his tongue in. He drew in a deep and shuddering breath, inhaling her scent, marveling at the softness of her lips, at the exotic, addictive flavor of her mouth. His groan rumbled from deep within him. It was eons old, that sound, of a male desperate for his female. His eyes burned so he closed them. All that mattered was this female in his arms. She threaded her fingers into his hair at the base of his neck. The feeling was sensational, making him shiver with need. Then she slipped her tongue into his mouth, past his lips, and he unraveled.

"Oyaz," she gasped when he feathered kisses along her jaw. "Please."

"What is it, beloved?" He raised his head to meet her gaze.

"Don't go slow, my Eth." She grinned. "I might explode if you do."

He jerked back, arching a brow. "Explode?"

"With love for you." She wrapped her legs around his hips, clung to his neck, and pulled herself up to kiss him. "Lots and lots of mini explosions." She peppered her words with short kisses. "You call them fulfillments?"

He growled and hurried to their bedroom to the sweetest music of all, her laughter.

Epilogue

Simone threw her legs off the side of the bed and stood. Five steps to the right, and she was in the quarters common room. Hand on the wall for seven steps to the comfy. With the cold fabric under a searching palm, she slid a hand down the backrest until she rested her fingers on the seat before she lowered her ass into it.

The conversation with Izzy haunted Simone so much that she couldn't sleep.

Her breath rushed out of her, and she couldn't suck in enough air to satisfy. Gasping, she pressed a hand to her chest and willed herself to calm. Izzy had always been there for her. And though Simone had resented it, the promise Dad had forced from Izzy had brought comfort. Blinded in a visual-orientated world was harder with no family.

The accident wasn't Izzy's fault, but Simone hadn't taken the time to convince her sister of this. She'd liked having someone to blame. And now Izzy was gone. Determination had saturated her voice. She wasn't coming back.

Added to the coldness inside Simone at having pushed away her last family member were waves of debilitating fear at the thought of having her eyes healed.

"Ensa?" Danic kneeled beside her, bringing his warmth and enticing cologne.

Throwing out a hand, she found his bare chest and splayed her fingers across it. "I'm sorry I woke you."

"What is it?"

She closed her useless eyes, as if bearing the pain with her eyelids open increased the intensity. In the same boat as Izzy at apologizing over and over, Simone yearned to undo her actions. She'd think twice before lashing out at Izzy, who'd wallowed in guilt for years. Or before swinging the shovel that had stolen two days of Danic's life. And the sweetheart had stayed with her when he realized she couldn't see. Out of pity.

"Just—" The sob squeezed her throat, and she curled in on herself, trying to stem the tears.

Forgive yourself first, Izzy.

Simone trembled. Demanding her sister forgive herself for something she didn't do was idiotic, but it was tied to Simone needing Izzy's forgiveness for making her believe it was her fault. The umbrella whack on her ass had stung, but it hadn't been hard enough to tumble her down the embankment. That she had done herself, chasing after a book.

Her fault her ankle had snapped.

Her fault she had slammed into the tree.

Her fault she was blind.

And now her fault she stayed blind.

Squaring her shoulders, she ignored the tears and wrapped her arms around Danic. "Please take me to Brynr. It is time to fix my eyes." Her nostrils burned with more unspent tears when he helped her to stand. This would be her gift to Izzy, to say sorry.

"You are in your sleep tunic, *ensa*."

She laughed between hiccups and sniffs, her heart lighter than it had been in years. "It's early in the morning, Danic, how many men will see me?"

Excitement swept through her, barreling over her twitching fingers, the hairs rising across her skin, and the dark whispers in her soul. What lay ahead for her, she couldn't say. But she did know, she would start with her sister and build the relationship they should have had.

The one Mom and Dad would have wanted.

But when Danic ushered her onto the cold, hard floor of the passage, she winced, wishing she had thought to wear shoes. He swept her into his arms, striding with enough force to whip her hair off her cheeks. She clung to him, burying her nose in the angle of his neck, needing his warmth to hold back the chill.

"You were right." She chuckled. "Clothes would've been wise."

"I can—" He hesitated, jarring her.

"No, it's fine. Let's do this before my courage fails." No man had held her in years, so being in someone's strong embrace was heaven sent. She cherished his hugs and touches. How did you two meet? She was so desperate for a hug, she hit the first man she met with a shovel. A giggle slipped free, more to do with her nervousness than the silly scenario she was imagining.

"Lady Simmy? Are you unwell?"

She wiggled for Danic to release her. His hold tightened before he huffed and lowered her feet to the floor.

"Medic Brynr, your offer to fix my eyes, is it still available?"

The male gasped, and she smiled, facing his voice.

"Of course, milady."

She held out her hand, and someone gripped it, tugging her forward with breathtaking gentleness. "Then, I am all yours."

Glossary

Etterians worship one God, one Maker, since the universes have only His fingerprint on all of it, a single golden thread through all of creation.

Tokens: intergalactic form of currency

Kliks: predetermined length of distance.

Hatimaye – To bring an end (Hutt-ee-my-ee)

Etterian

Alodon (A-low-donn): who accidentally shot his balls off with his own blaster.

Teacher: lima (lee-ma)

Great teacher: lima kuu: (lee-ma koo)

Directions: semit (semm-it)

Lemon: giyua (gee-you-a)

Young one: damu (daa-moo)

Heart: ensa (enn-sa)

Heart of my heart: ensa ra ensa (enn-sa raa enn-sa)

Beloved: thamani (ta-mar-nee)

Little joy: minus susa (mee-nas soo-sa)

Little cat: minus cesu (mee-nas sess-oo)

Large: magnus (mag-nis)

Orgasm: fulfillment/deite asteri (see stars) / released (day-ta ass-tare-ree)

Starfighter: asteri peju (ass-tare-ree pear-joo)

Collection of glass vials: virak (vee-ruck)

Scum of the galaxies: xemi (ze-mee)

Hair up: malia pa (Mar-lee-a par)

Hair down: malia pado (Mar-lee-a par-dow)

Lysaran

Visitor: kashi (Kaa-shee)

God: Kaiha (Kigh-haa)

King: Kuna (Koo-na)

Orange fleshy fruit: Lemte (Lem-ta)

White flowers: Myameru (My-a-me-roo)

Precious: Delica (Dell-ee-ka)

Sweetheart: Sali (Saa-lee)

Arum Lily-type flower: D'nastu (D-nass-too)

Love Blossom: aroa loulu (A-row-a low-loo)

Maloidian

Title of respect: lommia (Lomm-ee-a)

Stubborn, lethal tree: tewaa (Tee-wah)

Tokauri/Kulai

Blade – Sulac (soo-lack)

Bone – Ukog (you-cog) - bone from some dumb animal, probably an ukog.

Braided – Gisul (gee-sool)

Father – Danno (dan-no)

Heart – Kassu (cass-soo)

Maker – Mugbu (Mug-boo)

Mother – Manno (man-no)

Sapphires – Buha (boo-ha)

Shit – Saho (sa-ho)

Star - stuon (stoo-on)

Stupid – Ungog (oon-gog)

Vessel/ship - sakay (sa-kay)

Pronunciations

Names

Aaro - Ah-row

Adda – Ay-dah

Aldur - Al-durr

Alllero - A-le-row

Balllio – Bah-leee-oh

Bos - Boss

Bry-dar - Brigh-darr

Brynr - Brin-ner

Cales - Cale-es

Cento - Sen-tow

Citus - Sigh-tuss

Coldar - Coal-daar

Cria - Kree-ah

Eriz - Sigh-low

Danic - Dan-eek

Deeezo – Dee-zoh

Der - Durr

Diso - Dee-sow

Diyo - Die-oh

Eira - Eye-raa

Enyl - E-neel

Eriz - E-rizz

Garix - Ga-ricks

Gayn - Gain

Iddan - Ee-dann

Idon - Eye-donn

Illan - Ee-lann

Jarg – Jar-g

Jokta - Jock-tar

Kanzo - Can-zow

Keelu – Key-loo

Keryr – Kerr-eer

Ksal - Ka-sell

Lazu – Lah-zoo

Lurz - Lurr-z

Malo - Mail-oh

Matir - Mat-teer

Myan - My-ann

Myn-ras - Min-russ

Naio – Nay-oh

Nerx - Nurcks

Nuos - New-oss

Oyaz - Oh-yaz

Prex - Precks

Ronin - Row-nin

Saan - Sarn

Sena - See-na

Sy'mar - Sigh-marr

Syna - Sigh-na

Tamra – Tum-rah

Taro - Tah-row

Tenu - Ten-oo

Trav - Trahv

Tinh - Tin

Vytus - Vie-tuss

Vodin - Vo-din

Ulriq - Yule-rick

Vorn - Vawn

Vyar - Vie-arr

Xan - Zan

Xeus – Zeus

Zaro - Zah-row

Ziot - Zye-ott

Places

Argaxx – Are-jax

    Crustiiu – Criss-tee-oo

    Dyuqa - Dee-you-ka

    Etteria – E-tare-rea

    Galaza – Gah-Lar-Zah

    Gikaet – Gee-ka-ett

    Iphara = Ee-far-ra

    Kulai – koo-ligh

    Lysara – Liss-saa-ra

    Mascroba – Mus-crow-ba

    Resia Cay – Ress-Ee-ahh Kay

    Sarvis – Sarr-viss

    Sosu – Sow-soo

    Tokauri – Too-cow-ree

    Yithia – Yith-ee-a

Battleships

Chikara – Chee-kar-a - Force

    Gladio – Glad-ee-oh - Sword

    Kushin – Cush-shin - To Pierce

    Surata – Soo-ra-tah – Beginning

    Usaha – Oo-saa-hah - Endeavor

Shuttles

Celeeri – See-lee-ree - swift

    Denessi – Denn-ess-ee - sodge

    Eshima – Ee-shee-ma - respect

    Kevol – Kev-oll - agony

    Kuta – Koo-tah - modular shuttle.

    Liri-ny – Lee-ree-nye – freedom

    Misaia – Miss-aye-a - memory

    Sasay – Sass-ay - whispers

    Yakin – Yuck-kin - belief

Creatures

Asnu – Ass-Noo – buffalo/donkey

    Eiltur – Ale-turr

    Gracc – Grrr-ack

    Ilag – Ee-Lug– leggy slugs that feast on sol.

    Kreso – Kreh-soo

    Omeika – Oh-may-ka

    Pagsu – Pug-Soo - cocksuckers

    Reshy – Resh-Ee - huge, like the size of a kuta shuttle, with massive jaws and rows of sharp teeth.

    Sogair – Sow-gare

    Wilanegy – Will-anna-jee

ABOUT THE AUTHOR

Sevannah Storm is a fiction writer who immerses herself in fantastical worlds both magical and science fiction. She has a flair for the creative having studied art and interior architecture and spends her time drawing, oil painting, and writing. An avid reader from an early age, Sevannah finds her inspiration from various sources: games, novels, music, and the land of make-believe. The unique versus the practical has brought on numerous debates.

In her spare time, she does Krav Maga, CrossFit, and rereads novels that snatch her breath away. Having embraced the social media world, you can find her on most platforms.

Her home is a land south of Wakanda, where animals roam free. Born in Zimbabwe, she grew up in South Africa. The crisp blue skies with cotton-candy sunsets expand her heart and soul, encapsulating a sense of freedom.

Words she lives by: "Know your pothole and dodge it. Don't work in a pencil factory if you're a vampire."

Sevannah loves to hear from her readers. You can find and connect with her at the links below.

Website/Newsletter:

https://www.sevannahstorm.com/

Facebook:

https://www.facebook.com/sevannah.storm

Instagram:

https://www.instagram.com/sevannah.storm/

Twitter:

https://twitter.com/sevannah_storm

Thank you for taking the time to read Earth Forged. If you enjoyed the story, please tell your friends and leave a review. Reviews support authors and ensure they continue to bring readers books to love and enjoy.

https://sevannahstorm.com

SOUL FORGED

Know-it-all Oriana agreed to travel with aliens who need women. But she didn't agree to abduction, life/death battles, and escaping with a bossy, arrogant man. She was sabotaged, attacked, and kidnapped, but she is far from beaten. Forced to participate in an alien battle arena with no promise of freedom, she has to forget the loss of her family and focus on surviving.

Enyl has given up hope. His people are dying due to a genetic modification gone awry. Darkness is consuming his warriors, and his world, as he knows it, will end. His father, the king, has rolled out a plan to save them all. But Enyl doubts a solution will be found in time.

And when a compatible female is found...and lost, he must rescue her, a human female capable of surviving despite all odds. However, freeing Oriana serves to anger the aliens holding her captive. Ensuring she is cared for—as per Etterian protocol—he is stunned by the strong connection between the two of them. Such a bond was only experienced between Etterian mates.

Is she his salvation or is that wishful thinking on his part?

Read it here:

https://books2read.com/u/mlAWr9

FATE FORGED

SUN FORGED

The Gifting Series #3

Meeting a drop-dead gorgeous man, who falls onto a knee the first time they meet, sounded too good to be true for Ava. Of course, with her luck, he had to be an alien. Thrust into an unknown alien world, meeting weird and scary creatures, and fearing for her life, Ava tries to survive as best as a hairstylist can.

Kanzo never expected to find a life mate, a Dar Eth. Since he was young, he was taught that pairings were rare with fewer females born. The statistics on finding his Dar Eth would be slim to none. Instead of dreaming and longing for companionship, he focused on being the best male possible, to end his life on a battlefield with honor. But when he experiences the Ethera—the life mate force, and is blessed with his female, he isn't prepared for the level of pain, pleasure, and need she invokes within him.

Unable to save her as she's teleported from him, the dark consuming pain in his chest drives him into a blinding rage. With no idea who stole her or where to begin the search, he will scour the known universe to find her, to hold the female he never wanted.

Read it here:

https://books2read.com/u/3n5vaB

WAR FORGED

The Gifting Series #4

Being kidnapped by aliens does not sit well with Quinlan. Not only would her seven guardians give her hell if she doesn't attempt some sort of escape, but she refuses to be at anybody's mercy. With her practiced military skills, the help of an underground lounge singer and a personal assistant, she takes over the alien slave ship. Not knowing how to fly the damn thing, she sends a distress signal. ...The rescue comes swiftly in the form of a bronzed man with exquisite ice-blue eyes. Leaving her to ask the true question: has she just given up her newfound freedom for a gorgeous man who seems determined to have her for eternity?

As Elite Supreme Commander of the Etterian Forces, Xan answers a distress call in Earth English. That is all he did. The female who captured the slave ship shows remarkable skill, making her a warrior in her own right. Said skills should be respected and honored. Except she is his Dar Eth, calling forth the Ethera—the soulmate bond. How can he protect his female when she can do so herself? What can she possibly need from him? What can he offer a female, not Etterian but human? Not that he can think clearly in her presence when she scents so good and makes him want to kiss all of her.

Maker help him.

Read it here:

https://books2read.com/u/bz1QGD

STAR FORGED

THE GIFTING SERIES #5

Macy is feeling a little left out, as usual. Who would have thought moving from one planet to another wouldn't change that loneliness? She is never alone these days since Etterians guard human women with an urgency she understands. But the lack of companionship is like a dark aching abyss inside her chest. On some days, it threatens to implode, and Macy Mitchell would cease to exist. Looming is her impending meeting with King Xeus of Etteria. How is she supposed to keep her shit together when presented to royalty? Not after she ran from the last king she met.

For Xeus, the void expands daily. Duty, honor, concern for his dying people, and endless loneliness fill his life. Having decided to search for pairings among other worlds, he is pleased his son found his soulmate among human women. It doesn't mean that Xeus's loneliness and longing haven't ended until he stumbles upon a crying female. Meaning only to soothe, he is spellbound when her presence brings him peace. Unable to resist, he forms an attachment to a female he can never have

Read it here:

https://books2read.com/u/3nXgp5

SHADOW FORGED

THE GIFTING SERIES #6

Forty-year-old Caroline is too old to start dating and too bored with her vibrator, but what other choices does she have. On the day she burns her shirt and breaks a fingernail, she meets Etterian warriors. As part of her job at E.S.A. (Earth Space Association,) she must 'entertain' the hot-as-apple-pie Chief Engineer she suspects isn't who he claims to be.

Operations Commander Malo, Head of Espionage, must act as an engineer and ambassador, hoping to invite human females to visit Etteria and save his dying race. From Princess Oriana, he has strict instructions to distrust humans. What he finds he cannot trust are his emotions and his body whenever in the presence of the human ambassador, Caroline. She does not believe in soulmates or in a forever with him. Convincing her to choose him is the greatest task ever set before him, one he cannot afford to fail.

Until she is stolen from him. He calls in favors, utilizes all his resources to find her. And *when* he does, he is never letting her off his battleship...or his bed.

Read it here:

https://books2read.com/u/bPNd8j

LUST FORGED

The Gifting Series #8

Ex-socialite Leona wants nothing more than to enhance the mechanics within sex-cybs, not to mention improve their performances with their 'lovers.' It's a job where she's safe in an all-woman factory on Callisto, and far from her matchmaking mama. When the chief engineer is incapacitated, Leona's required to gift—her term would be pimp—sex-cyborgs to prospective clients. On an Etterian battleship, surrounded by gorgeous males, she tries not to think of sex when it's her work, especially with the Sub-Commander Aaro whose neon-blue eyes are the stuff of her erotic dreams.

As a diplomatic favor, Aaro must abandon his task to guard Earth, and perhaps find his Dar Eth or soulmate, all to protect cargo en route to many worlds, including the dangerous and unpredictable Yithia. Princess Oriana is most concerned for the two human female engineers determined to ensure the deliveries are successful. A simple enough mission until one human enters Aaro's cargo bay, dropping him to his knees.

But revealing to independent Leona that she's now trapped in a marriage isn't something Aaro can bring himself to do. He violates all he stands for, every ounce of honor by not telling her the truth. All in the hopes that she will choose to love him.

Read it here:

https://books2read.com/u/3LdA1w